One sunny day, in the Spring of 1938, some eighteen months before Adolf Hitler's storm troopers started their ruthless rampage through Europe in response to their leader's fanatical anti-Semitic persecution agenda, I was slowly wandering homewards, as a mere five year old, adjusting to the trauma of life at school. On this particular day, as I meandered along, happy to be released from another day's confinement in the still strange atmosphere of the classroom, I was confronted by a couple of slightly older boys from a rival school nearby. Halting me in my tracks, they proceeded to taunt me, and they jeered as they snatched my new school cap from my head and drop-kicked it over a high fence into what at the time were PRIVATE GROUNDS, strictly out of bounds to plebs like me. Then they laughed as they pushed me around – not because I was Jewish – but for being something which to them was equally odd, namely a *Catty Cat,* more conventionally known as a Roman Catholic. Eventually having exhausted their limited abilities to impose further humilities on me they allowed me to continue on my way, shaken and tearful.

Bigotry, I had discovered, early in life, was not the sole prerogative of the National Socialist Party in Germany.

When finally I arrived home, I was still in distress, fearful that I would be in trouble over the loss of my cap. To my great relief, my mother's anger was directed not at me but at the perpetrators of my misery, and after consoling me she then encouraged me to return to the scene - not to accost my erstwhile tormentors - but to creep into the private grounds, *'as any brave lad like me would'* and retrieve my cap! I felt my recent humiliation had quickly become a secondary consideration in her mind.

With time an opportunity to wreak vengeance came as when accompanied by an elder schoolmate, I encountered the same two adversaries, at pretty much the same point where our paths had crossed before. The elder boy, knowing of my earlier experience proceeded to challenge them, and since he was bigger and older than they, they cowered before him a little, scared of the drubbing they thought was coming. He then proceeded to humiliate them as they had me, not by inflicting pain or physically hurting them in any way, but by making them kneel together in front of me on the hard pavement, while I stood by, taking great satisfaction in their misery. He then made them declare that they were *Proddy Dogs* (Protestants) who could never get to heaven because they did not belong to the Catholic Church, the one true religion of Jesus Christ and the only one to guarantee instant access to eternal happiness when you die, assuming of course that you have led a proper and virtuous life.

I was as surprised as the *Proddy Dogs* were to hear him say this, and as he let them go, and they ran away terrified of the prospect of eternal damnation, I remember feeling quite sorry for them.

"That's the way it is" he said, in response to my question as to how he knew such a thing.

"Father Haggerty told us in class" he added, as we wended our way home again.

So I knew it must be true, the priest had said so!

As I advanced through these formative years within a Catholic culture, strong in political and tribal (Irish Catholic) traditions, I too was indoctrinated into the edicts of the 'true faith'. Although eventually, through living cheek by jowl with non-Catholic neighbours in the shared hospitality of a typical Durham County mining community, I realised that most in the Non-Catholic majority in our community had as good a chance of achieving salvation as any Catholic I knew, but it was only after I had witnessed the often damaging effects of the extremes of canon law, that I began to separate the underlying meaning of Christ's message from the literality of the Church's dogma.

Some prejudices, I learnt, were not confined to the Germans - or even the *Proddy Dogs*.

Down the years since I have perceived the limiting effects on good families that the strict tenets of any chosen doctrine can create. I have known parents deny their children when confronted by one who had lapsed from these doctrinal requirements; I have known fathers who have disowned their daughters and brothers who have disclaimed their sisters. I have known such sisters be denied the joy of a loving relationship with a partner because of the sense of inherent guilt their departure from 'the rules' they were taught during the formative years of their childhood invoked in them. I have witnessed the deep sorrow that such conflict of conscience can create, and I have been saddened by the fact of it.

This story contains all these elements to a greater or lesser degree, and while the persons and locations portrayed are of themselves totally fictitious, the essence of the situations portrayed are firmly based in fact.

Prologue

1988

The priest kissed the missal reverently and the altar boys intoned their Latin response, "Laus tibi Christe" they chanted in unison.

The old man turned slowly, and with rosewood cane in hand, tentatively descended the carpeted steps. The boys watched anxiously, alert in case he should stumble. He didn't, and smiled at their relief as he arrived safely at the bottom.

Before him the church echoed to the shuffling of feet and the clearing of throats as, gospel over, the congregation seated themselves in anticipation of the homily that was to follow. The church was full, for the celebration of the Tridentine Mass on the feast of Corpus Christi.

The homily would be given this day by Father Nigel Kirby, the newest in a long line of curates who had passed through St Hildreth's portals at the start of their ecclesiastical careers. Father Kirby had chosen to speak on the theme of *"Suffer the little children to come unto me and forbid them not, for of such is the Kingdom of Heaven"*.

He would stand, he had decided, not remote and aloof in the pulpit, but near at hand in the centre aisle that bisected the nave of the church. Smiling gently, he would, with relaxed familiarity, address the children in the first five rows, boys to his left and girls to his right. This special attention, he had decided, would be appropriate on the occasion of their First Communion. Father Kirby preened himself at this idea, which to him seemed singularly original.

Old Father Holland, in contrast to his young curate, had been a priest for some forty years at St Hildreth's in Eastinglea, and parish priest for most of them. He had seen many such Communion days and delivered many such sermons, in similar proximity to the young communicants.

Now as he lowered himself into the ornately carved sanctuary chair with its old velvet seat, he felt a pang of anxiety for these little ones. As the young priest started to speak, Father Holland smoothed down the apron front of his red chasuble and frowned his concern. Looking at the children, he saw in each young face an unquestioning acceptance of every word Father Kirby spoke. He recognised the simplicity and the eagerness with which they were ready to commit themselves to all that *Mother Church* would demand of them. These were Christ's newest disciples - the priests and nuns of tomorrow. Bright with the grace and fervour of innocent confession, they were ready to receive the Blessed Eucharist, like their fathers and mothers had done before them. They had reached the age of reason. They were seven years old and they felt grown up!

The old priest frowned more deeply as he pondered their futures. It would be later, years later, when they were full-grown and labouring under the burdens and responsibilities of their adult stations that the weeds of doubt would grow to smother the flower of the blossoming faith they now displayed, and which had brought them so happily to this special day. Most would survive the trials, but some would defect, and disillusionment and bitterness would fester in resentful minds.

Dermot Holland knew this with the certainty of a man who had spent a lifetime as spiritual counsellor to this flock of his. He knew his people and he knew his black sheep too.

He could recall each stray, each one of which he regarded as a personal failure for himself and his ministry. He remembered the manifold accusations he had sustained, the blasphemous outbursts against Holy Church. Being a priest in this hard working community carried no guarantees, and won no unearned respect. In his own case it hadn't even afforded him the approval of his own father.

At that moment the image returned. In his mind's eye he saw his father's face clear in every detail and smiling as always, but from eyes that were cold and unloving. He lowered his head sadly.

"Daddy, oh Daddy," he whispered.

Dermot covered his face with his hands to hide the tears that threatened to spill down his cheeks. He had carried the image through all his pastoral years, and in that time it had neither softened nor faded. Not since the first hurt-filled day he had experienced it.

Chapter 1

Dublin, Easter 1916

Tomas watched the battle fearfully from the upstairs window of the house opposite, and gasped despairingly as he saw the soldiers drag his father from the smouldering ruins into O'Connell Street. Wincing with pain, and with blood pumping from a gaping wound in his left leg Seamus staggered along, cursing his captors as he went. They bundled him down a cobbled alleyway into a warren of back entrances and warehouses, then prodded him at bayonet point through a gateway into the high walled obscurity of a backyard, where they pushed him to the ground. The ambiguous sign on the gate said *'Miller's Flour, The Flour Millers'*. The officer followed behind, casually slapping his thigh with his swagger stick as he strutted in highly polished knee-length boots with the arrogance of a man used to exercising unquestioned power over his subordinates, and more particularly over any who might be unfortunate enough to become his prisoner.

Tomas had wanted desperately to join his father in the Uprising, and he had followed him and his men to do so, expressly against Seamus's stated wishes. He had been angry when Tomas had suddenly turned up amongst them, and they had exchanged strong words before Tomas was eventually persuaded that his responsibilities, at least for the moment, were to his wife and his young family.

"There'll be time enough to fight later on," Seamus said, "once we've won this first one, and then you and a lot more like you will have to fight whether you want to or not, - but right now your duty is to Margaret and the children, their needs take priority. Now get the hell out of here! Go now!"

1

Tomas had left, feeling a little humiliated, and not at all consoled by the sympathetic looks of his father's men, but he knew that to stay and have his father worry, would make him more of a liability than a help to their purpose. So he left, but only as far as the house opposite, where along with other members of an astonished public he had watched the fire fight develop. Inevitably the battle was short-lived and as the superior force of British troops stormed forward in a hail of gunfire, acrid fumes, and smoke, it also resulted in his father's capture, when the soldiers blasted their way into the building and brought him down with a bullet that ripped open his left thigh as he fought a desperate rearguard action. By that time however, Seamus had seen his men safely away through the warren of escape tunnels that lay beneath the floorboards leading to the adjacent houses, which had been planned and constructed in advance of just such an emergency.

Now as he crept up the alleyway behind his father and his captors, Tomas heard the bolts rattle into place on the other side of the gate. He searched around frantically for a vantage point from which he could watch undetected, anxious to see what was happening. He squeezed through a gap between two loose planks in the railings of the adjacent yard, and once inside found slits in the separating fence through which he could observe everything. The Captain was standing over his father, his pistol in his hand. It was aimed at Seamus's head, who prostrate on the ground, glared defiantly up at the man. His situation was desperate in every sense.

The officer was interrogating him, but Tomas was having difficulty, trying to hear what was being said. He crept nearer, the better to hear their exchanges. With their backs to him and their attention focussed on Seamus, no one noticed as Tomas manoeuvred stealthily behind them, except Seamus himself. He flashed his son a warning look that said, *'Don't interfere!'*

The officer's tone became increasingly agitated as his questions met with no response. He was demanding names - of the "traitors" - he called them - who had evaded capture. His manner became threatening, and as Seamus remained obstinately silent, his demeanour grew ever more inflamed. He turned to his corporal.

"This man is not co-operating Corporal! What do you think we should do with him?"

The corporal's tone was conciliatory.

"The fight's over for him sir, he's just another prisoner of war now."

The Captain turned on the man furiously.

"What the hell are you talking about Corporal! He's no prisoner of war; he's a bloody rebel, a traitor! He's committed treason! He'll stand in front of a firing squad or my name's not James Spencer-Lambert, but before that happens I want the names of the others - his accomplices – and once I have them, they can all go to Hell together!"

As his agitation increased, the corporal grew alarmed. He tried to calm the situation.

"Yes of course sir. But he's lost a lot of blood sir. It wouldn't hurt to stick a dressing on that wound, just to keep him alive for further questioning - or to stand trial even - whatever you want to do with him sir."

Seamus recognised the corporal's concern, and shot him a grateful glance.

"I doubt very much that a trial will be necessary, Corporal," said the officer. His manner had momentarily calmed as he gazed at the gaping wound.

Then he added in a quiet and disturbing tone, "He doesn't seem to be bleeding too badly now, does he?"

Suddenly he walked forward, and stepping hard on Seamus's outstretched leg pressed down, leaning his full weight on the damaged limb. Blood spurted instantly from the dark red slash. Seamus let out an anguished cry and his face broke out in pain and sweat. Then mercifully he passed into exhausted oblivion.

The corporal stood aghast; the troopers were dumbstruck. Lambert took a step back, and gazed down at his captive, a malevolent smile on his face. Behind the fence Tomas cringed helplessly, enduring agonies at his father's misery, but unable to do anything. The Captain turned to his 'non-com'. His eyes were gleaming with malicious pleasure.

3

"Bring him round Corporal Roberts, stick a dressing on him, then we'll start again", he said.

The corporal's concern deepened as he looked at the unconscious man on the ground.

"Maybe the other prisoners will have coughed their lot by now sir; told everything. This man looks really sick; I do think we should get him to hospital sir."

The Captain snarled, "I'm not interested in other prisoners. I'm interested in this bastard, and he's not going to any hospital. For your information this is Seamus Mulholland, one of the more notorious rebels behind this fiasco. I've seen him before - him and his fellow riffraff - parading their bloody flags up and down the streets of Dublin. What he doesn't know about their organisations is not worth knowing. He's a Corps Commander in that ridiculous organisation, the so-called *'Irish Brigade'*. The man's a criminal, and he is not entitled to your sympathy!

"Now do your job, Roberts! Obey your orders and get him to his feet! Or I'll have you court-marshalled for insubordination! Do I make myself clear?"

His mood was as black as his face was red, and he was verging on hysteria. The corporal knew he was beaten.

"Yes sir, absolutely sir!"

He moved to revive his prisoner, who was still moaning on the ground in an unconscious stupor. He signalled the troopers to help him as he raised Seamus's head and poured water between his lips from a canteen. He wiped his face with a wet handkerchief. Seamus opened his eyes, as a soldier applied a field dressing to the weeping wound. Then they lifted him to his feet, where wincing with pain, he stood before his tormentor, a man supporting him at each shoulder.

As all this was happening Lambert stood casually by, impervious to his captive's distress. Now he stepped closer and legs astride faced his tortured prisoner. Seamus remained motionless, hanging between his guards, his head down, his eyes closed.

"Look at me, you contemptible Irish oaf!"

Seamus raised his head, and Lambert stepped even nearer, "One way or another you will tell me what I want to know. I want the names of your Field-lieutenants and the gutter rats that run with them. It's your choice Mulholland; you can make it very easy or very hard. I don't give a damn. You *will* name them though, let me assure you of that. Before I'm finished you'll be glad to do so, so I suggest you start now!"

Seamus spoke for the first time.

"Come closer Captain, I've something to tell you sir", he said in a weary whisper.

The Captain looked surprised. He hadn't anticipated any early response. He bent his head, keen to hear his prisoner's words.

Seamus pursed his lips and spat! A thick glob of spittle spewed out into the officer's face. Lambert staggered back, rigid with shock and fury. His scream of rage rent the air around him.

"That's everything you'll ever get from me, you English fuck-pig," gasped Seamus, shaking with pain and fatigue. Then exhausted by his efforts, he slumped at the knees.

The troopers tightened their grip on the falling man, confused as to what they should do. Corporal Roberts rushed to his commander's side, proffering the same handkerchief he had used on Seamus. The Captain snatched it angrily, and wiped away the phlegm. As he did so, a look of cold malice crossed his face. Stepping forward he slowly raised his pistol. The gun exploded once, twice, then a third time. Seamus juddered with the force of each impact, while his bewildered guards struggled to hold him. Finally as his life's blood spread in a dark stain across his chest, they laid him on a pile of old sacks behind them, and watched helplessly as, with his breath rattling in his throat, Seamus Mulholland died.

For a few seconds that lasted an eternity, nobody moved. Then a second scream rang out, tearing the silence asunder. Bellowing out a barrage of tormented profanity, Tomas wrenched at the planks of the fence that separated him from his murdered father. The startled onlookers, slow at first to react, turned in alarm to see him struggling in the narrow space he had ripped open. But before Tomas had forced himself fully through, a trooper, now alert to what was happening, stepped forward, raised his rifle and brought the butt down hard on Tomas's unprotected head. He fell unconscious into the yard at the soldier's feet, where he and his companions gazed at him in shocked surprise. As realisation dawned that before them was a witness to all that had taken place, they looked around apprehensively, first to each other and then to their leader.

James Spencer Lambert walked over and looked down at the still figure on the ground whose interference was complicating an already difficult situation. For a moment he looked unsure.

"Who is this clown?" he asked, but no one knew.

His men watched anxiously, waiting to see what he would do. As he held up his pistol, they stiffened instinctively, but were surprised when he made no move to fire it. Instead he opened the chamber and emptied the remaining rounds into his hand before putting them into his pocket. Then kneeling down he pressed the empty weapon into Tomas's open palm. Standing up and turning to his men, he appeared calm and in control again.

"Pay attention, and listen carefully" he ordered. They did so in focused silence.

"You will recall - I've no doubt, each one of you - how I was robbed of my weapon during our recent skirmishes."

He paused to allow his words to penetrate, as he fixed each puzzled man with a challenging gaze. Then pointing to Tomas, he continued, "You will recall - I've no doubt - how this man ran off with it - while we were subduing his accomplices."

He paused again to let his words sink in.

"Do any of you have a problem with these recollections?"

There was a tone to his voice that precluded objection and evoked a mumbled acquiescence from all, but their confusion persisted.

"Good" he continued, "Then you will have no problem verifying it to the police when they get here. Furthermore, you will confirm how we pursued this pair, and arrived at this yard to find them in a quarrelsome shoot-out, which we were unable to prevent, without incurring unnecessary risk to ourselves that is, and which resulted in the scene we have here before us now. Our sole

contribution, you will say, was to overpower our murdering friend here."
Again he pointed to Tomas.

"Remember to tell them that - exactly as I am telling it to you now!"

They looked at each other, unconvinced.

"I can assure you, thin though this story sounds, it will be accepted without serious question. After all, the police are on our side against these criminals."

The ensuing silence signified no disagreements. The Captain looked around them, and then satisfied they would comply, turned to his corporal.

"See to it Roberts. Leave a man to take care of sleeping beauty over there, take the other men and go find a policeman. I want this business cleared up fast. When you are finished, report back to me at HQ."

To the others he said, "I should not need to remind you that I don't expect any of you to reveal anything of what has happened here today. If even a word leaks out I'll hold you *all* responsible, and I will act accordingly. You are all from the North of England, where you will return soon, and I need not remind you that my family exercises much control in those counties, particularly with regard to employment there. Do I make myself clear?"

The reply was unanimous; there were no dissentions.

"Get on with it then." He turned and marched briskly out of the yard.

The corporal turned to his men, "Smithers", he barked, "you stay with the prisoner. You lot, come with me"

❦

When they had gone, Smithers walked across to where the unconscious Tomas lay, and nudged him with his boot. Tomas moaned, but remained face down on the ground, motionless. Smithers looked at him and decided he was going to be out for quite a while yet.

"Sorry Ah hit you s' hard mate" he said, in his colloquial North of England slang. "But if ya'd been conscious when the Captain looked ya ower, like as not he'd 'ave shot ya. So mebbe Ah did y'a favour efter all."

He smiled with amused satisfaction, and paused as if expecting an answer from Tomas. Receiving none, he shrugged and turned away to await his companions at the gate.

He reached into his pocket withdrew his cigarettes and lit one. The harsh smoke of the Woodbine burned his throat and he coughed as he blew it out in a slow cloud. He gazed down the alleyway, looking for sight of his comrades returning with the police. After a minute or two, impatient with waiting, he wandered away towards O'Connell Street, out of view of his prisoner, whom he assumed to be still unconscious. It was a mistaken assumption. Finding no sign of them he wandered back, and resting his rifle against the gatepost, stood at the doorway smoking, gazing out impatiently, his back to the yard.

As Tomas came round, he was befuddled and unsure of his whereabouts. Holding his throbbing head, he scrambled slowly and unsteadily to his feet. The pistol in his hand and the sight of his father's body lying still on the sacking brought him starkly to his senses. He looked around anxiously for his guards. He saw the rifle leaning against the gate, and heard Smithers coughing outside. Sticking the handgun into his pocket, he moved swiftly, and when Smithers turned at the sound of a weapon being cocked, he found himself gazing down the barrel of his own gun. Before the trooper could react, Tomas reversed it and struck him hard in the face, snapping his head back on his shoulders and cracking his jaw. The man fell with a grunt, still and insensible. Tomas paused only momentarily, unmoved at the sight of him. Dragging him into the yard, he bound and gagged him securely with strips of flour bag sacking.

Then he turned and looked at his dead father on the ground. With pain and grief etched on his face, he bent and lifted Seamus firmly in his strong young arms. Holding him close he spoke in sobbing anger, "If I wait fifty years to do it, Dadda, that man will pay for what he has done this day! I swear this on my life, and the lives of my children!"

Then with a heart torn with grief, Tomas carried his father out of the baker's yard into the protective obscurity of Dublin's high back streets.

Chapter 2

Respect and Disrespect

Many of those who came to the house that evening to pay their respects in prayer were rebels already, or rebels in the making, The failed Easter uprising had not quenched the spirits of these men, and given the same call they were ready to fight to a man once more. Most however were not fighting men, but simple cotters - family friends and neighbours - to whom Seamus was a hero, the one who had had the courage and the determination to fight and die for his convictions. His actions and his words had inspired in them a belief in the justice of the struggle, particularly when he had spoken out openly against the landlords, '*whose incontestable power is rooted in the ownership of the very soil our livelihoods depend on*' he had declared. Seamus was their role model, their champion, and their respect for him was immeasurable.

Also present amongst them that night were some who were strangers, men who had arrived unannounced from undeclared locations. Two enigmatic young men in particular, whose city clothes betrayed them, stood out among the general assembly as they prayed with them around the open coffin.

To the Army Council of the decimated *Irish Brotherhood,* Seamus was a soldier, who had fought with the group near Bowlands Mill before scattering and seeking refuge in O'Connell Street, where for his defiance he had paid with his life in a baker's yard, murdered by his captors. The strangers were there to honour Seamus and the two men were the official, but anonymous face of the Republican movement. To all these people Seamus was the quintessential Irish martyr, who had stirred in them a pride that had for too long been dormant.

Now they came together, soldiers and civilians, men and women in common purpose, to pray for the soul of a man they mutually revered.

Only one man stood apart from it all, refusing to be sucked into what he described as "the ill-fated philosophy of armed rebellion". Father Theodore Mathew O'Malley was the parish priest at St Joseph's in this small and unremarkable market town in the county of Monaghan. He was fifty-six years old, a portly man, with cropped black hair that surrounded a balding crown. Though not an imposing figure, he exuded that pretentious air of authority often assumed by people of small stature, who finding themselves in positions of social or religious ranking, benefit from an authority and respect born of their status, which of themselves they could never hope to achieve.

For Father Theodore, St Joseph's was his pond and he was the big fish in it. On this sad evening he had decided to exert this unwarranted authority by laying down what he regarded as the ground rules of church ritual and proper behaviour in the funeral service at which he would officiate the next day. He had determined that he would dowse the heated republican fervour around him, which to him was an anathema, by imposing his own regulatory values upon the proceedings. As he concluded the evening's rosary and prayers with the Sign of the Cross, he turned to face the gathering while their attention was still with him. He looked around their faces with a domineering air, and as he spoke he did so most sombrely.

"I have something to say to you men and I want you to hear me clearly." He paused for effect as his listeners waited curiously. Turning to the women who were gathered together in a communal group, he bestowed on them his most patronising smile, "If you ladies will excuse us, 'tis to the gentlemen gathered here that I now address myself", adding with ill-grace "You girls might want to go to the kitchen and prepare some tea."

The women looked somewhat slighted, and ignoring his directive stayed put. Unabashed, Father O'Malley turned his back on them to face his chosen audience. Then in a challenging voice, accompanied by unequivocal and accusatory stares into the faces of the two young men from Dublin, he started to speak, grimly and in confrontational tone.

"I am as Irish as the next man," he said "And I also believe that Irish politics are in need of change. But contrary to most of you here, I believe that the Home Rule policy, pursued in the London Parliament by that noble Irishman Sir John Redmond is the one to be applauded; and it is proper, it is legal, and hence within the law!

"Since I know many of you can't read or write, and therefore aren't likely to understand what the Home Rule Policy entails, I'll try to enlighten you, so that you too will see the value of accepting it as it stands.

"William Gladstone himself, was the first man to try to correct the wrongs that English law has imposed on Ireland, but he failed. He once said 'It is my intention to pacify Ireland.' He failed because the House of Lords vetoed his bills – he had two tries, but failed on each occasion. Charles Stewart Parnell was the next to try, - and him a renowned follower of the Protestant doctrine at that - but he failed as well. I'll not bore you with the details, except to say that it was the House of Lords again that did the damage. Since then, right up to a few years ago successive governments have fought shy of dealing with the legitimate claims of the Irish people. However today we have Sir John Redmond who has successfully persuaded the Liberal coalition, under the leadership of Mr Herbert Asquith, who although lukewarm to the idea, needs the support of the Irish Nationalists at Westminster to stay in government, to acquiesce and support the Home Rule Policy. If you do not already know, it went into the statute books in 1914, to the great chagrin and consternation of Mr Andrew Bonar Law and his Protestant-based new Unionist Party, I might add. Its passage through government was also helped by the fact that the House of Lords has been unable to exercise any veto because it is no longer in its power to do so!

"What does this new Home Rule mean to you and me then? I'll tell you, shall I?"

Without waiting for a reply he continued his diatribe.

"It means that we will establish an Irish Parliament, here in Ireland, based in Dublin. It means that all matters governing our everyday life will be decided here at home. Of course major items affecting England as well, such as Crown matters, the armed services, foreign policy and civil service will be still decided in Westminster, - but don't forget Irish Members will still be allowed to sit in London. That for me is a satisfactory solution to the Irish problems and gives no justification or reason for the recent rebellion in Dublin."

When he had finished talking a resentful hush settled momentarily on his listeners, till a neighbour and close friend of Seamus's spoke up,

"Are you saying we are better off as we are, remaining under the English as servile subjects, than we would be in a new Republic as free men in our own country? You are crazy! Good god man, don't you know; they've suspended the bloody Home Rule Act already – they make the excuse it will have to be held back till their war's completed. They need us Irishmen to fight for them, and they want to make sure nothing prevents them calling us to arms if they need to. Then when their bloody war is over, they'll find another reason not to implement it. It's what they always do. Where's the bloody freedom in that?"

Without waiting for an answer the man continued, "Are you telling us our dear friend here, lying dead because of a murdering Englishman's bullet was a traitor? I'll not listen to such insults, not even from a priest. Seamus was and will always be a genuine son of Ireland, a true hero, and I'd rather starve as a free man on my own land than be a well-fed slave for an English landlord. My family have worked our land for generation upon generation, but who owns it, not us, a bloody Englishman we never see - he doesn't even live here, he lives in his big house in England! All we ever see is his bloody agent - usually when he calls to tell us the rent's gone up again!

"I've heard enough of your sycophantic codswallop about the English and their lawful rights! Long live the Republic, I say! Now I'm leaving before I do something I regret."

Turning to the other friends he said, "Gentlemen I'll be taking my leave of you all."

With a courteous nod to the group of ladies, he gave a brief "Goodnight" and left.

His departure was greeted with murmurings of agreement and approval, which Father O'Malley rapidly hushed by resuming his loud bluster.

"Despite our friend's unwarranted outburst, Home Rule is the way forward for Ireland, and it is a legitimate and moral aspiration which we should all support. Rebellion and revolution are certainly not!"

Before him the disagreements became louder, as did his voice in response.

"The path of the rebel is a sinful one, which must inevitably fail, just as this most recent fiasco has failed, and I for one will have no truck with it, or with those who promote it."

There was open dissension now, which became argumentative. It was at this point that he chose to drop his bombshell.

"To that end, I will not allow tomorrow's *Requiem Mass* to be hijacked and militarised by anyone here! There will be no parades or displays, no flag-waving interludes, and there will be no acclamations, eulogies, or other mumbo-jumbo talk about causes and brotherhoods! Not in my church; not in my services!"

The young men from Dublin bristled visibly, and the guests protested loudly in shock and astonishment as Father O'Malley continued undeterred, "Let me remind you, in case you have forgotten, His Holiness - the Pope himself - issued a decree not yet one hundred years old, condemning secret organisations as ungodly. The *Ribbon Men* of yesteryear and the *Irish Republican Brotherhood* of today fall directly into that definition. Archbishop Walsh of Drumcondra is also on record as saying that violence against the British Government is a mortal sin, and can never be justified.

"If you are the God-fearing Catholics you should be, you will obey your Church; you will heed Her advice, and put all sinful ways behind you. For my part, I'll not have you using God's house as a Republican platform - a failed cause if ever there was one – and the very reason we are here tonight is witness to that fact!"

The atmosphere was thick with suppressed resentment as he continued, "This is the last sacrament the soul of Seamus Mulholland will ever receive, and I intend to do my best to get his wretched soul into heaven. This funeral is a spiritual affair, so remember that all of you."

Looking around he concluded, "Do I make myself clear?"

There was hostility, there was offence, but no one spoke out further against him.

"I'll take your silence as agreement then" he said rigidly and turned to remove his stole and surplice. The mutterings of discontent and suppressed unease continued behind him.

"Now he's drawn a well-defined line in the sand, hasn't he" whispered the taller of the two Dubliners to his partner, and his grey eyes blazed in his long face.

"A clerical clown if ever I saw one," replied his companion with contempt.

It was at that moment of tension that Seamus's widow Mary entered the room, on the arm of Tomas her son. She carried herself before her compassionate observers with a composure and dignity that shone through her grief. She had been forced to absent herself from the prayers earlier, when pain and heartache had seized her and overwhelmed her spirit. Now as she returned, the earlier tensions in the room evaporated, giving way to the good manners and respectful sympathy that was proper to the occasion. All eyes were focused on her, as she too prepared to address her guests.

"My dear friends" - her voice quavered as she spoke, "I want to thank you all for being here tonight; your presence is a great consolation to myself, and to Tomas and Margaret. I particularly want to thank those of you who have travelled far to be with us, and more particularly you two men from Dublin. I regard your presence here as an indication of the respect in which my husband was held within the *'Organisation'*."

Then with firm determination she stated, "Let me say to you, my son Tomas has already vowed to fill his father's place, so that this Mulholland family will continue to stand up and be counted as long as there is a fight to fight."

She turned to her son, "Is that not so, Tomas?"

Tomas stood straight and proud as he replied, "It is that, mother. I'll fight, like my father before me, till every Englishman is driven from the blessed turf of this beloved land. And I will find his murderer too. He will pay for his crime, I promise you that."

His expression took on a look of ruthless determination, "I know his name! I know his face! I saw him do it! There will be no trial. He's already guilty; he's already condemned. I'll find him, no matter how long it takes, no matter where the search for him takes me!"

There were general murmurs of approval all round at Tomas's emotional outburst, and no one there questioned his right to dispense his own justice against the man who had so callously murdered his father. They had all heard the circumstances, and no one there doubted that justice in this case meant an eye for an eye - except of course Father O'Malley, who at least in this moment, felt discretion was the preferred option in the presence of his vengeful host.

"I think the tide has just washed out that line you mentioned," whispered the second man from Dublin.

The tall man smiled, and the assembled visitors exchanged meaningful glances, while carefully avoiding the eyes of the priest who stood alone, silent and bewildered by the sudden turn of events.

Unaware of the effect her contentious words were having, the widow Mulholland continued, and changing the subject she lapsed into more conversational tones as she relaxed into a role more familiar to her, "I know a lot of you are anxious to be on your way home now, some of you have far to travel and you may not be able to return tomorrow. We understand that, and we are grateful for your presence here tonight, but if there are any who wish to stay, then there are plenty places prepared for you, some here and some with our generous neighbours, so if you want to stay you may do so."

Her guests gracefully acknowledged her words as she added, "Now there's hot food for all in the other room, so I want you to go through and eat it."

Turning to the priest she said with a light smile, "There's even a bottle of the good stuff for you Father, if you'd like a drop"

The heavy animosity that hung in the air towards him was broken when the priest, sensing that he had outstayed his welcome spoke up hastily with some embarrassment, "Not tonight Mary, I must get back. I have things to do before tomorrow, so I must decline. Maybe after tomorrow is over we can share a drop together." His words were hurried and ill considered.

"All right then Father, we'll do that," his devoted parishioner agreed.

She walked him to the door as people around jostled past, heading for the other room to partake of the light supper awaiting them. On the doorstep, the priest shook her hand rather clumsily and bade her an awkward farewell, 'Goodnight and God's blessing,' he said brusquely.

As Mary watched him go, hurrying away into the night, the spiritual comfort she took from what he represented was replaced by a returning sense of unhappy loss. A cloak of deep sadness enveloped her once more. Tomas and Margaret came up behind her, and sensing her mood placed comforting arms around her shoulders. She reached up and clutched their hands tightly.

Later, after the remaining people had departed, the tall stranger from Dublin prepared to leave also, for the warm hospitality of a neighbour's bed. He spoke to her softly, "I loved Seamus as a brother, Mrs Mulholland. He was my mentor. We fought together in the Uprising. He was a brave patriot and a treasured friend. I will always remember him. We all will."

He took her hand and kissed it. Then wishing her a peaceful night he left. Mary and Tomas watched him go. As he disappeared, she turned to her son quizzically, "Who do you think he might be, Tomas?"

"If I didn't know he was in a Dublin gaol right now mother, I might be persuaded to believe that man is Eamon De Valera himself."

Behind them a voice spoke quietly, "Perhaps what we think we know isn't always correct."

They turned in surprise to look into the smiling face of the other Dubliner, as he too waited to take his leave of them.

"The Germans have a word for it," he said softly, "I learned it recently on a submarine, Doppel-ganger! Look it up when you have a chance."

He too kissed her hand, as he bade them goodnight.

Chapter 3

The Wake

The following morning was cold and overcast and the wind from the northwest was cutting. The small church quickly filled to capacity, even the organ gallery was full. The congregation had wrapped up well, more for December than May. They had come from all around, from the villages, and the remote surrounding farms. The news and manner of Seamus's death had reached them all. Many had travelled far to get here, some by "jonty" cart, along narrow rough roads.

Father O'Malley, robed in the black of a requiem mass, stood at the door like a sentinel, ostensibly to meet the mourners, but in truth to scrutinise each arrival for flags, insignia, or other manifest displays of Republican sympathies. Most guessed his intent, but apart from some mumbled dissent, could do nothing to thwart his purpose. As for the priest himself, if he noticed their disapproval he gave no indications of it.

Eventually the cortege arrived, led by a funeral director who walked ahead of a gleaming hearse with polished trims and shimmering glass, pulled by two cockaded black horses. Following behind were two Hackney carriages, bringing the immediate family and friends. Behind followed a host of sympathisers on foot.

Tomas sat in the first carriage with his mother, while opposite him sat Margaret consoling a maternal aunt. Tomas held his mother's hand firmly, as she struggled to control her grief; Margaret and the aunt watched her, stiff and red-eyed themselves. The second carriage came behind with the pallbearers, each personally selected by Mary, as Seamus's best and most trusted friends. At the rear, the general assembly of mourners walked in sorrowful procession, huddled together against the cold, many clutching wreaths and floral tributes which themselves seemed to wilt in the morning air. Outside the church the carriages stopped and their passengers alighted at the steps. They lined up behind the coffin as it was lifted out of the hearse, to be borne shoulder-high by the friends.

The priest approached, blessing the coffin with holy water and incense as he walked around it, accompanied by two cassocked altar boys carrying long candles whose spluttering flames threatened to die in the gusting wind. This ceremony completed, he turned to lead the solemn line up the marble steps, reciting the first prayers of the service as he went. Immediately behind the coffin Tomas supported his trembling mother, while his maternal aunt leaned heavily on Margaret. Relatives and friends followed on, and at the rear the Dublin men, darkly suited and wearing black ties under winged collars, took their places in the last row behind the assembled mourners.

As the service began, a crowd stood outside where they hopped from foot to foot in the cold, because there was not enough room for them in the small church.

The requiem proceeded steadily in the true Catholic tradition, a ritual of candles, flowers, and incense. Prayers were chanted in sad unison, and hymns were sung to the unhappy accompaniment of sobs and tears. Eventually the time for the eulogy arrived, and Father O'Malley ascended the steps of the pulpit to stand before the gallery of mourners. He gazed at them all in a moment's silent wonder, contemplating what it was about this man that evoked such respectful response, when all he was, in truth, was a law breaking rebel. He felt he had a message to deliver.

He started politely enough by praising Seamus as a man of high Catholic principle, which he had practiced and upheld all his life. He offered his deepest condolences to Mary his wife, and to Tomas, as a loyal and obedient son. He praised the Catholic heritage they had enjoyed together, and he congratulated Tomas and Margaret on the way they too upheld the principles of the Catholic family. He also sent his blessings to their children.

He would have done well to have left it there without further comment, but he didn't. Instead he chose to extend his discourse with a sad but damning indictment of the futility of Seamus's demise, and an unambiguous condemnation of the circumstances that had led to it.

"I could not help but be saddened", he said, "by the misguided principles that have culminated in this untimely death. I urge you all to take heed of them, to learn from these mistakes, and to put aside the populist trend for rebellion that caused them, and which ended in the tragedy you see here before you. I would be failing in my duty as spiritual counsellor to this parish and community, if I did not denounce rebellion as irresponsible and a sin before God. I repeat what I have said so many times before; we have a duty to support the principles of legitimate government and the rule of law, and to denounce those who would seek to overthrow it."

They waited in stunned silence for him to continue, hoping he would at least assuage his harsh comments with a call for justice against Seamus's murderers. They waited to hear him denounce the manner of his death, not just the cause, but he did not. He denounced no one. He merely re-iterated the hollow words of sympathy he had already uttered, and calling for a final hymn, turned back to the altar to conclude the service. Around the church, astonishment turned to barely suppressed anger, and dissent rumbled through the benches. Tomas's clenched knuckles gleamed white through stretched skin, and his breath hissed loudly through gritted teeth, as beside him his bereaved mother sat shocked and ashen-faced unable to believe what she was hearing. Her priest, her link with God, had maligned her husband - at his funeral! The combined pain of bereavement and the public denouncement of her husband's death as misguided folly conspired to crush her beneath an unbearable burden of shame and hurt. She closed her eyes and slid sideways in an exhausted faint.

❧

At the graveside, people jostled gently for position to participate in the final ritual, while those at the front struggled not to fall into the gaping hole.

The pallbearers placed the coffin on the boards that straddled the cavity. Beneath it dangled the ropes, ready for the lowering into the final resting-place. The priest took his place at the head, and the final prayers began.

In the carriages that waited at the roadside, her son and daughter-in-law were tending to Mary. She was sipping hot tea prepared for her by a kindly gardener. She had recovered now, and was composed enough to protest her desire to be at the graveside for the last devotions. Tomas was quietly adamant that she should not expose herself to further distress, and insisted she should listen and pray from the warmer comfort of the carriage. He had spoken little to anyone since his mother's faint, and his concern for her welfare had outweighed the anger and animosity he felt for the priest. There would be time and opportunity later, he had decided. Then the prayers stopped, and their ordeal seemed at last to be over. They waited expectantly for the crowd to disperse.

At the graveside Father O'Malley prepared to leave, but strangely the throng around him made no move to depart, and he found his exit barred.

"It's time to go now" he said, "We can do no more here. He is in God's hands."

He spoke with firmness and self-assurance, confident of being obeyed, but still no one moved. Only the flickering fingers and the muted prayers of a few at their rosaries disturbed the stillness that had descended.

"Let me through now" he said with some irritation, but no one stepped aside.

His young acolytes looked confused, and the priest's face reflected a growing annoyance, which almost immediately gave way to apprehension as the Dublin men eased forward to stand directly in front of him.

The tall man spoke, standing close to the priest who stepped back a little, uneasy at his proximity.

"On behalf of Mrs Mulholland and her family Father, - and The Army Council of the Irish Volunteers - I want to thank you sincerely for what you have done this day, both here and in your church. Your meticulous ministrations will, I'm sure, have secured the reward of everlasting happiness for Seamus, and the heavenly glory he so richly deserves."

His words were sincere, but his quiet tone seemed to hold menace to the increasingly nervous priest.

"So now that his soul is safe for all eternity, we would like to accord him the respect and recognition he has so valiantly earned in his mortal life. And since we all co-operated in the spiritual rites you have so efficiently administered, I would feel gratified if you would agree to spend a little time longer here with us while we conduct our temporal tributes. Now would you do that for me Father?"

The question was rhetorical, and spoken with an air of authority that annulled the priest's earlier influence, as he now struggled to control his jangling nerves.

"Good" said the Dubliner, as the priest stood dumb and downcast.

"I'll take your silence as agreement then!" he said, re-iterating the priest's high-handed language of the previous evening.

He turned to face the gathering, and ignoring their smiling endorsement of his table-turning tactics, signalled to his partner with a curt nod. He in turn called out a sharp command, apparently to no one in particular. The response was instant.

From out of the assembled crowd stepped forward six young men, heavily dressed in mourning black. They arranged themselves in two rows of three along the sides of the coffin, then at a quiet signal, each drew a pistol from beneath their long overcoats, which they held across their chests. Finally they came smartly to attention. Two more young men stepped forward, and between them draped over the coffin the new flag of the infant Republic as they walked smartly down each side of it. Then they too took their places and stood at attention with guns drawn, facing the now traumatised priest and his awe-struck acolytes at the other end of the grave. The tall man and his partner watched all this in silence next to the priest, whose discomfort was plain for all to see, and who had now abandoned all hope of departing the scene in which he found himself trapped.

At that moment, Tomas and Margaret appeared with their mother, who was being led gently forward by yet another anonymous soldier, who had been despatched to bring them to the graveside. They gazed at the scene

21

in amazement. The tall man moved to welcome Mary, and took her hand courteously.

"Mrs Mulholland, dear lady," he said gently, "I hope you are recovered now."

She nodded silently that she was.

"Well enough to grant us your permission to continue with our ceremony I hope," he continued, "Because without it, our presence here would be nothing less than an unwarranted intrusion."

He paused allowing himself a brief but encouraging smile,

"It is our most fervent wish to accord your husband Seamus the military honours to which he is so rightly entitled, but we can do this only with your complete agreement and consent. I apologise for the dramatic way in which we seem to be springing this on you, but I'm sure you realise that keeping as low a profile as possible is an essential precaution that we who remain active in today's struggle must observe. I offer you my sincerest apologies for its necessity.

"Would you grant us this privilege, ma'am", he concluded gallantly.

Mary hesitated in slight confusion as she gazed at the scene before her. She glanced at her son for re-assurance. Tomas beamed back his delight, and Mary turned back reassured, a glint of hopeful joy on her face.

"I don't know who you are sir, nor your colleagues for that matter, and I will not embarrass you by asking your names. I am satisfied that if you thought it safe to do so you would have told us them by now."

She spoke with cautious pleasure.

"What I do know though is that by your presence here you have identified yourselves as friends who have come to pay tribute to my husband, and your behaviour has been both courteous and gallant since you arrived. After the requiem service in the church I had thought that all honour was to be denied him, but now..."

She gazed with gratification at the coffin draped in its flag of tribute. She smiled her pride, "Of course I want my husband to be honoured. It will please us greatly, and salve our pain, so please go on - with whatever it is that you intend to do."

The tall man bowed a salute to Mary before turning to address the assembly of mourners, who stood in silent anticipation waiting for him to speak.

"My Friends" he said, "I would like to start by telling you something of what has been happening most recently in our fight for Irish freedom. All of you understand what it was about, but not everyone knows all the details of what has been happening, so please bear with me if what I say sounds familiar to some of you.

"During the last few days, things have happened in Dublin that both thrill and chill those of us who took part in them. The brave uprising of the *Irish Volunteers*, and the declaration of a Republic, embodied as it was in the seizure and subsequent siege of the Post Office in O'Connell Street and those other strategic sites around the city is over."

Stark silence greeted his bland statement.

"On the face of it this was, as Father O'Malley here would have you believe, nothing more than another futile act, ill conceived by fools, and with no chance of success. Sadly, the bare facts of that opinion are true! The rebellion was doomed from the outset! Things went wrong, but even if they had not, then the concept of rebellion, in the face of the overwhelming odds against it, was ill timed and should perhaps have been postponed to a better day.

"However a lesson has been learned. The pity is that it has been learnt at an unaffordable cost, because it was paid with the blood of good and honourable men who trusted us to do better. Men like my dear friend Seamus Mulholland here, whose passing I shall forever mourn."

He paused in momentary distress before continuing, "So what was it all about? Just another sad episode to be added to Ireland's sorry history, now to be lamented in song and spoken of in legend only, by generations yet unborn? Is this Irishman's curse, you might ask - to fight and to fail! Some will tell you *Yes*! That's the way it is! That's the way it has always been!

"Well I tell you *No!* This is not the case today! I tell you this apparent failure is a beginning – *the beginning* - of Ireland's freedom! This rebellion has caused shock waves that are still reverberating round the halls of power in Westminster, the like of which have not been felt since the days of Cromwell. The bravery of a few Irish patriots, who held back the might of the world's greatest empire with nothing but a few rifles and their dauntless courage, has changed the face of Irish politics forever. By their sacrifice over seven glorious days, they have proved that the British can be challenged - and should be challenged. By their sacrifice they have shaken the foundations of established imperialism in Ireland. They have planted doubts in the minds of the complacent, and fear in the minds of the guilty.

"'The guilty? Who are the guilty? I hear you ask. I will tell you, my friends.

"The guilty are those who have served themselves during this conflict, and in so doing have plundered our country and destroyed our heritage - they are the guilty. They are those who have sponsored injustice and corruption in the institutions of government - they are the guilty. They are those who have become rich and powerful on the backs of the farmers and cotters that have worked their lands conscientiously for them, but yet remain impoverished - they are the guilty. They are those who have evicted honest men and their families from lands rightfully theirs, because they could not meet the impossible burdens of taxes and rents laid upon them, taxes and rents that reduced them to penury and homelessness. All of these people are the guilty.

"And yet worst of all, there are those who are guilty of murder!"

The tone in his voice had hardened and now they could detect anger, "It's May 7th today. Our comrades surrendered on April 30th, to save lives and prevent further bloodshed once they knew the fight was over. A lot of fine Irishmen died in this conflict, decent ordinary men who sacrificed themselves to their ideals. Future generations will honour them and rightly so. Many of their commanders died with them, but of these leaders, most were taken into custody that same day.

"I have to tell you three of those captured were put to death only three days later!"

A ripple of shock flowed through his audience, "These men got no trial; they were allowed no defence; they were given no chance to speak! They were simply murdered!"

A stunned silence prevailed as he continued, "Patrick Pearse, Thomas Macdonagh and Tom Clarke were taken out at dawn on the morning of May 3rd and executed in front of a firing squad. They were gunned down like animals one after the other. They had barely time to make their good-byes to their families and their peace with God.

"These were men of substance, and many, among their accusers even, spoke of them with admiration. Let me tell you who they were exactly, and just as importantly, who they were not, for they were not criminals to be callously cut down by the so-called advocates of British justice. No - that's certainly not who they were.

"Pearse was a headmaster, a barrister and a poet. He was a natural leader, who spoke vigorously of the right to self-determination and freedom. *'You cannot conquer Ireland, you cannot still the tide of freedom that will sweep all opposition before it,'* he said.

"He was right and he died, firm in his belief that right would prevail, even though sadly, he himself would not.

"Tom Clarke - skinny Tom - skeletal almost! He already knew what it was to be persecuted for the Cause, for he had already served sentence in Portland jail in England, where time after time he was thrown into solitary confinement. But seldom was he left alone there. Repeatedly he was subjected to cruellest ignominies and degradations that would have broken a lesser man in months – and Tom was there for six long years. With time in Chatham and Pentonville as well, his incarceration lasted a full fifteen and a half years in all. He knew he could never survive a jail sentence like that again. Now he doesn't have to!

"Thomas Macdonagh, ostensibly a renowned university lecturer, had a passion for Ireland's freedom that even surpassed his fervour for his academic vocation. This passion cost him not only his career, but his life as well.

"Who was it then that took upon themselves the right to terminate these men's lives? What authority decided that these honourable men were such a threat to the great British Empire that they had to be eliminated?

"Was it the judicial system? It was not! Was it the parliamentary government itself? It was not! Who then wielded the power of life and death over these patriots for freedom? I'll tell you, shall I?"

His listeners cried "Yes!"

An expression of angry frustration passed over his face as he continued,

"It was the military men at the height and heart of the mighty British war machine, led by no less a person than the C. in C. of His Majesty's Armed Forces in Ireland, General Sir John Grenfell Maxwell himself. He and his cohorts were given carte blanche to "sort out the rebels", in whichever way they thought fit, while the politicians to whom they were accountable turned their cowardly backs and looked the other way. These 'Soldiers of the Empire' are the guilty ones; there is blood aplenty on their hands. And to compound their crimes, they even refused to return the bodies of their victims to their families, denying them the right to Christian burial, and their loved ones the right to mourn their loss! Instead they buried them in quicklime!

"They could not risk them becoming martyrs in the eyes of the Irish people! The fools didn't recognise that by executing them so cruelly that's exactly what they have become!

"These murderers should fear for their lives, and in truth they should fear for their souls! They should tremble at the thought of the day when they have to face their God!"

As for a moment he paused to collect himself, the emotion in his voice evoked a murmur of response from his attentive audience, but when he spoke again his anger had gone, and in its place there was controlled composure.

"But today my Brothers and Sisters, thanks to his own son's swift initiative, we are able to mourn one such man of substance, our own dear friend and brother, Seamus Mulholland.

"We are here together to pay him tribute as one who decided 'enough is enough', and then stood up to be counted! We salute him as a soldier of our new Republic. For he and all others who died in this revolution have started a movement that will not be stopped. A movement which we, who survived the carnage are duty bound to carry forward, and establish as a living breathing reality in this land of ours. And let me reassure all of you, this we will do! We of the *Irish Republican Army* promise you, we will make it happen!"

He waited till their enthusiastic clamour had calmed, then he continued solemnly, "I will ask you now dear friends to observe two minute's silence, as we give our final tribute to this noble man."

Then standing firmly upright he addressed his men with authority, "Soldiers of the Irish Republic!"

They brought themselves to attention with a smart click of heels that produced a knock-on effect among the assembled watchers as men straightened their backs in instinctive response.

"Present Arms!" The guns were held aloft in straight-arm formation at forty five degrees.

"Fire!"

The explosion of eight guns echoed as one around the cemetery. Six times they fired before lowering their weapons. The gardeners lowered the coffin into its final resting place, and for the next minute, total silence ensued, in stark contrast to the thunderous detonations beforehand.

Later, as they drifted off in quiet order, moving in the direction of the Mulholland home, they left behind them the lonesome figure of an Irish piper, whose plaintive lament followed them on their way.

When they finally arrived at the house after a cold and wearisome walk, the welcoming smell of hot broth, mutton stew and newly baked bread assailed their senses and stirred their appetites to make their bellies rumble. Prepared for them by kind friends who had chosen not attend the funeral, but instead had stayed behind to prepare it all; it was a practical display of neighbourly hospitality, expressed in the preparation of a hot meal with which to nourish the hungry guests on this cold day. Additionally a plentiful supply of beer was arrayed across the sideboard inside, while for the abstemious, hot strong tea stood ready.

As he left the cemetery, Father O'Malley was in anguish, at odds with himself as to what he should do. Having been publicly humiliated by the Dublin men and their henchmen - hardly soldiers he thought, - skulking like cowards in the crowd around them, he was totally unsure of his next move.

Face! How to save his face! Revenge even, if that were possible! These black thoughts crowded his mind as confused and sullen, he wandered along in the wake of the now distant crowd, his acolytes trailing behind him.

As he approached his carriage, he looked up to see the tall man awaiting him, leaning on the open window of the carriage door - like a labourer whose lost his shovel - thought the priest ungraciously. What does he want now!

The Dubliner spoke, "Let me help you in Father." A slight smile stretched the corners of his mouth as he held open the door. The priest made to reply, but before he could the man continued,

"Will you be joining us at the house Father; the widow will surely be expecting you?"

The priest looked appalled at the idea and struggled to control his angry confusion. The thin man saw his anxiety and made to calm him, "Don't worry, I'll be there to support you, you have nothing to fear."

"Fear!" snapped the priest instinctively, "I'm not afraid of anyone. In this parish these people fear me, not I them! I have friends in high places I'll have you know sir! People of power and influence! I'm scared of no one!"

The tall man was tempted to challenge the priest about his social allegiances, but he refrained. 'Power and influence' suggested persons unsympathetic to all that he and his men represented.

"I'd re-think your last remarks if I were you Father. Whether you like it or not you have some fences to mend with the Mulhollands, and with your parishioners as well. A large number of them heard your insensitive discourse and more than a few were unimpressed. If you wish to retain any loyalty at all in this parish you will turn up at the wake later and make your apologies when you get there. It's not yet too late to undo the damage, but it will be if you are not seen to present yourself in a sympathetic mode. I'd be there within the hour if I were you, before the liquor takes hold and loosened tongues get malicious."

He paused before adding impishly, "At least this way, when the Bishop hears the story he might have some sympathy for your point of view as well as theirs"

"The Bishop!" spluttered the priest bewildered, "What's this got to do with the Bishop?

"Well he is a sympathiser now isn't he?"

The priest looked mystified.

"To the *Cause* Father, didn't you know?"

Father O'Malley looked dumbstruck, and as if in a dream climbed into the cab and slumped down in a corner with the air of a defeated man. The tall man closed the door quietly behind him and spoke softly as he leaned through the open window, "Obviously you *didn't* know, did you Father!" The priest sat shaking his head silently, watched by his fascinated acolytes.

The driver snapped his reins, clicked his tongue, and the horses moved off.

The Dubliner watched them go, then turned and headed towards the Mulholland home.

"I could be wrong" he mused, "Maybe it's the Bishop of Cork I'm thinking of," and the smile on his face broadened wickedly.

As he approached the house, he heard the sound of a concertina and a fiddle floating strains of lively music on the air, a backdrop to the buzz of happy chatter, which carried towards him as the guests celebrated in true Irish tradition the passing of a dear friend into the presumed joy of his eternal reward.

He entered, and a jolly-faced woman in a blousy dress welcomed him with eyes wide in awe and admiration. She thrust a pot of black beer into his hand. As he smiled his thanks, she quickly pointed across the room to where Mary was seated, flanked by her attentive son and his wife and a crowd of caring friends. The strain of the past days was noticeably absent from the widow's face as those around tended her every wish, distracting her from her grief, if only for the moment.

He edged his way over to them and after paying his respects, joined in the general small talk, awaiting an opportunity to introduce the subject of the priest's impending visit. It came unexpectedly, and at a time when the atmosphere was most relaxed and the family at their most receptive.

Tomas was relating tales of happy times spent as a boy with his father. He was regaling the company with a story of his father's relationship with

Father Brendan, Seamus's life long friend and priest of the day at that time in the parish, when as young men they were both full of fun and more than their fair share of mischief.

"They would go to the *hurling* every Saturday" he said with enthusiasm "but not just to watch the game. They were just as keen on getting into Murphy's afterwards, where I might add they were known to indulge more than a little in the "*divil drink*", despite Murphy's many attempts to control them.

"The first time I was there, I was fifteen, and while I was quite used to see my father a little inebriated, I had never seen Father Brendan the worse for wear before. I couldn't believe my eyes - or my ears!"

Tomas chuckled and paused to take a drink himself in concert with his tale.

"It was when my dad questioned Father Brendan about his sins of intemperance that my jaw fell open. But when he went on to suggest they should hear each other's confessions, I thought a bolt from heaven would strike us all dead!"

He laughed loudly and they laughed with him.

"The conversation went something like this", he said, '*You can't hear my confession, Seamus, you are not a priest*'

'*We're both fathers aren't we, so I'll forgive you and you can forgive me. Get down on your knees and I'll start now! Confess your drunken ways!*'

'*I repeat, you can't hear my confession, Seamus, you've not been ordained*'

"My dad got a bit miffed at this, and became a little belligerent", '*I don't have to hear your sins anyway, I've been with you all day; I know what you've been up to*'.

"His sober logic belied his intoxicated condition," laughed Tomas.

"'*I can hear yours though,*' continued the priest ignoring my father."

'*You don't have to hear mine either. For the same reason, we've been together all day! Your sins are my sins and that's that*'

"The argument was incontestable.

'*Just forgive me*' he hiccupped

"Father Brendan gestured a wavering blessing and slurred his way through the Latin words."

'Ego te absolvo pecattis tuis.........'

"*'Ditto'* was my dad's reply"

"*'Ditto!'* said Father Brendan in astonishment and then he reached out for the bottle between them,"

'What do you mean, ditto!'

'The Ego thing - Ditto, from me to you'

"*'You can't ditto me'* insisted Father Brendan,"

'You're not a priest!'

'The church says we must forgive. So I forgive you'

"Dad's logic was slipping"

'That's different Seamus'

'Why'

'I can't remember but it is'.

"Father Brendan was as hazy as the smoke all around him"

"*'Some priest you turned out to be. Always knew you couldn't keep two thoughts in your head, you were the same at school'*

"*'If you are going to insult me I'm leaving'* said Brendan and made to rise."

'Go on then, get petty! Feck off if you must!'

"I was flabbergasted, but bursting to laugh as well. I just daren't" said Tomas,

"*'Who's paying for the whiskey'* said Father Brendan ignoring my father's obscenity.

"*'I'll pay'* said Dad, *'but if I do I'll have no money for the collection tomorrow;'*

"*'So I pay - one way or the other'* said the priest.

'You can't have your cake and eat it'

"*'We haven't had any cake'* said Brendan, and he looked as though he would love some. It was hilarious, it really was. Dad said,"

'If you don't get back to the presbytery, you won't have any tea either'

"*'I've got confessions at seven'* said Father Brendan,"

"'Don't start that again' said my Dad".

"'God bless you Seamus' said Brendan, and got up to go."

"'God bless you Father. See you tomorrow'. Then as an afterthought Dad said,

'Try not to breathe on anyone during Confessions!'"

Tomas was beside himself with laughter as he finished the story, and all around him people were laughing with him. His mother looked amused, but pensive.

"I was fifteen" he repeated, "I couldn't believe it"

The Dubliner saw his chance

"Seamus was a wonderful man and a devout Catholic, Tomas, was he not?"

"He certainly was" mused his son, still smiling at his reminiscences.

"What about you Tomas, are you still the god-fearing Catholic man your father taught you to be? Do you still respect your religion, the Church - your priest?"

"What does that mean?" said Tomas, defensively.

"Simply this, Tomas. Your father would not be happy to see his son in confrontation with the Church he loved and respected. Nor with its priests."

Tomas's mood darkened.

"I've not quarrelled with the priest. What are you trying to say?"

"Only this Tomas. For the sake of your father's memory and what you know his wishes would be, in the interest of your family's good name and your mother's peace of mind, you must put aside your anger at this time, justified though it is."

Then he added gravely,

"You must forgive this priest and make him welcome in this house."

Tomas looked sternly at the Dubliner who remained calm as they searched each other's eyes.

"If my mother doesn't forgive him, why should I?" he said finally.

"Your mother has already forgiven him Tomas"

Tomas looked hesitant, as the Dubliner explained, "She needs her priest Tomas, good or bad, he's part of her life's purpose, as is the Church. She's forgiven him already – why don't you ask her."

Tomas hesitated and his brows creased as he considered what he was hearing. Then he turned to his mother who was engaged brightly with her guests. He bent down and whispered a question in her ear. They talked briefly in undertones as the room chatted around them. Mary's face took on an anxious expression as she looked into her son's eyes and nodded.

Taking only a second to gaze at her, Tomas put his arms around her, and hugged her where she sat. After a moment she relaxed again, and Tomas stood up to face the Dubliner.

"You are a very astute man sir," he said "One day I believe you could become a great leader in this land of ours, and I for one shall look forward to that. You are right! My mother does want to put the shock and sorrow of today behind her. She wants to forgive and forget. So that's how it must be.

"For my part however, I cannot and will not forgive that man for the insults he has heaped on my father's memory, and the pain he has caused my mother. But I will make my peace. If he comes he'll be made welcome in this house."

"He'll come," replied the Dubliner, "but before he does, I have something to give you Tomas, and something to say."

He held out an envelope, which Tomas accepted with great curiosity.

"You have made a vow to avenge the murder of your father Tomas, and there are few here who doubt your sincerity. But vengeance is a fickle emotion born in the heat of pain and sorrow. It can cool with the passage of time, when people forget or even doubt their own motivations as wounds heal. This is not so with justice, which must always be served whenever possible. An injustice today is an injustice forever, until it has been righted. This letter is to help you in this regard. If ever you wish to forget the death of your father and the way it was brought about, then so be it."

He held up his hand to quell Tomas's protests,

"If you think you will never see justice done in this matter and are unable to complete your vow, then that is alright too. But if as time goes by you find need to refresh your belief in the righteousness of what you have sworn, then this might help you to sustain it.

"It is your authorization to act in this matter on behalf of the Army Council of the IRA, the movement your father served so well.   Read it whenever you need to. This is not a matter for personal vengeance. You act for the *Cause* Tomas; you are a soldier."

They paused in silence and gripped each other's hands tightly in mutual friendship.

"Put it away now before the priest gets here," said the tall man.

Tomas mumbled his uncertain thanks, took the letter to the bedroom, and carefully secreted it away among his personal papers, still unsure of its precise contents. He would read it at his leisure. Then he returned to the living room, and took his place among his guests. Almost immediately, there was a hum of surprise, followed by an uncomfortable silence, as the priest appeared at the doorway.

❧

The atmosphere chilled, like a cold mist over a lake, as the priest stood and scanned the faces about him, uncertainty in his eyes. Tomas stiffened instinctively, and his mother's recent peace faded to be replaced by her earlier anxieties at her son's hostile demeanour. The tall man appraised the situation quickly and acted.

"Father O'Malley" he said lightly. "You came. Look Tomas, Father O'Malley is here."

Tomas reacted to the prompt instantly, and restraining his animosity, forced himself to relax. His mother smiled encouragement to him and as his tension eased, she relaxed with him. He spoke, loud enough for all to hear, as he went forward to meet his scarcely favoured guest. He proffered a reluctant handshake.

"Come in Father, you're welcome in this our house." He turned towards his wife.

"Margaret, will you get Father O'Malley a drop of the good stuff and something to eat."

They shook hands and smiled wanly at each other. Margaret also smiled, with amusement at their expressions, but pleased to oblige she went to get the drink. The room relaxed, and people resumed their previous chatter.

"I'll not need the food, Tomas," said the priest" "But I'll gladly accept a drink. I've come to pay my respects to your mother, in my capacity as a family friend you understand, not as your pastor. So a drink will be most welcome and I thank you for your hospitality."

It was formal and a little stiff, but it served to melt the ice between them. Father O'Malley felt re-assured again, as he made his way across to where Mary was seated, his composure returning with every step. As he approached she made to rise.

"No Mary, sit you back in your chair. You don't have to stand up for me." He was back to his patronising best again.

Margaret returned with the whiskey, which glistened in the glass, amber and inviting. The priest was known to have a weakness for good Irish whiskey, and he beamed his pleasure as Margaret passed it to him. His gratitude was genuine enough.

He sat next to Mary, in a chair readily proffered by an attendant companion, who then moved off to engage elsewhere, and together they talked in pleasant but subdued tones. He chatted kindly though in a condescending manner, his words laced with clichéd platitudes, but Mary did not seem to notice and she was consoled, as always, to have her chaplain beside her.

As the afternoon wore on, the visitors from far away began to depart to their homes, blanketed against the cold that would descend on them as they retraced their weary paths along the same long roads that had brought them here. A daylight start at this time of year was still advised to avoid the chilly discomfort of the night air.

Those who stayed continued to gorge themselves on the food and the drink that was constantly replenished by the anonymous neighbours who inconspicuously provided it. As the drink flowed the noise increased, and the conversations began to be boisterous. The men had polarised into groups of common interest. A couple of livestock farmers were arguing heatedly about animal husbandry, while another group discussed the unlikely expectation of extending their small dairy herds. In a corner two farriers were forging improbable tales of difficult horses they had shod.

Meantime, the women, led by Mary, had sensibly retreated to the kitchen to gossip more discerningly and circumspectly than their noisy partners.

The biggest group of men had formed around the Dubliners, who managed to divert probing questions about their identities but failed to achieve the low profile they would have wished for. Surrounded by an enthusiastic crowd of admirers, they were plied with a barrage of questions. Their affiliations, their plans to fight on, their belief in freedom for Ireland were typical topics of frequently repeated enquiries. They managed to answer most of them with necessarily vague generalisations and diplomatically obscure promises for the future, but as the drink went down the questions became more and more probing, and even the faint-hearted became emboldened.

"Did you know Patrick Pearse?" said one to the tall man's companion

"Very Well"

"Did you know Roger Casement?"

"I did"

"Will they execute him?"

"I hope not, although I fear they will."

"Is it true he was queer?"

"I wouldn't dignify that question with an answer. What I will tell you is that Roger Casement – Sir Roger Casement – knighted by the same government that now holds him in prison while it besmirches his name before they brand him a traitor and kill him, is and always will be a true friend of Ireland, and the concept of an independent Irish Republic is near to his heart. He is one of us, a member of the Irish Volunteers for the past three years. He looked for support for the *Cause*, and when he couldn't find it among his English peers in Westminster, he turned to Germany for help in the form of guns and people. It all went wrong for him, they supplied him with nothing more than a token handful of weapons, and the Irishmen he courted in their Prisoner of War camps refused to join the fight for freedom. He got caught when he returned to Ireland, some say he was betrayed, and now they hold him in Pentonville gaol, where one day they will surely hang him."

His now enthusiastic interrogator switched focus,

"Do you think the Fenians will get that Maxwell bastard? Will they kill the satanic sod?"

It was at this point that Father O'Malley, overhearing this remark, chose to intervene. He had excused himself earlier from Mary and her companions, and graduated towards the noisy circles of men. Having been afforded the hospitality of the house and having appropriated the whiskey bottle, he proceeded to move around quite relaxed, quietly confident in his restored station as spiritual counsellor, and convinced of his status in what after all was 'his community'.

Mary had smiled with amusement as she noted that he had secured the whiskey and now carried it with him, topping up his glass as required, while reluctantly dispensing only the most meagre of measures to others who had the audacity to approach him for refills as he wandered around from group to group.

"I really don't think this is the time or the place for demonising anyone," he interjected with characteristic smugness, in answer to what he perceived as an unkind denunciation of General Sir John Maxwell.

"And especially against a man who, in carrying out his duty, managed to restore order out of anarchy." he pontificated.

"No matter what your politics might be, no one should wish ill on another human being, and certainly not his death? Charity must prevail above all. We are all God's children, from the best to the worst of us. We are all sinners, and we must forgive those who sin against us, - assuming that is, that we have been sinned against at all - as indeed God forgives us"

He spoke with a slur in his voice and a slight smile that flew in the face of the mood of the conversing protagonists who turned on him with some animosity.

"This is a political discussion - a temporal matter Father, not a spiritual one. I suggest you keep your religious psychotherapy out of it."

It was the second of the Dublin pair who spoke very sharply.

"Because we fight oppression and search for liberty does not mean we are godless men."

The priest failed to acknowledge the menace in his tone, an inane smile across his now ruddy complexion.

"I have spoken earlier on these matters, and you know my thoughts. You heard them today. You could do well to listen to them," said the priest, sounding slightly drunk, slightly loud, and exceedingly pompous.

"I think it's time you went home Father O'Malley," said the Dublin man coldly, "before you offend your host"

"Why should I be offended?" said Tomas, who had come up behind, unnoticed.

They hesitated to reply.

"Tell me!" Tomas insisted.

"Father O'Malley has had a drop too much, Tomas. He's just leaving."

Tomas bristled instantly.

"Have you said something to insult my father again?" Instantly his anger flared, and he had to battle to contain himself.

"I have said all I need to say on that subject, I will not repeat it all again" slurred the priest, striving to maintain his equilibrium.

Tomas lost control completely.

"Get out of this house, you contemptible little fraud! You're so full of shit it's a wonder you can stand your own smell! It's hypocrites like you that betray the Irish people. Priest of God! Man of the people! My arse! You're nothing but a black suited impostor! You'll get in where a rat won't, - with the bloody squire - and his high and bloody mighty cronies, the very people who are suppressing us!"

He waved an encompassing arm around the room.

"They are suppressing all these people! Your flock - your people! You should be on our side, you bastard!"

Tomas was becoming increasingly inflamed.

"You make me sick! You're nothing but a self-seeking, self-centred bigot! The worst kind of charlatan! Get out of this house! If you ever come back in here again I'll kill you. Get out!" he yelled.

He was seething and lunged towards the priest with menace. The Dubliners restrained him, as the priest shied away, first in shock and then in anger.

The tall man's partner then took hold of him by the shoulder and forced him towards the door, but he resisted and shook himself free.

"I'll have my say", he said, and his anger had sobered him somewhat; his fear had faded.

"You are like them all round here, Tomas Mulholland. You are a malcontent," he hissed.

"You just can't accept that people like you are born to *serve*, not to lead. Your father's mistakes will be perpetuated in you for sure and probably in your sons."

He turned his attention on the Dubliners and snarled,

"As for you brave heroes, criminals more like! You teach hatred and promote anarchy against the right and the righteous, because you are filled with envy. Yes envy! Envy against those who are born better than you, richer than you, with more authority than you. You don't fight for an ideal. You fight for yourselves. You fight to take what you can never otherwise own, and you don't care too much how you get it, just as long as you do get it. And the same goes for these others around you. All of you! You're not patriots, fighting for freedom and justice, you're just small time gangsters and thugs, fighting to line your pockets and your reputations, so that when your "war" is over and the English have gone, you can be the new masters, and the people will rejoice in your success, and the blood the pain and the heartache will be forgotten, and you'll all be rich. Some hope!

"Well you won't succeed, 'cos you haven't got it in you to succeed! None of you! All you will achieve is to keep Ireland down - in the bog, while the bloodletting goes on. I hope you get caught, and I for one will do all in my power to see that you do!"

He turned on his heel to leave.

In a fit of blazing anger Tomas shrugged off the men holding him, and raged forward. He struck the retreating priest on the back of the neck with a heavy blow that felled him instantly. The little man crumpled and crashed to the floor with a thud where he lay still, his eyes closed, his head at an incongruous angle.

For a long time no one moved, they stood gazing at the fallen priest in silent horror, till eventually the tall man slowly bent down over him, close to his face. He raised an eyelid. He listened to his heart and his breathing. He felt for a pulse. Then he shook his head. He rose slowly. He looked at Tomas, who stared back at him, grey with shock, his mouth hanging open.

"He's dead, Tomas, his neck's broken." He spoke in calm but grave tones.

Tomas stood benumbed, his shoulders heaving.

"He can't be dead; I didn't hit him that hard," then questioningly,

"Did I?"

He paused, ashen faced, as no one answered.

"Oh God, what have I done! I didn't mean to kill him; I really didn't mean to kill him. What will I do?"

Word of the incident travelled swiftly to the kitchen. Margaret came rushing through and gasped at the sight before her, her fist clenched in her teeth to stifle the scream that fought to escape. Behind her Mary followed with the remaining women. She stood stiffly and swayed slightly when she saw the prostrate figure on the floor before her.

"What happened?" she whispered. "Who did this?"

"It was an accident, an unfortunate accident," said the second Dubliner, less than convincingly, and his voiced trailed away as he failed to find the words of an acceptable explanation. Tomas spoke up.

"It was no accident, mother," he choked.

"I hit him, he fell, and he broke his bloody neck. Jesus, I didn't hit him that hard!"

He moaned slightly and shook his head as he gulped air into his heaving lungs.

"I'm a bloody murderer!"

He grabbed at a chair for support.

Margaret rushed to her husband and clutching him to her, held him tightly to her in an attempt to console him. The tall man ushered them away from the scene into an adjacent bedroom, and as he did so he signalled silently to his companion to take the immediate matter of the fallen priest in hand, before closing the door behind him to exclude the horrified onlookers.

Mary moved over to face her son. As she spoke her voice was tight, but composed.

"You are no murderer Tomas, but they will say that you are. They'll come for you. You can't stay here. You must get away and you must go quickly! If you stay, you will be arrested and they will execute you, as surely as they executed your father."

She was shaking as she spoke.

"I didn't intend to kill him!" pleaded Tomas, desperately seeking to rationalise things in his mind.

"There are people here who heard you say you would kill him, Tomas," said the tall man, as he placed a hand on his shoulder.

"Your mother is right, you must go. If you stay, you will be arrested and tried. Father O'Malley had, on his own assertions, powerful friends in this society, and many of them are English. You cannot risk being tried by any court in this area. You wouldn't stand a chance."

Mary spoke up again, and there was a note of urgency in her voice.

"You must go away to England. There's work there, in the coalfields, and you have your cousin Michael there to help you. I have his address."

Tomas listened to his mother as if in a dream with child-like attention, saying nothing.

Mary turned to Margaret who was in better control of herself.

"You must leave too, Margaret. They will come here looking for all of you, so in the meantime you must go to Dublin and lose yourselves in the city until Tomas has found work and a place for you and the children. We have plenty relatives there to hide you, and you will be safe till Tomas sends for you."

Margaret nodded,

"We'll do that mother," she said, "But what about you. You must come with us; we can't go without you. You can't live here on your own?"

"I'll be fine, they won't bother me. I'm an old woman. There wouldn't be anything for me in England."

"I can't bear to think of you without us around you" Margaret said, "I hate the thought of you being alone. You belong with us, we must stay together."

Mary shook her head,

"I have my friends nearby, and my sister is not too far away. I'll be fine. You must go. You have a life to live and a future to make for the children. Unfortunately that future can no longer be here. I must stay here, where Seamus is."

"What will we do about Father O'Malley?" asked Tomas, still traumatised.

The tall man spoke up, "We are taking care of him." he said firmly,

"Once you have gone, his body will be returned to the church for a proper burial. By that time you must be well away from here, because as soon as they put two and two together, they'll come after you Tomas. Your mother is right. You must prepare to leave in the morning – with us!" He glanced towards his companion, who had entered to join them. He nodded his agreement.

"Take only a minimum of what you need, even for the children. We will leave at daybreak. By the time you are on the ferry to England, we will have returned the body. And by then Margaret and the children will have disappeared into the Dublin suburbs."

Margaret and Tomas went to Mary and for some few minutes they hugged each other tightly. When Mary spoke again her eyes were full and glistening.

"We must try to rest now. Sleep may prove difficult, but we must rest nevertheless. You have a long journey tomorrow."

She paused, and for a moment she looked helpless and confused, like a child.

Margaret looked at her with an aching love and a yearning desire to take the sadness and bear it for her. Mary seemed to have grown old in this instant, and her anguish was clear to see.

This woman had been her mother since she was six years old. She had lost her own parents to a winter plague of pneumonia, all those years ago, and she herself had almost died. Seamus had brought her home, an orphan child, to his house, sickly and weak. Mary had nursed her day and night through two weeks of intense fever, feeding her on beef tea and "hot sweet milky *boily*", a hand-me-down potion that only she could prepare, and slowly Margaret had improved. She grew stronger daily and eventually the fever left her. Since that day she had lived with them, and with them she had blossomed into beautiful womanhood.

Tomas had protected her as his little sister when a girl, and then fallen in love with her as a woman, and they had married – but only after confusion over the requirements of Holy Church's law on *Affinity*, and the granting of a necessary dispensation by the bishop of the diocese. Margaret had given them their grandchildren, who they adored and now she belonged to them wholly and entirely, and they belonged to her. And she had wished for nothing more, she was content with her lot. Now as she spoke it all seemed to be lost,

"We'll send for you," she said in a voice tinged with desperation.

"You can come and live with us in England, - at least for a while - a holiday! We'll all be together again! Soon!"

They looked at each other, knowingly, recognising that this was an unlikely prospect, but Mary nodded,

"Of course dear. Soon." she said with quiet resignation.

Tomas took his mother in his arms, hugged her again for a long time and cried softly on her shoulder,

"I'm sorry mother, I'm so sorry" he sobbed.

ᴄꙬ

They left the next day at first light, accompanied to the train by their tormented mother. They travelled by cart to the railway station, escorted by the Dubliners who with their "soldiers" stayed long enough to see them board safely, before all but one vanished into the countryside, as mysteriously as they had arrived those few ill-fated days previously. In a state of emotional turmoil Tomas and Margaret hung from the open compartment window to make their final goodbyes, before the train shuffled off along the narrow track, one single carriage for passengers and the regular two old box cars for the milk run, carrying the daily yield to the factories which churned out the cheeses and butters so famous and familiar across Ireland, and equally so in most of England's suburban homes.

So much of our lives are tied to England, reflected Tomas, as he cradled the sleepy forms of his two sons under his arms, and gazed across the fields that passed too quickly by. Will we ever be free? Can we ever lift this yoke? His heart was heavy for he feared that this was his last view of his beloved country. He felt sure he would never return. As his anguish possessed him further, he vowed that no matter where they settled in England, he would teach his children their heritage, and preach to them that above all things they were Irish, first and last and always. Margaret bit her lip and pulled her baby daughter close to her, as across the carriage she watched the pain etched on her husband's face, suffering it all with him.

Behind on the platform, Mary stared in anguish as the train rattled its way out of sight round the first bend in the track, and then strained her ears to capture the last sounds of its fading departure. When there was nothing more to hear, she stood motionless as the silence on the air enveloped her like a shroud and filled her with a desperate sense of isolation. Then aching inside, she turned and left the empty station, and her new companion followed closely behind her.

Chapter 4

They came in the night…

They came in the night, and hammered on the door. Mary woke with a frightened start. Tomas sprang immediately to mind. They had come for him! She had barely time to light the lamp beside her bed and pull on a robe, before the door burst open under the rain of their rifle buts. Mary held up the lamp to gaze into the red face of a khaki-uniformed sergeant, sporting a black Glengarry cap.

"We've come for your murdering bastard son!" he snarled in a threatening Scottish accent,

"Where is he?"

His eyes scanned the room and seeing no one but Mary, waved his troops forward to search the house. They pushed unceremoniously past, and set about their task with wild ferocity. In a wave of unrestrained vandalism they overturned tables and chairs, tossed linen to the floor, smashed crockery, and pierced the mattresses on the beds with their bayonets. They tore the doors off cupboards and wardrobes, and they ripped the shutters from the windows. Only the rafters above them were strong enough and remote enough to resist their wanton destruction. Through all of it Mary stood silently watching, covering her ears against the noise and the foul and abusive language that assailed her. In less than an hour they had finished, each one shrugging a futile gesture to the sergeant who paraded amongst them, while glowering in angry displeasure at Mary.

"Where is the bastard?" he snarled at her.

Mary said nothing as she glared back defiantly.

"If you don't tell me where he is, I'll burn this house to the ground."

For a moment a flicker of fear showed in her face before she regained her composure.

"As you have found out for yourself, Tomas is not here," she managed to say. He is safely away, from you and your kind. It matters little where that is, since he is well beyond your reach. You people murdered my husband, but you will not be able to do the same to my son. He is free of you all. As for me you don't scare me. It will serve you neither profit nor purpose to harm me, but do whatever you wish, I cannot stop you."

The sergeant stepped close, and raised his hand as if to slap her. She glared back without flinching. His men watched impassively, but their attention stayed his hand.

"Torch it" he said and stalked to the door. "Burn it to the ground!"

The soldiers lit papers and scattered lamp oil over towels, sheets and blankets. The fire took hold quickly, and the flames leapt high to the roof and the thatch. As the soldiers hurried outside, one of them turned to Mary.

"Better get out now missus, this place is like a tinder box, they all are. Believe me we know. We've burnt a few, I can tell you!"

They gathered outside and watched the fire spread, then they stood frozen when they realised that Mary had not come out. Looking back at the house, they gazed in subdued silence at the sight before their eyes.

Silhouetted against the raging flames, Mary stood at the window and prayed, passing her rosary beads through the fingers of her right hand, while in her left the silver figure of Christ Crucified on a cross of black ebony, appeared to take on a life of its own, as it reflected the shimmering flames around her. They stepped back as the fire gathered ferocity, and suddenly above her the turf-covered roof erupted in a ball of flame. As the air rushed in the heat intensified to an unbearable level, and Mary raised her hands to protect herself, and fear was suddenly etched across her previously calm face. Almost immediately the rafters caved in on her and she was felled by a blazing beam.

Outside they continued to watch, stunned by what they were witnessing. No one moved at all, and for a moment a flicker of concern crossed the face of the sergeant as he gazed at the scene before him, but then it passed as he commented,

"Well that's one less Mick to worry about," he said with heartless indifference. "It should help smoke out her son when he hears about this." But when he laughed at his own joke, his false bravado drew no response from his men, whose contempt was conspicuous in the glances that passed between them.

In the dawn light, all that was left were the gable ends and the dying embers of the burnt out rafters that crackled and hissed as they spat out small tongues of angry flames. The lowing of unattended cows in the shed nearby sent a mournful lament across the fields and the bogs, heard in the early mist by only one man, who stood crying as he gazed at the ruins before him. Slowly he slumped to his knees, and his wretched sobbing continued.

❧

Tomas stirred to consciousness in his chair on the deck of the Liverpool bound steam packet as it cut a channel through the dark choppy waters of the Irish Sea in the cold of the night. He felt chilled, but the chill inside him was only partially related to the windy blast that cut across the deck, causing his fellow travellers to huddle down further into the thin protection of their ship's issue blankets. Steerage passengers had to rough the conditions on deck, and try to ignore the sounds and smells of affluence that emanated from the better class quarters below.

Tomas's chill however was more a sense of foreboding, which had possessed him as he contemplated his distant wife and children, and the image of his mother, which had so vividly sprung into his mind at that moment. He tried to sleep again, but did so only fitfully, and his unease was still with him when they finally docked at Liverpool.

❧

The sergeant stood to attention before the officer seated behind the large oak desk and prepared to report. He was ready to lie to save himself from the wrath of this officer known to his men as the *'Psychopath'*. He would tell him what he wanted to hear, because to tell him anything less could bring down vengeful response that at best would cost him his stripes, and at worst could see him in the "glasshouse" - for a very long time. Captain James Spencer Lambert was a man you didn't cross, not at any price.

"Mission accomplished, sir. Mulholland is dead. Burnt to death in his own house, with his mother, sir. We caught him just before he was about to fly the coop, sir. Wouldn't surrender sir, even when the place was on fire, and his mother wouldn't come out either. Didn't find the wife and kids though, they must have left beforehand, sir."

"You are sure it was him sergeant."

"Yes sir, that's if his name is Thomas, 'cos that's what she called him sir - his mother."

He watched and waited as Spencer-Lambert considered what he was hearing. He wasn't totally happy with the sergeant's report, and for a moment he stared at him solidly, watching his eyes, looking for an indication that he might be lying. The sergeant stared straight past him, remaining firmly at attention. His face did not flicker. Finally Spencer-Lambert spoke,

"OK sergeant, you may go now."

The sergeant snapped to attention, saluted sharply and turned to leave.

"Sergeant" said the officer stopping him at the door, "You will be sure to tell this story to others exactly as you have told it to me, won't you?" There was an undercurrent of threat in his voice that the sergeant didn't miss.

"I wouldn't like to hear later that you and your men used unwarranted force in trying to apprehend Mulholland. The fire *was* accidental wasn't it, Sergeant?" His comment lacked sincerity, and the sergeant was quick to recognise it.

"Absolutely sir, they must have knocked a lamp over in their anxiety to escape sir." He smiled cynically at Lambert who nodded back with a degree of satisfaction. He waited uncertainly while the officer studied him closely again. He found his gaze unnerving, but then the Captain spoke again.

"Sergeant, he said, "When you leave the army, look me up. I might have work for a man of your talents, someone who can enforce authority. Have you ever considered taking a private security job in civilian life?"

"Not really sir," answered the sergeant, surprised at the line of questioning.

"Do you think you could persuade men to live up to their responsibilities, say miners acting unofficially, striking unlawfully in pursuit of unreasonable wage demands and the like? Could you help the police evict such people from their tied cottages, if necessary?"

"I'd revel in a job like that sir, I really would!" replied the Sergeant enthusiastically.

"Good. Then look me up when you are discharged. As I say, I can find work for someone like you. "You may go now – till we meet again!"

"Thank you sir, thank you! I'll be out within a year!" He threw up a second salute, and then he turned and marched smartly from the room, a broad smile on his face, his eyes bright with excitement.

Chapter 5

Durham County

The journey from Liverpool was long and tedious and it was a weary Tomas who embarked on the final leg to where his cousin would meet him in Eastinglea. He boarded a train in Durham City, and slumped wearily into the corner of the empty carriage. With a sigh he settled back and attempted to sleep. As the train jerked into motion, he awakened. Opening his grit-filled eyes he gazed languidly out of the window at the passing scene outside.

As he train moved faster, it spewed behind it a trail of white smoke, that reached backwards towards the majestic structure of the great cathedral which rose high above the city below, where narrow winding streets twisted through buildings of classic architecture, and the colourful shops were already busy with the day's trade and customers. To Tomas it all seemed strange and unfamiliar. The carriage rocked rhythmically as the train chugged onwards to Sunderland and points east, and the sight of beautiful Durham vanished from sight.

Almost immediately the train ran into a succession of mining villages, each with a defining pithead, and grimy streets of terraced houses lined up in monotonous rows, surrounded by ugly slagheaps, which towered darkly over everything in self- defining purpose. Tomas felt apprehensive and fearful of what he saw. He felt unhappy about surrendering himself to such an environment - a coal dependant economy. He yearned to be able to turn back the clock - just a few short weeks - so he could make things happen differently. This was a journey into a world from which he might never escape, and which would determine the future not only for himself, but his wife in Ireland, and the children he and Margaret had been blessed with.

Though in the moment it was a thought Tomas refused to accede to, subconsciously he knew it was unlikely he would ever return to his beloved Ireland.

Eastinglea station was a miserable affair, two flat open platforms on either side of the track, with only a small wooden shelter on each side. His cousin was nowhere in sight, as he stepped off the train, so he retreated to the shoddy protection of the sad little shack to wait for him. He pushed open the door, and immediately a sulphurous grey-green cloud spewed out from a coal-packed fire, assaulting his eyes and nostrils, and those of the other waiting people within, polluting the entire atmosphere in the seconds it took him to shut out the draught as he struggled to close the ill-fitting door behind him. The blandly decorated room boasted only a brown fitted bench seat, which ran round the entire interior, save at the entrance, and the place where the black cast-iron fireplace was fitted into the chimney wall.

Tomas moved up to the dully-glowing coals, where two other men stood similarly seeking comfort from its limited warmth. They glanced briefly at him before resuming their conversation in language that fell strangely upon his ears.

Standing with his back to the fire, he gazed out through rain spotted, grime smeared windows towards the more conspicuous comfort of the brightly illuminated pub just beyond the boundary fence of the railway premises. He wondered if he dared go there to wait till Michael appeared to take him in charge.

That Michael was not yet here to meet him was typical of the man, thought Tomas, for as a boy, he was notoriously late for everything, except his meals. He smiled as he concluded that life's adult responsibilities had obviously not changed this particular characteristic. He decided to stay put, worried that he might not recognise Michael from inside the *"Station Hotel, Eastinglea"*.

It was then that the door rattled open again, and as another cloud of obnoxious gas assailed them, a tall young man entered. It was Michael, looking hale and hearty, and easily recognisable by the impish grin and the laughing eyes, in the now older and leaner face of a handsome mature man.

"Good God Tomas, you've aged," he said provocatively in a stentorian voice tinged with that unfamiliar dialect Tomas had just heard from the two others present, which reminded him instantly of the soldiers in the Dublin baker's yard who had been party to his father's murder. It shocked him somewhat, and he retorted with some resentment,

"Are you so happy to be in England Michael, that you have discarded your Irish tongue already?"

Michael laughed, "Tomas, Tomas," he said, "I haven't seen you these past five years, and already you're fightin' me."

He smiled mischievously below thick eyebrows raised in mock offence, as he strode forward and embraced Tomas enthusiastically.

"Let's go have a pint in the pub there, before we get into the arguing, man."

Tomas was suddenly embarrassed, and smiled sheepishly at the watching strangers who were taking a quizzical interest in their conversation.

"Sorry Michael, I'm sorry. Let's do that. A pint will be most welcome," he said apologetically.

"Good! Let's go!" Michael bent to take Tomas's suitcase, but Tomas stopped him.

"All I've got in the world right now is in that bag, Michael, so I'll take care of it. It's not heavy and I've become very attached to it since leaving........."

"Belfast!" interrupted Michael loudly. " Since leaving Belfast! Of course, I understand, how is Belfast?

"Let's go have a pint in the pub there," he repeated, " You can tell me how the old city looks these days."

A bemused and confused Tomas took a seat in the bar of the Station Hotel, utterly flabbergasted by Michael's strange reference to Belfast, and their rapid departure from the smoky waiting room. Michael brought the pints to the table and sat down. Then anticipating Tomas's questions said,

"It was the Colliery Agent, Tomas. Mr Simon Perkins - there in the waiting room. He works for the coal owners. He's a most powerful man He was taking more than a just a passing interest in our conversation. He was aware of your Irish accent, and alert to what we were saying. He's a bible-punching bigot, one of the worst anti-Catholics you could ever meet round here. And when it comes to working, he is the man who has power to hire and to fire. You don't want to get on the wrong side of him on your first day here."

He took a sip of his beer before continuing. Tomas copied his example, and was surprised how good it tasted, even though it lacked the rich flavour of the black beer he was used to. Michael wiped away his frothy moustache and continued,

"The mine managers are not too favourably inclined towards the southern Irish right now, not since the Uprising. They see every Paddy as a potential troublemaker. His Lordship lost quite a bit of money on his properties in Dublin, and that pleases him not one jot! If you are to get a job here, Tomas, you are going to have to change your place of birth. The Northern counties have the only acceptable Irish flavour right now, but since the English can't distinguish one Irish dialect from another, they'll gladly accept any hometown you offer them - so long as it's from the north. Belfast is a sure thing. You'll stand no chance if they think you have Republican sympathies, and if you say you are from Dublin, well, you might as well get back on the boat now."

Tomas frowned as he listened.

"I'm not sure I'm prepared to deny my birthplace"

"You'll have to do more than just that Tomas!"

"What do you mean?"

"You'll have to change your name!"

Tomas looked ready to explode, as he hissed his answer at Michael.

"Why should I do that, I'll not deny my father's name! I will go back and that's a fact. I'll never deny my family line!"

Michael's tone was steely and blunt.

"Have you forgotten why you came here Tomas? You're a bloody fugitive, remember! You killed a man! You can't go back and you won't be safe here unless you change your name."

They faced each other in tense silence. Then Michael spoke again in a conciliatory manner.

"They have black lists Tomas, and if your name is on them, and it surely is or was, not only will you not work here, as like as not you will finish up in Durham jail, awaiting a visit from the hangman."

"Why would my name be on their lists? They don't know I killed the priest, not for certain they don't."

"They know Tomas, but they also think you are dead, and as long as they continue to think you're dead you will be safe. The search for you has been called off, but if you turn up at the nearest pit, - an Irishman looking for work, - called Tomas Mulholland, then you could well resurrect their suspicions and in no time at all you could be in deep trouble. All it takes is for some bright spark to put two and two together and your game is well and truly up. You must change your name and you must change your origins."

Tomas shook his head in dismay and incomprehension.

"What do you mean they think I'm dead? How the hell can they come to a conclusion like that?"

Michael's face and mood changed dramatically and his voice fell to a whisper. He leaned forward as he spoke, his face up near to Tomas. "I have something to tell you; something difficult Tomas."

"Then bloody well get on with it Michael, what is it, man?"

Michael took a deep breath.

"They went hunting for you after the priest was found. They went to your mother's house, Aunt Mary's. They broke in while she was sleeping and ransacked the place, looking for you. When they didn't find you, they tried to get Aunt Mary to tell them where you were hiding. She wouldn't talk Tomas." He drew a deeper breath. " She wouldn't talk so they burned the house down around her."

"My God," Tomas said in fear filled panic "How is she? Is she safe? Is she well? Who's looking after her?"

54

Michael looked at him and paused a moment.

His face told Tomas there was worse to come.

"She refused to leave with them Tomas. She died in the flames."

He stopped, and bent his head hardly able to look his cousin in the face. When he did look up the sight he saw tore at his heart.

Shock and pain were seared across Tomas's face. All colour had drained from him, and he looked ready to collapse. His breath came in desperate gasps.

"Jesus man, I'm so sorry," was all he could manage to say.

He reached across and grasped Tomas by his lower arms, gripping them firmly in an attempt to steady his shaking frame. Tomas's strangled sobs drew the brief attention of the domino players, but they soon returned to their game with only a few mumbled comments about emotional drunks. The cousins sat still and gradually Tomas was able to regain some composure. His breathing slowed, his body calmed and he was able to re-focus again. Then his mood slowly darkened. He looked at Michael with ice-cold eyes that would have struck fear into the bravest of hearts, but only Michael was watching, and he did not fear Tomas. He felt only heart-rending compassion for him.

"I had to tell you Tomas. I wanted you to know and to have a chance to take it in before we went home. Everybody at home is waiting to give their support to you. We want to help you through this whole appalling thing."

Tomas appeared not to hear him, lost in his own private torment. Eventually he spoke.

"How do you know this has happened?" he asked quietly.

"We got a call from Dublin. We are in constant touch with all that's happening over there. After you and Margaret left, and unbeknown to either of you, the men from the Army Council, those who you met at your father's funeral, had left a man behind for a while to help your mother through. What with you leaving and everything, they felt it was essential to have someone on hand if she needed anything. They also felt that somebody should be around to see her through the hoo-hah that was inevitable once the priest was found. They planned for their man to stay in the house with her, but Aunt Mary said that would not be necessary. They said she seemed a little embarrassed at the thought of having a stranger living in with her, so soon after all that had happened. They pleaded with her to reconsider, but independent soul that she was, she insisted that if he were to stay at all, he should stay at the pub in the village where she said he would have a lot more convivial company than she could provide. It was a compromise they didn't like, but she was adamant, and it was better than nothing.

Garretty, - that's the soldier's name, promised to be at the house each day, and to stay each evening till she was settled and secure for the night. He was there that night, before it happened. He was making his way back to the pub after saying his goodnights to Aunt Mary, walking the last half mile from the outskirts of the village, when a truck full of British soldiers passed by him heading back up the road towards your mother's place. They almost knocked him into the ditch they were travelling so fast. He was sure they had all been drinking. And it bothered him a lot, seeing them like that, enough to make him turn and go back. It's a long way to run back to your house, Tomas, about two miles I'd say, but he did it, he ran all the way. He was too late. When he got there they were assembled outside, so he stayed hidden."

Michael pause and drew breath, when he continued his speech thickened with emotion.

"Then from his hiding place, he, like them, watched the house burn. He heard them talking about her, saying how stupid it was, - her staying inside. Some were arguing they should have dragged her out. But the sergeant, merely shrugged his shoulders and said,

'Good riddance, her choice to stay! One less to worry about! Let's go. We've finished here.'

Garritty stayed hidden. There was nothing he could do that would change anything - except cry that is! He stayed all night and when the next day those at the pub discovered he hadn't come home, they searched for him. They found him, still at the house, still outside on his knees, still crying."

In the moments that followed, only the raucous laughter from the domino table broke the silence around them. Though it irked Tomas, in the end it served to break his mood.

"Who did this Michael, and I don't mean the bloody soldiers. Who went hunting for me - on whose orders? And why me?"

"It's a long story Tomas, but I might as well tell it all now.

"When Father O'Malley's body was eventually found by the local police where the soldiers had placed it, so that it would be found, they realised at once there was a connection to the 'Army', and they didn't feel competent to deal with it on their own, so they passed it up the line. The Dublin Police, in turn, passed it over to the British army, for much the same reason. Even in Dublin they didn't want to get involved with the republican movement without support from the military.

"A guy called McRory, Sergeant Robert McRory, ex-Black Watch, assigned to 'special security duties', which means cleaning up after the Uprising, was called in to investigate. He's a brute of a man, a Scotsman, well known to the Council in Dublin for 'crimes against the cause'. Works with a bunch of thugs, hand-picked by himself. They didn't take too long to piece the bits together. You were a suspect from the outset, being Seamus's son and all, and once they had talked to a few who had attended the funeral, plus others who were at the wake, it was an easy thing to confirm you as the main suspect. The fact that you were nowhere to be found made you "prime"!

"McRory informed his Captain of the facts, and the captain told him to find you at all costs. He warned him not to return without you, under threat of demotion to the ranks. Our friends back home got that from a couple of McRory's men in the pub one night, when they were all well in their cups. They also said that some of the men he currently commanded would give a *Private McRory*, demoted to the ranks a very hard time. Apparently a lot of them had serious personal scores to settle with him.

"We aren't entirely sure of the details that followed, we don't have anybody that close enough to the captain's office or his staff to verify the facts. What we understand is that McRory told his boss that you had perished with your mother in a fire, which he claimed had started accidentally. The surprising bit is that Lambert seemingly accepted McRory's story without verifying it with his men, and the search for you was called off. McRory was moved out soon afterwards, but we are not sure where or why."

Tomas suddenly alert, looked at Michael. "Lambert, you say? Tell me it's not Captain James Spencer - Lambert?"

"Yes," said Michael surprised, "That's him, son of Lord Lambert here in Durham. He's the coal owner's son! How did you know his name?"

Tomas looked frightening as he answered coldly, "He killed my father..." and his words hung in the air, as he added "....and now he's killed my mother!"

It was Michael's turn to gasp. He looked at Tomas appalled, and he was filled with a burning anguish for his cousin. They sat together for long minutes, silently looking into their beers in dismay and confusion. Eventually Michael stirred, and when he spoke it was with fervent love and sympathy,

"Let's go home Tomas, for this is surely your home now, here with us. I will be your brother - not just your cousin, and we will help you, and Margaret, and those fine children of yours. We are your family now."

Tomas looked at Michael with calculated candour as he asked him slowly, "If you will be my brother Michael, will you help me - as a brother?"

He watched the question seep into Michael's understanding before he continued, "Will you help me kill James Spencer - Lambert?"

Chapter 6

"Of babes and Sucklings"

During the weeks that followed the news of his mother's death, Tomas wandered through the streets and countryside around Eastinglea in a state of inner turmoil. His aimless meandering sometimes took him along the beach that stretched out past the colliery standing on the cliff-tops above. Walking past, he gazed up at it resentfully, ever aware that it belonged to the man responsible for all his families' sufferings. His bitterness festered into pure loathing and his need for vengeance developed inside him with cancerous progress. During all this time his adopted family watched him anxiously as he struggled to come to terms with his new existence. He shut out the care and love which they tried to bestow on him. He mourned alone for his parents. He was their only son, and he could not share this pain.

When Mary had given him life those thirty odd years ago, she had sustained complications, which had rendered her unable to bear children again. He had no brothers, and in reality no sisters either, and though he had often felt a need for both before, that need was never more intense than now. Only Margaret could share this pain, only she would feel it and understand it, for in all but blood she was not only his wife but also the sister of his youth. He longed for Margaret to be with him, but Margaret was in Dublin, and she would remain there until he had a home for her, and he would not have a home until he had a job, and the only job was at the pit. With the job would come the house, a colliery house! The thought depressed him. His inner self was in turmoil, as his common sense battled with his emotions.

It was in this continuing mood of depression and indecision one clear bright day, that he took a seat in the park, a little Eden in Eastinglea, which Tomas frequently headed for when seeking escape from the black industry that otherwise scarred the landscape all around him. On this day the golden glow of the spring daffodils blended with the multi-coloured tulips, that grew wild along the grassy banks that swept down to the ponds below. There, two boys shouted and balanced precariously on the edges, engrossed in their quest to catch the ponds' *"tiddlers" and "sticklebacks"* in the jam jars dangling from strings, that they trawled through the moss-covered waters before them. Tomas listened to their chatter as they played, distracted from himself by the happy intrusion of their voices with their pronounced accents that he was now beginning to understand a little better.

"Me dad's tackin' us to the beach tomorrow, Ah'm ganna catch crabs and shrimps. He says he knaws where to get loads, and we'll pick willicks an' all."

Tomas wondered what 'willicks' were and was tempted to ask, but the second boy pre-empted his question

"Wat's them?"

"They're like sea-snails, man. Hev ye niver heard of willicks before?"

"Noah" said the second boy *"Ah hevn't."*

"Some posh people call them whelks. Me dad sometimes brings them yairm when he's been to the docks. Ah dinna like them much, but me mam eats a lot o' them. And me dad says they are good for ye."

"What's it like to hev a dad?"

"It's good. Where's yewer dad like?"

"He got killed in the waar, Ah canna remember him really. Ah wish he was still here."

"Me dad's a hewer at the pit, but he's off work today with a bad back. That's why he can tak us to the beach. D' yea want to come?"

"Aye, ah would. D'ye think ah can?"

"Ah'll ask him. Ah think he'll say aye."

"Ah wish ah still had a dad."

"Sh'rup man, you can come with us. Anyway, it's dinnertime. Ah'm gannin yairm, Ah'm hungry!"

They raced away on muddy shoes, with jars full of fish and pond water, which slopped out as they ran up the banks and across the fields towards the curling columns of smoke that rose from the chimneys of the town's grimy houses.

Their departure left Tomas pensive, and the fatherless boy's words echoed in his mind. There was a message there he could not miss. He decided it was time to bring his family to England, and face the future as it was. He rose from the seat and walked purposefully back towards the smoking chimneys.

Michael met him at the door, before he could go inside.

"You and I need to talk Tomas, I have a lot to say to you and you are going to listen. We'll go to the 'George', I don't want the family to hear our conversation."

"Sounds serious, Michael, what have I done?"

"Nothing, and that's the problem. Let's go."

They walked in comparative silence the half-mile to the pub, their regular local. They bought their beers and sat down together. Tomas felt he knew what was coming, as Michael looked at him gravely.

"Tomas," he said, "I am concerned for you – we are concerned for you – all of the family. You have been here quite some weeks now, and even allowing time for you to pick yourself up after the terrible shocks you have had, we think it's time you got yourself together again. You appear to have lost all interest in everything. You haven't even attempted to contact Margaret and the children. You avoid us most of the time, and you have expressed no interest in finding work, or bringing your family to England. What the Hell's going on, man? I think you owe us an explanation, don't you?"

Tomas looked Michael squarely in the eyes, and paused before answering.

"I agree with you Michael. You are quite right, and I'm sorry. I owe you all an apology. I have been floundering in an ocean of self-pity, and I have neglected my family while I wallowed in it. That's over now. I'll grasp the nettle; I'm ready to start again. I'll be seeking work at the colliery tomorrow, and I'll be sending for Margaret and the boys immediately. If that's alright by you, and you meant what you said about helping us to get settled."

A broad smile lit up Michael's face.

❦

The Colliery manager had the agent, Mr Simon Perkins, brought in during the interview. Tomas recognized him from the casual glimpse he had had in the waiting room on the day of his arrival. The thin-faced man made Tomas feel very uncomfortable. His questions were pointed and deliberate, and directed at determining Tomas's religious and political background.

"So you are from Belfast, Mr Holland?"

"Yes sir". The lie made Tomas want to retch.

"But you are Catholic are you not? So you'll probably have Catholic relatives in the south, haven't you? Are you a papist? Do you support Irish Nationalism?" Tomas ignored the 'relatives' question.

"My name is Holland, sir, that should give you all the indications you need of my allegiances."

"Nevertheless, you are a Catholic, am I right?"

"I was born a Catholic, but I have long since ceased to practice my religion. I find it difficult to believe that any supreme deity - especially the loving god that the churches promote, can, with the perceived omnipotence we are expected to believe in, watch the pain and strife of his "beloved children" with what is nothing short of total apathy and indifference."

He regretted this outburst of anti-religious rhetoric, which might threaten his application for work in front of such obvious pillars of local society, and the look of anger and outrage on the face of the agent confirmed that he had indeed antagonized his prospective employers. He almost snarled his disapproval.

"I am a god-fearing man, Mr. Holland, Presbyterian as it happens, and such an atheistic outlook is repugnant to me. People like you disgust me!"

His vehemence only provoked Tomas into defending himself further.

"I don't think being irreligious will make me any less a good miner," he replied with conspicuous animosity.

It was then that the Colliery Manager intervened, to halt the deteriorating exchange between the two men.

"No, I suppose not, Mr. Holland. It isn't a requirement to be of a particular faith to work in this mine, but political allegiance to the Republican movement would prove to be a very different kettle of fish."

He looked at Tomas with piercing intensity, who felt compelled to defend himself further.

"There are many Irish Catholics in these coal mines, are there not?" said Tomas defensively, "Do you suspect all of them of being Republicans?"

"We question only those who recently arrived from Ireland, like yourself, Mr. Holland. We feel it is reasonable to examine these matters with them."

His quiet summation restored a tacit calm to their discussions.

Then as Tomas and the agent silently watched him, he entered some brief notes into a file with which to initiate Tomas's employment record. He continued,

"Right then. I think we all understand each other. You can start tomorrow Holland. You will work *on bank*. See my clerk outside; he'll explain everything to you."

The clerk explained to him that he could not immediately be employed underground. He would have to work on the surface - on bank - in the parlance of the pit yard - till he had been through the basic training necessary prior to working underground. He would meet the Training Officer when he started work the following day, and he would work initially on the *screens* where they separated the worthless slag and stone from the coal. His time on the screens would also be used to induct him into the requirements that would later make him a collier.

Later as he left the office a silent Mr. Simon Perkins watched him from the window, and his dislike was conspicuous in his tight face.

Tomas told Michael the news, adding with some bitterness that Perkins might have to be included in his list of people he wanted to dispose of. To his surprise, Michael responded defensively, chastising him for his manner.

"Listen Tomas" he said, "You are going to have to change your attitude a bit. Yes Perkins is a bastard, but the people you will be working with are the salt of the earth. Like us, they've suffered hard times at the hands of the landed gentry in this country. All the bad stuff wasn't confined to Ireland you know."

"Then they'll understand *my attitude* as you call it."

"Maybe they will and maybe they won't. You are a foreigner as far as they're concerned and they may well close ranks if they hear you mouthing off against what they regard as their country and heritage. Even if what you say is all true. Patriotism is like family loyalty; if you challenge it, then you could find yourself in a minority of one – on the outside. For my part I have a great deal of time for these people and mining history makes absorbing reading."

"Tell me about it!" said Tomas, sarcastically.

"OK, I will! You get the beers in. This might take a while."

Once Tomas had returned to his seat Michael continued,

"When you were in Durham, if you had had the opportunity to go to the Cathedral, you would have seen the Memorial there to the Durham Miners. I went, and I saw it, I found it very moving. It bears a simple but compelling message that says,

'Remember before God the Durham miners who have given their lives in the pits, and those who work in darkness and danger in those pits today'.

"That prayer is for you now Tomas, so keep it in mind". Tomas looked at him with unfeigned indifference.

"I'll go there and look, first chance I get," he said without conviction. Michael was unmoved by his cynicism.

"Do, Tomas. You'll get your chance. At the next Gala Day, once the war is over. It's held every year in the summer. All the miners from across the County get there. It's known as *Big Meeting Day*. Party politicians abound, waving and 'speechifying' from the hotel balconies and on the racecourse, people like Ramsey MacDonald, the renowned politician, and Robert Smillie, President of the Miners' Federation of Great Britain. Banners flutter and there are bands from every Union Lodge. They play "Gresford" a hymn of

Remembrance, and you can hear a pin drop while it's playing. People are dressed in their Sunday best.

There are fun fairs, dancing in the streets, ice cream, lemonade, and picnics by the riverbanks, the works. And of course the beer flows like water. By the end of the day it tastes like water! Straight out of the river most of it! But by then nobody cares."

He looked wistful as he spoke,

"It's the bonding of people you notice most, everybody in harmony with each other. At least for one day, the mining families are together in common understanding and unity. It's awesome really."

"You really have become one of them, Michael, haven't you?" Tomas's tone was matter of fact, and slightly hostile.

Michael seemed not to hear him as he continued,

"Did you know Tomas, that since 1850, to date, 31,000 men and boys have been killed in the Durham coalfields, and across the country the price of coal today costs the lives of 1000 men a year. Did you know that? Of course you didn't. Why should you? I didn't know it either till I read it, but the more I read, the more I admire mining folk. And Tomas, I intend to be a part of the fight for a better deal for the miners. I am putting myself up for election into the local lodge, and hopefully I'll go beyond that to do great things in a great cause."

He looked at Tomas and Tomas could never doubt the commitment he saw in Michael's eyes.

"Then my question to you about James Spencer Lambert becomes irrelevant, Michael. You won't want to dirty your hands seeking retribution for the death of your Aunt and Uncle, will you?" His challenge was unmistakable.

"I'll help you seek justice Tomas, of course I will", replied Michael firmly.

"I'm still Irish, and Ireland's just cause remains very important to me. It's my just cause as well as yours! There is no conflict of interest."

Chapter 7

1923

"Dermot Holland, will you get down these stairs this minute. You'll be late for your own funeral and that's a fact!"

Margaret Holland stood arms akimbo, at the foot of the broad staircase that rose to the landing above, where sunlight from the stairhead window mixed with the russet patterns of the rich wool carpet. Her voice with its mellow Irish brogue carried upwards to the bedroom at the end of the hallway.

"Coming mammy, I'm coming!"

The boy looked into the long mirror of the old '*clothespress*', one of the few pieces of furniture that had travelled successfully from Ireland all those years ago, before he was born, when the family had been forced to seek promise in a new future, and for his father, vengeance for an old past.

Today Dermot felt proud. He was wearing a clean white shirt, a red tie, short grey trousers, grey knee-length stockings, and shining black shoes. On the bed lay a new navy-blue blazer. His fair hair gleamed brightly in the warm light that filled the room. He looked as fresh as *Easter*, as his Aunt Sarah was apt to say.

Dermot loved his eccentric aunt. She fussed over him and made him feel very special when they met regularly outside church each Sunday morning after mass. She always gave him money; she sometimes gave him sixpence! It was his birthright, she claimed.

"Any child who survived your start to life is entitled to privileges", she insisted.

"You're a walking miracle, a walking miracle and that's a fact". Then turning to the nearest parishioner she could capture, she would recount to them the story of Dermot's birth, those seven short years earlier.

Sarah was not a qualified midwife, having had no formal training, but she took every opportunity to be present as an enthusiastic amateur at each confinement that occurred within her circle, particularly with family and friends. Over the years she had developed her birthing skills to such an extent that she was now sought after, rather than resented by the nursing attendees - as originally she certainly was. Even the local doctors called for her now, on occasions when the district midwife found herself over-stretched in the rapidly expanding community that was Eastinglea.

Margaret Holland was forty-three when Dermot was born, and the event proved to be a difficult experience for both of them. Not of course that Dermot was aware at the time, but as he listened enthralled to Aunt Sarah's graphic account, related repeatedly to her post-mass captives each Sunday morning in all its lurid details, he felt he was experiencing each perilous moment as a conscious happening that was taking place, even as she spoke.

"He was thought to be stillborn you know; discarded at the bottom of the bed - wrapped in an old copy of the Daily Express. How absolutely embarrassing, the Daily Express for goodness sake! And it was I, his aunt Sarah who saved him!"

Each Sunday hostage would respond politely at first, displaying the right degree of contrived shock and appropriate approval as her dramatic tale unfolded.

"I saw him" she would continue, "out of the corner of my eye, just a flicker of movement, but enough!

"He's alive!" I said. "I saw him move!"

"In a second, Mary and I - Mary was the midwife, you know - had him out of that Tory rag - I don't know why Thomas Holland allows it to fall through his letter-box, I really don't - and we were blowing air down a paper tube into his little lungs, till he gasped. Then we smacked his tiny backside, and stuck him under the kitchen tap!"

The question framed on the face of her now bewildered listener would go unasked, as with impeccable timing Sarah continued,

"To baptise him you see, otherwise it was Limbo for all eternity if he died. We didn't give him much chance of survival at the time. Scrawny little bag of bones he was - like a skinned rabbit," she added wistfully.

"When we showed him to Dr Mealing - God rest his soul - he muttered something about an awful lot of trouble to deliver such a miserable little runt, then went back to helping his poorly mother. I was left to tend to Dermot........." At this point she would turn to admire him, like a prize possession. "... and look at him now."

Dermot's embarrassed blush was not devoid of some pleasure as she chucked him lightly under the chin.

At this point the befuddled listener often managed to slip away, while Sarah wrapped in her reminiscences, continued her diatribe to her nephew, who was still young enough to be enthralled by the frequently told tale, and which through its persistent repetition he became able to recount himself, - word by Aunt Sarah's word.

Finally, remonstrating with him gently, that he had not been round to visit her and his Uncle Michael of late, and assured by his promise to do so, Sarah would press the customary coin into his hand before turning away in search of another parochial neighbour with whom to wend her way homewards - engaged in what she felt confident was convivial and engrossing conversation.

"I won't tell you again Dermot, get down here immediately!"

The boy was jerked out of his reverie by the sound of his mother's voice, which now had an edge to it that could not be disregarded. Grabbing his jacket from the bed, and with a last glance in the mirror, he skipped lightly down the stairs and into the kitchen, where he found his mother tidying away the breakfast dishes.

"Will Daddy be at the mass, mammy?" he asked, absent-mindedly dipping his finger into the small glass dish that served as a saltcellar, and licking off the salt that stuck to it.

"Your father's at the pit, and right about the time you should be stepping up to receive the Blessed Sacrament, he'll still be on his way out from the coal face. He said he would try and get out early today, but he's not home yet, so I don't see him making it now.

"Your father has never darkened a church door since the day your granddaddy was buried, and he only did it then out of respect for his father. Believe me, if your granddaddy hadn't been the devout Catholic he surely was, he wouldn't have gone then either. The sad part is that he has trained your brothers to think the same as him. You'll have to make do with Uncle Michael, Aunt Sarah, your sister Bridgett and me for your family. It's a sorry day when I have to rely on our other relatives to swell the family presence at my son's First Communion, but that's the way it is."

Dermot felt hurt that his father was not going to be there.

"Why does Daddy not like me, Mammy?"

"Don't be saying such things now" his mother replied sharply, "Your father loves you and that's the God's truth. It's the Church he can't come to terms with, not you."

Dermot didn't know why, but he was less then assured by his mother's words. Nevertheless his spirits stayed up, in anticipation of the day's excitement. He knew he would be richer for one thing. Once he met up with Aunt Sarah and Uncle Michael there would be more pocket money in it from both of them. He felt suddenly guilty as he remembered he should be thinking about receiving Jesus in the Holy Eucharist, so he tried to switch his attention to that. Then he remembered! Fasting from midnight! With the sharp tang of the salt still on his tongue, panic gripped his young soul. He turned to his mother in dismay.

☙

In the vestry, Father Docherty smiled at her concern as he put on the red vestments that grace the celebrant at all masses for the feast of Corpus Christi.

He explained to the worried mother that dipping a finger absent-mindedly into a saltcellar and licking it, hardly constituted a breach of the Church's edict on fasting from midnight before receiving the Blessed Sacrament. Only by deliberate intent could Dermot have barred himself from taking the Eucharist, he declared.

"Go to the altar with God's blessing my son, and I hope every child that receives the Sacrament this day will be as prepared for it as you are. Indeed we'll have a fine crop of young Catholics if they are, the sort that will become the great priests and nuns of the future." Then with an impish smile he added lightly,

"I don't suppose you would like to put your name down now Dermot, would you, - to be a priest I mean?"

Dermot paused, his forehead screwed up in serious deliberation as his mother and the priest exchanged amused quizzical glances. Then with a look of deep sincerity he said,

"Yes Father, I would like to put my name down, because one day I will become a priest!"

Margaret Holland looked at her son incredulously. All her life she had prayed that God would bless her with a husband who would return to the church he was baptised into, and a son with a vocation for the priesthood. She had long since come to terms with the fact that the first of these two hopes was not in God's plans, realising that even He would need some degree of cooperation from Tomas. The second dream she had retained much longer, but as each of her boys matured to embrace the godless ranks of their father and his deep-rooted contempt for the Church and its ministers, this hope too became a fading candle in her heart. Now suddenly, she was hearing her youngest expressly stating his intention of becoming a priest, and by doing so rekindling in her a flame that she thought had long since been extinguished.

Father Docherty looked at Dermot solemnly, before he spoke,

"If you still feel like that when you are a few years older my boy we'll talk about it some more. Now run along and join the other children in the church. You'll take at least one more sacrament yet before we get to Holy Orders."

Then turning to his mother and seeing the expectant surprise on her face, he said firmly,

"Don't be making plans for Corshaw College just yet Margaret. He'll want to be a footballer tomorrow, and fly an aeroplane the day after that. Boys his age have a remarkable capacity for adventure and romance – unfortunately it's usually accompanied by the mental focus of a butterfly."

"You're wrong there Father," Margaret replied firmly, "Dermot is very constant about the things he says. You can see it in his face if you look. It was there right now." She nodded wistfully for a second, then turned abruptly to follow her son into the church.

The priest shook his head sadly as he completed his preparations. It saddened him that such a good woman should have to live a life of hardship and haplessness, void even of a partner who would stand with her in the light of God's grace and goodness. He resolved to make a special invocation for her each day that her faith and devotion might reap its deserved reward.

Later, as the children collected their medals and Communion Certificates at the end of the celebration breakfast at the school, the tall figure of a man, in flat cap, with blackened face and blackened hands, reached upwards to peer over the windowsill of one of the high Norman windows that lighted the old hall. Tomas Mulholland grunted disagreeably as he recognised the scene and the participants inside. Just up from the pit, where he had spent the previous twelve hours directing repair operations in a five-foot coal seam, he had been wending his way home tiredly, when he remembered his promise to attend his son's Communion day. Not the mass, he had insisted, just the breakfast. Now he was late, but consideration for his wife's wishes made him change direction and pass by the school in the hope that he might at least accompany his family home.

He saw Dermot moving up the line towards the priest, and he wondered about the boy. He was seven now, but still lacked the signs that showed he would develop into what Tomas thought to be a "proper" boy. He rarely got into mischief, was never rude, and didn't play with the other kids in the street. He had been a problem from birth - hadn't they both nearly died - and

Dermot surely would have, had it not been for Sarah Railley's sharp eyes, Maybe that was what was different about him. He had had a bad start, but time would change that. Tomas felt he loved all his children equally, but the boy baffled him, they just weren't close like they should be. Now as he watched him beaming with delight, with his red-ribboned medal gleaming round his neck, and his parchment certificate clutched in his hand, resentment welled up inside him, bitter at the control the Church exercised over his son's young mind. He turned away, and cursed aloud.

Chapter 8

Corshaw College, 1927

As Father Domingo led Dermot and his mother towards the chapel, a sense of affinity for the place stirred inside the boy, and a feeling of belonging came over him. He walked slowly up the steps, and passed expectantly through the double doors that led him into the body of the church. The beauty of the interior enthralled him and he gulped audibly. Beside him he heard his mother whispering her prayers, in deference to her surroundings. Father Domingo smiled as his guests looked around at the imposing scene before them.

Above the high altar the magnificent stained-glass window depicting Christ in majesty surrounded by all his disciples shone gloriously in the afternoon sun, and cast radiant colours over the pews and floors below. Intricate paintings of the Resurrection and Ascension decorated the walls behind the altar table which itself was draped in fine white linen delicately edged in hand embroidered lace.

A silver crucifix inset with blood red stones, stood in the alcove over the tabernacle, where – for the faithful – Jesus Christ reposed in the Holy Eucharist, his presence implied by the ornate lamp, which, suspended on golden chains glowed red and constant over the sanctuary below. In front and to the left, the lectern stood on a marble floor, a masterpiece of wood and metal, complete with sculptured eagle, with wings spread wide as a missal stand.

The adjacent Lady Chapel almost hidden in the shadows to the left was illuminated by a single candelabrum set before a statue of the Blessed Virgin.

All around, the furnishings and the brass work gleamed and twinkled in the changing light, enhancing the peace and splendour of the whole interior.

"We are truly in the house of God," thought Margaret Holland, and she was filled with a profound sense of Faith.

They walked slowly up the centre aisle and for a while stood together in silence before the sanctuary, absorbing the quiet ambience. Eventually Father Domingo spoke, addressing himself to the boy in a firm but kindly tone. Mrs Holland stood behind her son, listening attentively, with her hands resting protectively on his young shoulders.

"This is Saint Aidan's Chapel Dermot," the priest said, "and we are very proud of it. We make a point of showing all new boys around here on their first visit, because this chapel embodies what Corshaw College is all about. Our job here is to nurture boys like you into Christian manhood, then to convert those young men into priests of the Catholic Church. That is our purpose, and St Aidan's is the very essence of that purpose. If you decide to come to us you will spend much of your time in this chapel praying to God. You will pray to Him more intensely and frequently than you have ever prayed before. He will be your *raison d'être*, as the French so aptly put it, your reason to be. Your life will no longer be your own; you will belong to Him."

He paused to observe the effects of his words. Dermot looked impressed, his mother looked overawed.

"Every minute you are here you will work to a timetable dictated by the College, and you will obey every legitimate instruction without question. Discipline will be your watchword. There is no place in Corshaw for disorder or for those who would promote it." He paused again, before continuing,

"You must think very carefully about these things Dermot, and if you have any doubts at all about coming here you must tell us today. We don't wish to hear some months down the road that you have changed your mind. That would be a waste of time and money, and such wastages are not acceptable-either to your parents or to us. While we are walking around, think about these things, and make up your mind to be honest, not just with me, but also with yourself. I will ask you again before you leave if you still want to come here, and you must give a firm answer one way or the other."

Dermot interrupted in a rush of words, "I do want to come here Father, I really do. This is where I want to be!"

Father Domingo smiled indulgently, and glanced towards Dermot's mother with a collusive expression that presumed her concurrence with his preconception on the fickleness of adolescent fervour. However before he could speak on the matter, she did,

"You are the second priest to question the sincerity of my son's motivation Father, and I'll tell you the same as I told that gentleman those four years ago. When Dermot expressed his desire to become a priest he did so without coercion from anyone. It was his decision and his alone. He made it, and he has stuck by it. He's waited since he was seven years old to come here, and he's never wavered for a moment. He's been scorned and laughed at, even by members of his own family, but he's as resolute now as he was then. And that was on the day of his First Communion, Father. Now if that's not a call from the Almighty himself then, I don't know what could be!"

The Irish lilt to her voice softened the challenge in her words, and Father Domingo smiled comfortingly.

"Dermot's sincerity is not an issue here, my dear Mrs Holland, but I would be failing in my duty if I did not raise these serious points at the outset. The priesthood is not for all boys; in fact it is as you state yourself, a calling for a selected few. There must be positive indications of a serious vocation and assurance of continuing support from each boy's family. It has been our sad experience that this is not always the case. For some parents, having a son studying for the priesthood represents a personal status symbol, that sets them above their social peers, and some have been known to send their sons to Corshaw for their own personal image rather than in response to the boy's vocation, or indeed to the needs of the Church itself. These cases are few, but they can result in great unhappiness for the boys concerned. By asking questions now, we hope to avoid such mistakes, and we would be sadly lacking were we not to do so. It is not our intention to doubt - either parents or sons - merely to clarify what is being undertaken."

He leaned forward a little as he finished, his hands clasped in front, and smiled gently at her, "I am satisfied in this case that both parent and child fully understand and accept the responsibility of the undertaking."

Margaret felt uneasy at her outburst` and embarrassed by the explanation, for she was plagued with doubts of her own. She felt unsure of her motivations, and fearful of her husband's reaction when he was made aware of what she was doing. Her secret had so far remained hers alone, although Father Docherty had expressed reservations about the deception she was carrying out on her husband and the other members of the family.

Nevertheless for Margaret the idea of having a son ordained priest overcame all her uncertainties. It was the culmination of a lifetime's dream for her, and now at the weekly parish meetings of the Catholic Mothers Union she could take quiet satisfaction when she detected admiration, tinged with a little envy, in other eyes that in different circumstance might give her not as much as a second glance. She felt she must justify herself to the kindly man before her, and allay all doubts.

"You are right Father. Dermot's always been determined to serve god as a priest, and nothing will change him. Of that I'm certain," she added firmly, stifling the doubts that made her words sound hollow in her own ears.

"Good" said Father Domingo, " then we shall say no more about it. As you are aware we do counsel the boys at regular intervals to make sure they haven't changed too much." Turning to Dermot he said cheerfully, "Now young man, let me tell you a little of the history of this splendid establishment.

They left the church and crossed the quadrangle towards the Refectory. They entered a light and spacious hall with oak-beamed ceilings and high panelled walls on which were hung a vast array of imposing portraits. Brightly curtained windows overlooked an arrangement of tables and chairs at which, during the academic year, several hundred students were sustained three times a day from the College's large kitchens.

Just inside the entrance, a life-sized figure of St Joseph gazed up the body of the hall from a high podium, watchful and aware it seemed, of all that took place within. Now, in the quiet emptiness of the summer recess, his attention seemed focused on Dermot, causing the boy to feel a little disconcerted. The bright eyes seemed to follow him everywhere he went as he and his mother followed Father Domingo, who continued on his way, outlining rules, traditions and required behaviour, seemingly indifferent to the watchful attentions of Christ's stone foster-father. On their way out of the building, Dermot glanced nervously up, and felt sure he detected a twinkle of amusement in the corners of the great saint's eyes.

They wandered progressively through the college's imposing buildings, which were to play such a major part in Dermot's formative education. Father Domingo waxed knowledgeably as they went, taking great pains to expand upon the details of the development of the seminary.

He explained how Corshaw found its origins in the Reformation period, at a time when Catholicism was under threat of extinction in England and Wales, and the need for a continuing supply of priests became of paramount importance to the survival of the Church.

He told how it was that young men of noble heart, and often of noble family, exiled themselves in France where they studied intensely, either to receive the Catholic education they were denied at home, or to follow a vocation to the priesthood and thereafter return to defend the Faith of their fathers in England. These young crusaders of Christ travelled secretly and in disguise, in constant peril of their lives. Hidden by loyal Catholic families from their persecutors, they were often delivered up by informers, who, Judas like, frequently betrayed them for little more than a handful of silver. Over two hundred such priests were executed as agents of Catholicism, and the Church ultimately acknowledged their sacrifice when it declared them martyrs - albeit a few hundred tardy years later - as the priest added somewhat wryly.

With the due passage of time however, the persecutions slowed down, and the religious climate improved to such an extent that Catholics were once more allowed to celebrate mass, and when their rights of land ownership were eventually restored, the rewards for informing on them were simultaneously abolished. Coinciding with this, war with France made it impossible to continue training priests abroad, and two seminaries were re-established in England. One of these was located at Corshaw in the mid-nineteenth century.

But as Father Domingo went on to explain, the troubles were not yet entirely over...........

After the persecution by the state had ceased there followed a natural enemy equally insidious with similarly devastating consequences - disease - in the form of Typhus! It killed several of the first influx in the College's very first year. Then followed a series of fevers at various intervals and in the first fifty years of the young college's existence some forty students died. Their graves the priest explained soberly could be viewed in the College Cemetery at the northeast corner of the gardens.

Since these times, Father Domingo continued, the College has progressed steadily growing in size and importance as the demands for priests hastily increased. More buildings were added to accommodate the increasing numbers, which rose to between three and four hundred by the turn of the century. First came the Chapel, then the infirmary, followed by the now expansive library, each of these accompanied by concurrent expansions in the accommodation, kitchens and educational facilities. The recreational services include a swimming pool, which he said, Dermot would probably discover featured prominently, if unofficially, in the initiation rituals of the college. He smiled at Dermot who gave him an anxious glance.

During this protracted period of change and development, the objectives of the college remained constant - to provide the best possibilities for the development of boys of eleven and upwards to the highest standards of classical education and seminary training.

With this final pronouncement Father Domingo concluded his long and mobile discourse. Over tea and crumpets, he thanked them for attending the interview and preliminary induction, before leading them to the gates to say goodbye.

Thus Dermot became aware of Corshaw, and Corshaw became aware of him. He was completely enamoured of it. As he and his mother travelled home by train through Durham's rolling countryside, hardly a word was spoken between them as they separately contemplated the day. Dermot rejoiced within, in a state of ecstatic reverie as he gazed dreamily out of the window seeing nothing of the fields and meadows, the farms or the colliery villages that passed swiftly by the window. His mother, in deep contemplation saw nothing either. She was lost in her concern for her son's unknown future, and it was conspicuous in the lines that creased her face.

❧

Margaret had revealed nothing to Tomas of her plans to guide Dermot towards the priesthood. Since his first Communion Day, and the boy's declaration to Father Docherty, (which Tomas had so harshly dismissed as childish fantasy), she had spoken no more of it. She had merely kept her own counsel and developed her private plan, knowing that she must proceed on her own initiative, without moral or financial support from her husband. She did so with a stubborn determination that had been absent on those previous occasions, when he had similarly heaped scorn on her vocational aspirations for their elder sons.

Now, each week, she secreted away a portion of the generous monies that Tomas allowed her for the household. As a result, over four years of disciplined frugality, during which time Dermot grew to a strapping eleven year old, she had accumulated enough to kick-start her son's ecclesiastical career. The recent visit to Corshaw Catholic Seminary with Dermot had shown her, that it was, as reputed, the most prestigious institution in the Northern Counties, and she felt assured that it was in God's great plan that Dermot should pursue his vocation to the priesthood under the guidance of the College's great teachers. And other than her priest, only her bank manager was aware of her secret.

As he had said with pun-laden humour, at one of their rare meetings,

"Your cache is safe with us Mrs Holland - or rather- your cash is in our safe with us!"

He laughed heartily at his own joke, but Margaret, never comfortable in the presence of bureaucratic administrators, remained unamused, sure that this was a line often repeated to customers such as her, and with the same honeyed patronisation. She merely re-iterated her concerns about absolute confidentiality.

"Under no circumstances whatsoever" she said, "must anyone ever reveal any knowledge of these savings to my husband."

No one did, and the money grew steadily, in preparation for the day that was now upon them. It was the new term and the new intake of seminarians would take place tomorrow.

She considered these things as she ironed Dermot's clothes, silently preparing for the journey to Corshaw. Tomas watched her curiously from his armchair through the haze of smoke that rose from his briar as he relaxed with his newspaper. Nearby the gramophone was playing a selection from Gilbert and Sullivan, which next to his dormant compulsion for vengeance against the English, was his most consuming passion. He wondered vaguely why she was pressing the boy's new trousers, and was that not also a new tie, he thought, a school tie in fact! He put down his paper as realisation began to dawn.

Down the year's Margaret had always argued against Tomas's religious intolerance, and stated her opinions vehemently on those rare occasions when they had cause to talk "matters of Church". Now she was forced to argue again, but this time over their son. She did so with the diplomatic skill and forceful persuasion that only wives can muster, but in the face of her husband's stubborn inflexibility, only the ultimate threat of her leaving him forced Tomas to give way to her demands over their youngest son's vocation. Such unhappy compromise was a distressing experience, which they had never before faced in their marriage, and the emotional wounds of it went deep, and stayed with them even after they had stopped arguing. Later that night they lay in bed with their backs turned to each other - something they had never done before, and a tear trickled down Margaret's cheek as she held back a sob, while Tomas fought hard to stifle the rising lump in his throat, and yet harder to avoid audibly sniffing his hurt. From that night onward they always slept apart from each other, and the cherished intimacy that so embodied the beauty and strength of their marriage slowly drifted away from them.

In the days that followed, Margaret reflected on the reasons for it all, and wondered why chance and circumstance had so cruelly damaged their lives. She had always understood the pain he suffered – and identified with it – but she felt helpless to comfort him. She believed sincerely that it was the Church's ministers, not the Lord Jesus himself, he was at odds with, and in her heart she harboured an undying hope of reconciliation for him; a return to the faith into which he was born. She yearned to comfort him in his anguish, for beneath his anger there was deep distress. Tomas, when devoured by his demons, was inevitably plunged into a trough of despair, which always ended in a drunken stupor that dragged him back to the Wake, *Seamus's Wake*, that is! Margaret remembered it all so clearly.

Father O'Malley was at the root of it all! He had surely started it, and what he had begun, had ended in deep tragedy. And the guilt of it stayed remorselessly in Tomas's mind, degenerating with time, which for Tomas proved to be no great healer. The passing years served only to distort the events, such that, what at its inception had begun as fear and guilt over a tragic accident, he now perceived as justifiable retribution for insult to his father's honour. Furthermore, he now judged the circumstances of both parent's deaths as raging injustices that demanded equal resolution. In truth, Margaret reflected, the misguided beliefs of a self-opinionated, none too intelligent country priest, had changed her husband from a man of high principle into an embittered bigot with an irrational resentment of both Church and State. And in reality, wasn't it all down to the drink, she thought. Margaret shook her head in frustration at the memory.......

Chapter 9

The Seminarian 1927

Dermot arrived at Corshaw on Saturday September 27th 1927. The bus rattled its way up the hill from Durham City and stopped in a fusillade of backfiring and blue smoke, almost opposite the entrance to the college. Three other new boys in conspicuously new uniforms alighted with him, and after exchanging brief smiles and nervous hellos, during which they cautiously appraised each other, they turned their joint attention to the college itself and the imposing entrance before them.

The freshly painted wrought iron gates were supported on both sides by two stone pillars, upon each of which was perched a huge concrete ball, put there, thought Dermot by no less a person than Atlas himself. To the side of the left pillar was a shining brass plate, boldly pronouncing the name of the college and its purpose. Beyond the gates was a gravel driveway, which ran past the Lodge House on the right, so defined by a small notice stuck in the front lawn, which said, 'TO THE LODGE', but sadly pointed downwards to the grass.

"It would have been better if it read 'Keep off the Grass, don't you think?" said the red headed youth, who had surreptitiously attached himself to Dermot.

Dermot murmured a subconscious word of agreement as he surveyed the view in front of him.

To the left a cobblestone yard opened up to outhouses and workshops, which he concluded were there to serve the college's storage and repair requirements. The driveway meandered onwards past rhododendrons and laurel bushes to a terraced front before an impressive building some four stories high, which had a high-arched four-pillared propylaeum in front of the large open doors of the entrance hall.

Summoning their collective courage, Dermot and his new companions passed through the gates, and exchanging only a few nervous quips moved in reluctant unison towards the doors before them. They gazed ahead at the hustle and bustle in progress, overawed by the procedures they could see being conducted inside the open entrance, where administrative officials and school staff busied themselves with introductory formalities for the considerable numbers of new entrants who like themselves had arrived at the appointed hour to present themselves as candidates for their new life ahead.

Dermot wondered if these new boys had - like him - visited the college before, assured and encouraged at the time by the presence of parent or guardian. They - like him - he thought, would have been free of the nervous fear that now clutched at his stomach, and by the looks on the faces around him similarly afflicted his new companions. Together they walked cautiously into the entrance hall in an uneasy bunch.

"This way, boys," an anonymous voice commanded, "Line up at the desk in front, and try not to make too much noise!"

❧

"They say the first three days are the worst," said Jackie Quinn later, the redhead who had so tenaciously attached himself to Dermot, and had taken the bed-space next to Dermot's in the dormitory.

Jackie had never left Dermot's side throughout the initiation procedures, and Dermot had taken comfort in his companionship, though his constant chatter left him somewhat bewildered in the light of the frequently barked commands for silence by the staff in charge of their inductions.

"You there! Stop your blathering boy!" was one reprimand directed his way by a staff member who they would later identify as their Latin master. He was to remember young Jackie's first day down the years on repeated occasions, as he summoned him to use his 'loquacious talents' - as he called them, to read and translate the more difficult passages of Virgil's *Aeneid*, before a class of his amused peers.

Jackie in the meantime had continued his non-stop talking through 'supper', a misnomer for a meal that had consisted of nothing more than bread and butter and a cup of hot cocoa from a large urn, which tasted of tea, and was excessively flavoured with both milk and sugar.

"Those two older students we met are to usher us around tomorrow," Quinn continued. They said they would take good care of us all", he continued with unwavering enthusiasm. Dermot pondered the implications of the latter remark.

It was then that the door at the end of the 'dorm' opened, and a voice, firm in authority, boomed down at them,

"Be quiet in here. If you have anything to say, say it to me or quietly to God, otherwise shut up, get into bed, and get to sleep!"

Silence in the college was a rigidly enforced discipline they would have to learn to live with, Dermot thought.

But he smiled to himself as he climbed into bed, for already he had realised, that this indeed was the beginning of real life for him. This was exactly where he wanted to be, and his deep satisfaction with his newfound situation was equalled by his underlying certainty that he would see it through. The next fourteen years of his life would take him through adolescence to manhood, and to that special day when he would be ordained priest in the service of his Lord Jesus Christ. He drifted into sleep with this unwavering conviction firmly entrenched in his young mind.

His confidence was only slightly dented by the events of the next day, when he and "Quinnie", and an accompanying mass of unruly novices, embarked on three days of the college's official induction procedures, guided by senior students, their appointed mentors, who, allocated to advise and inform, simultaneously subjected their charges to a series of unofficial though traditional hazing rituals.

The flour bagging was a nuisance, albeit somewhat amusing, watching those who were unfortunate enough to snort the powdery cloud deep into their bronchia, causing spluttering, coughing, sneezing, and near asphyxia in some cases. Dermot was lucky enough to escape with whitened hair and a dusty blazer. "Quinnie" was equally fortunate. However both of them were then forced to endure the indignity and discomfort of "Chinese burns" and unrestrained arm-twisting, from which, when it ended, release came as a blessed relief. Then they were shown the swimming pool, and it took only a second to realise that this was to be their next humiliation; it was then that Dermot remembered Fr Domingo's warning!

As they climbed out dripping wet, they were ordered to waste no time getting dried as there was much they needed to do before the day was ended. Dermot and Quinnie exchanged knowing glances with dismay.

Next they were herded, like sheep through a dip-trough, into the "Black Hole Of Calcutta", a narrow cul-de-sac bounded by the high walls of the college building. Once assembled, they stood trapped while rather large youths charged and crowded them backwards into the corner, pulverizing the unfortunate individuals at the front till they became howling wrecks, while those at the back, jammed and crushed, became sweaty, claustrophobic and panicky. The remnants of flour in Dermot's wet hair took on the odour of fermenting dough.

Eventually they were released to clean themselves up before the evening prayers and dinner, but with the morrow came the dawn, and with daylight came their ultimate humiliation!

During the morning, Dermot and Quinnie were separated from the pack by their personal mentors to complete their more personal induction procedures. They were lead around the remaining buildings hitherto not visited, and given what Dermot considered was a much less polished description of the colleges history and purpose, than that which he had received from Father Domingo on his visit with his mother.

As on that previous occasion, a walk round the college's boundary limits took them through the fields that surrounded the outer perimeter. It was there that it happened! With no warning and with complete surprise they were suddenly grabbed from behind and amid hoots of unrestrained laughter from their erstwhile guardians, were unceremoniously dumped into the one of the many clusters of gorse bushes that dotted the fields around. They were forced to endure this torture not once, not twice, but three times in all.

Later as he painstakingly and painfully removed gorse needles from his bleeding palms and the exposed areas of legs that showed whitely below their short knee-length uniform trousers, Quinnie ruefully remarked,

"I wondered why there were three of them today, they needed two to throw us in, and one to stop the other one running away", he surmised ruefully.

Dermot gave a grunted response as he pulled a well imbedded needle from his knee with an anguished grimace, and dabbed a spot of blood with one of the iodine soaked swabs, they had been given afterwards by their latterly compassionate tormentors.

The third day the hazing stopped; the tortures were over, and their mentors, who told the boys they may refer to them by the bizarre title of *"old cods"*, adopted a conspicuously more friendly approach to their young charges. Just before they released them that evening, Coughlin the senior of the two, even showered them with praises.

"Well done you two. You are a pair of fine lads. You have borne your trials and tribulations over the last two days with a fortitude and dignity, which went way beyond that shown by most of your contemporaries. Tomorrow your formal studies begin."

Then with an abrupt "Good Luck", a brusque handshake, he and Morrison - the other *"old cod"* - left.

Dermot and Quinnie watched them go, before turning to each other with an incredulous snigger and a considerable degree of relief.

"I'm glad my mother can't see the state of my new clothes," said Dermot.

"Me too" said Quinnie, "and it will be Christmas before we can get them properly sorted out."

This wasn't strictly true, for they were to discover that the college laundry was very adept at restoring the ravages of the annual hazing rituals, at only a modest charge from each boy's allowance.

"Well it's classroom C12 for us tomorrow, Quinnie," said Dermot

"Let's hope it's better than the last few days," replied his friend as they headed off to the 'dorm' to prepare for dinner.

Down the years that followed Dermot thought it strange that he never found cause to speak to either one or the other of their initial mentors again, beyond a passing smile and an occasional "hello". Then one day they were gone, priests off in pursuit of their lives, each in their personal vocations, as indeed Quinnie and he would do themselves one day.

Before any of that could take place however, there was not just water to flow under his personal bridge; there would be a river.

ℰℐ

For "*new cods*" the first seminary year started at six-thirty a.m. After washing and dressing they assembled for prayers, which were led by a "*Divine*", one of the select group of very senior students who were in the final years before ordination. Mass followed, and with the completion of these spiritual observances, the temporal needs of the body were then addressed. Breakfast was served!

On their very first morning, the hungry new boys, Dermot, and Quinnie among them, marched eagerly to the refectory, anticipating their first meal. A few days later all anticipation had waned, although the appetite remained - as acute as ever. To these young boys breakfast had hitherto been a major expectation, awaited avariciously, but at Corshaw, the monotonous repetition of the fare served up, blunted all pleasure in its consumption.

"I'm starving!" was an exclamation heard widely across the breakfast table each day, but the sight of the food being served was enough to dull the cravings of most.

Porridge with treacle, a portion of bread and butter, and tea inevitably pre-flavoured with copious amounts of sugar and milk, did nothing to stimulate their young appetites; it merely served to assuage their bodily needs. The tea was provided in the same urn as the previous evening's cocoa, and it needed a discerning palate to detect any significant difference in the taste of either. Soon breakfast became no more than the necessary refection the college intended it to be, an essential but unexciting consideration in the daily routine.

It was commonly believed that serving bland meals was a deliberate philosophy, its purpose to mould young minds on matters spiritual rather than temporal, while at the same time inducing the sense of self-denial deemed so essential to their priestly formation.

Dinner proved to be almost equally predictable, for although differing in content on a day-by-day basis, it was recycled week by week against a preset menu. This was printed and displayed on the refectory notice board, where it was ignored completely by the students, who could repeat it from memory within a few weeks of being there without need for further reference.

'Meat and veg' were served from Monday to Thursday, with boiled cod on Friday the abstinence day. Roast lamb on Sundays was a fixture, and Saturday's 'meat and veg' was served with *mashed* potatoes instead of the whole variety. The 'sweet' course fluctuated between rice pudding, apple pie, and a fruit pudding, which resembled a plainer variety of its Christmas equivalent.

In the following fourteen years, the time that it took Dermot to complete his studies and training, the same sheet hung on display. It turned yellow and curled up at the corners till eventually it became as brittle as an Egyptian papyrus, but somehow it survived, and so did the meals it listed.

Though the food was monotonous, the manner of its serving was a fascination that amused Dermot from his first day to his last, and which he and "Quinnie " derided continuously as hilarious, inefficient and unnecessary. Their many attempts to have it changed however proved all to no avail.

The food was carried, 12 plates at a time, on large stout wooden trays by two robust lads, who virtually raced to and fro between the service counter and the aisles between the tables. The awaiting students on the alleyway side of the tables grabbed two plates each as the bearers passed by, handing them across the table to the boys opposite who were always served first. This procedure was repeated until all the boys had been served at which point the exhausted carriers were allowed to join the diners. Then before starting to eat the fast cooling food, grace was recited by the presiding prefect, who delivered the prayers in Latin. This procedure, like the menu sheet, persisted down the years.

The school years that followed were progressive if uneventful. The Seminary, which was separated from the college except for meals, introduced the young students to the mysteries of Latin, Greek, French, Maths and the Classics. The General Science lessons scratched at the surface of everything, but in essence taught little of anything.

These studies occupied the minds of the young students up to the age of twenty when they entered a different and more pertinent phase of their training. They studied Philosophy for two years and having survived this experience entered into the serious business of fulfilling their long awaited purpose. They joined the "Divines" and spent their final years studying Theology in all its expansive detail.

It wasn't all work and no play however. They went swimming – twice a week – in the college's excellent pool, and they played seasonal football and cricket. They also sweated and toppled around in the gymnasium under the watchful eye of one of the only two 'lay' instructors employed in the school.

Pat O'Neal was an Irishman whose heritage shone like a beacon from within. He was the consummate joker, and in his day played football for his country. He had a tender side to his nature, which became conspicuous when he refereed their football matches. He did not like to see losers, and would frequently award a struggling team an unjustified penalty kick or two in order to balance up the scores. Equality achieved, he would then blow the whistle before full time to complete the game while honours were still even. The groans from the better players and the better teams only caused him to chuckle with delight.

"Two's each apiece, bhoys!" he would laugh, before congratulating everyone on a "foine sportin' contest"

There were the annual summer field sports too, with trophies - silver cups and shields, which were competed for at the end of each scholastic year and many students took the tradition very seriously, training every evening for weeks beforehand, some even throughout the winter months beforehand.

Radley, a fellow of Dermot's year always came first amongst his equals. He jumped higher, ran faster, and hurled a cricket ball way beyond the attainable limits of his fellows. It was inevitable that as he matured he would become "Victor Ludorum" of the whole college - and he did, once he had reached the ripe old age of 15. The irony was that he trained only a few nights before the games, for just a couple of hours at most! His athletic prowess was truly a god-given talent.

The second lay teacher was Mr John Herberts the Music Master, whose sharp features and aquiline nose gave him a rather severe image, which totally belied his true aesthetic nature. This he displayed eloquently in the expressive beauty of his piano playing. Dermot would listen to him playing for hours with a profound pleasure, which later developed into a mature appreciation of the musical classics that stayed with him into his latter years. John Herberts, for his part, was always pleased and ready to oblige any admirer by playing for him, and their relationship developed into a mutual friendship, which lasted for all of Dermot's college life.

And so the years moved on, and Dermot grew in mind and body, and with each passing year his mother's joy and pride in him was clear for all to see. In contrast, his father became increasingly aloof, and with his parents so visibly polarised over him, life at home suffered badly. Their transformation from a close and loving family unit to a household in strife became conspicuous to both friends and acquaintances alike. And all who saw it were saddened. It was also during this unhappy time that Bridgett left home, and it was not till decades later, when she was with Dermot as his housekeeper that she told him why she had gone away. It was a sad tale of conflicting loyalties as such tales often are, in which young love suffered most.

In the interim, George and Padraig married, set up homes for themselves elsewhere, and left the family nest. To Margaret it seemed that the house now echoed with coldness and emptiness, as Tomas spent more and more time with his friends at the "Catholic Club". For Dermot holiday periods at home became more and more difficult.

Eventually his time at Corshaw was fulfilled, his priestly training was completed, and the day of his ordination finally arrived. All his family, with the conspicuous exception of Tomas, attended the ceremony in the beautiful St Aidan's chapel. The *Class of Twenty-Seven* that he and "Quinnie" had joined were all ordained. There were no dropouts. They had entered as boys and emerged as priests. "Quinnie" became Father John Quinn, and almost in an instant changed into a restrained mature adult, a distinction that had up till then eluded him throughout the long years of his pastoral studies.

Afterwards, when the pomp and ceremony were over and the time came for then to leave to their new lives, the two friends faced each other, darkly suited and pensive in the stiff white collars that now defined their status.

Dermot felt he was losing a brother. The new Father Quinn would eventually join the Dominican order, to serve god as a missionary, a vocation he had developed over the latter years of their formation.

Dermot on the other hand had been appointed locally, as curate at St. Leonard's in Satsworth, not more than a few miles from his home.

"God bless you, and go with you, Dermot," said his much-loved companion

"And with you, dear friend" said Dermot sadly. Then on impulse, he stepped forward and taking the new priest into his arms hugged him fiercely.

"I will never forget you as long as I live, and I will pray for you daily" he said huskily.

"And I you, Dermot ……and I you" replied Father Quinn with emotion. Then without further ado, he turned and walked away. Dermot watched him go with a heavy heart, till he vanished behind the gates through which they had entered together those fourteen years before. He never looked back.

They would never meet or communicate again.

❧

Chapter 10

"...to a greater glory"

The Democratic Cooperative Working Men's Institute was located in the middle of a terraced street of residential houses, consisting in itself of two of those houses, which had been modified to purpose some many years before.

"Knocked together on the cheap by a couple of local navvies," is how club steward Martin Gilpin defined it.

"Later they extended it at the back a bit," he would add with dismissive understatement.

In reality it was a formidable structure, spacious and comfortable, which more than met requirements as a social centre and alehouse.

It stood a hundred yards down from the local police station, across the road from the offices of the Urban District Council's Water Department, and it laboured alternately under the nicknames of the "Demi" or the "Catholic Club".

The latter name was the more commonly used, due to the fact that the long-serving membership was predominantly Catholic. The name was further compounded by the fact that St Hildreth's Catholic Junior School, designed for children between the ages of five to ten years also stood opposite, next to the Water Department's offices, where it served the joint objectives of introducing the children of the club's members to the three "R's", while simultaneously indoctrinating them into the tenants and dogma of the Roman protocol.

The club's narrow entrance with its plain grey door created minimal expectation for anyone contemplating entry for the very first time, but opened surprisingly onto a long brightly illuminated hall, along which ran a flower-patterned carpet that stopped abruptly at the foot of the staircase that led up to the steward's private apartments. A quick turn right then sharp left for a further five yards led to the two steps down into the salon which formed the main bar and games room.

The snooker table was set centrally in the room, and usually occupied by players whose moderate skills were invariably subjected to caustic abuse from the critical steward as he polished glasses with a clean white towel behind the bar, when not otherwise serving beer to his thirsty customers.

On opposing walls hung two dartboards, with mandatory chalk and slates for marking scores. Each was set amidst a plethora of plainly framed sepia photographs depicting scenes from Eastinglea's past, which contrasted incongruously with the elaborately gilded coloured portrait of the club's founding fathers hanging proudly over the marbled fireplace.

Below in the hearth, the fire irons and the polished copper bucket brightly reflected the glow of the blazing coals.

It was a good club, and it enjoyed a popular notoriety in the community which benefited frequently from the morale boosting social activities that were so often inspired and activated by the club members and in particular by those who subscribed to the activities of *The Christian Men's Charitable Society*, which used the club's facilities as the meeting point for all its activities. Their numbers were small and membership was exclusive to only those whom the President selected, and the President was Thomas Holland.

They had been operating through all the war years and their reputation was built on the help that they provided through the good times and the bad. Typically they organised sports days for the schools and swimming competitions in the local docks – conditional only on the tides and the weather – with a fallback plan to go to the baths along Newcastle Road in Sunderland, when thundering waves over the unfenced pier made the dockside an unsafe haven on which to assemble. Not all pursuits were hazardous however, most were placid and humdrum, but of equal importance to the participants. There were picnic days, afternoon teas, and hot suppers for the old aged pensioners, to which the club steward and the other members also contributed with enthusiasm. They took the old folk on days out to see the local sights and beauty spots. They even hired a boat to take them up the river Tyne where they enjoyed lunch at a prestigious hotel by the riverbank. They made hospital visits to the sick, and home visits to the housebound. After all as they told everyone repeatedly, "there is a war on and we all have to pull together to keep our spirits up". It is fair to say that morale throughout the community remained on a high, due in no small measure to the work of the *C.M.C.S.!* And they paid for it all from monies donated by the local public. Popularity in Eastinglea loosened the purse strings of even the most frugal amongst the people, and generous gifts from the local council and civic dignitaries came pouring in. The *C.M.C.S.* was not an impoverished organisation.

And when they were not engaged in charitable works of mercy, they were at the Drill Hall, learning the art of killing as soldiers in the Territorial Army and the Home Guard!

On this particular Tuesday night, in February 1941, quiet as always by weekend standards, and more so than usual in the freezing cold of the winter's evening, the members present were variously engrossed in heated discussions about the war, the weather, racing and football, as they perused the assorted newspapers spread across the tables before them. The discussions became louder as pint glasses were repetitively raised, stimulating the essence of their conversations. An ever-thickening cloud of blue smoke from cheap cigarettes hung heavily on the air.

Back up the hallway towards the entrance, in the room to the right known respectfully as the "Committee Room", a group of some sixteen men met in conclave behind locked doors. Huddled together in close council they talked in subdued tones. One man was the focus of the gathering, and his companions deferred to him respectfully, as they took their places. He was Tomas Mulholland, now respectfully established in the community as Thomas Holland, the "Irish Overman".

This night he would speak to them of murder and treason!

⁊

Tomas had started his working career as a miner, *on bank*, as the manager had indicated he should, working on *THE SCREENS* where raw coal just out of the pit was graded before shipment. The Screens were housed in an overhead shed to which a moving belt conveyed the mixed coal for sorting and grading. It then passed onwards to men lined up on each side of the belt. Their task was to remove the unwanted stone content, discarding it down rectangular funnelled chutes into wagons standing on the tracks below. Once full, the wagons were shunted away, and emptied onto nearby slagheaps, which mushroomed daily around the pit's perimeters, and could be seen from afar as scars on the face of the surrounding countryside. These ugly black hills defined the common profile of every mining town across the County, and their unsightly existence symbolised the economic dependence of these communities on the all-embracing coal industry - and its masters.

Tomas found screen work unchallenging, and financially unrewarding, and determined that he would get below ground as quickly as possible, where 'the real money' was to be earned. So he applied himself with dedication to his work, ignoring the sullen resentment displayed by his younger workmates, callow youths who with little heart for the job and even less responsibility, sneered at Tomas's diligence and work ethic. In stark contrast, they directed their own energies to further advancing their already entrenched malingering practices. Tomas paid no heed to them, and since their personal animosity did not extend to deriding him within earshot, he remained largely unaware of their juvenile ill will.

Eventually his conscientiousness paid the dividends he sought; his supervisors noted his efforts, and within a few short weeks they brought him his just reward. He was recommended for underground work in the pit.

Once there, he committed himself to his new challenges with equal fervour, and rapidly earned the unspoken respect of both masters and fellows. He started initially as a *'putter'*, - moving the heavily laden coal tubs out of the workings and empty ones in, to the men labouring in short face areas known as *bord and pillar* workings. Tomas worked diligently at his task and quickly graduated to join the *Stonemen*.

Stonework was an activity, which demanded muscle, skill, and an awareness of danger from those whose job it was to develop the roadways behind the colliers, blasting down the overhead roof section - the *'top caunch'* - as it was called - that was left hanging behind each advancing coalface, and lifting the *'bottom caunch'* too, the stone beneath, which remained once the coal had been extracted. Tomas's strength and work rate impressed his new companions, as with relative ease he manhandled heavy timbers into place, and packed more stone into the side walls than any among them could match, despite their long years at the task. So these new mates, or *'marras'*, as they were known in the underground parlance of the pit, quickly accepted him as a man among equals.

However, it was not to be his physical prowess that would ultimately establish him in their eyes, but a singular act of bravery that saved the life of his own particular *'marra"*, Big Jim Lewis.

Big Jim was a tall, lean, and muscular man, whose lithe and sinewy frame had been shaped over years of continuous labour as a collier. He was a veteran of his trade and an ideal working partner, and Tomas was very grateful to be teamed up with him. Stonemen mostly worked in teams of three, occasionally four. It was a specialist skill with specific hazards for which each man cultivated an instinctive alertness and respect, but only after continued years of exposure to them. Big Jim had the experience and was considered by all to be the complete stoneman. Nevertheless it was considered remarkable that after only a short working span together, their partnership had developed so well that Jim and Tomas were allowed to continue as an exclusive two-man team. Their earnings went up accordingly, and many of their colleagues regarded them with silent envy, but silent it remained, for none could equal their strength, their stamina and their output.

The shift had started well that night, with good humour and banter in the *cage*, the shallow steel box, which, suspended on thick steel hawsers and held vertically between heavily greased runners hung over the open pit-shaft, where it acted as the hoist both for man and coal. It would, at a given signal from the *banksmen* to the *engine room*, carry them down into the dark recesses of the pit below. The *'tub-loading'* or repair shift - Dead Man's Walk - as it was sometimes called, started at ten o'clock in the evening. It was not a popular time to start a shift, but stonework was self-defining as repair work, and for Tomas and Big Jim that was their task that night as on others.

There were only five of them in the cage, four workmen and a supervisor, standing crouched in the low confinement of the half-lit box, waiting patiently till the 'banksman' secured the doors and signalled the 'engineman' to thrust them down below.

Matt Brownlie was the *'Deputy Overman'* in charge, a title that was invariably shortened to *Deputy*. More usually officials were addressed only by their first name, - titles and formalities underground were regarded as unnecessary, the common yardstick being a man's competence rather than his job title.

It was Matt's turn to take the flak that night, to be the butt of the jokes. Notorious as a dedicated gardener, he had a proclivity for exaggerating his horticultural skills and the produce that resulted from them, and that evening it laid him open to the incisive wit of his companions.

"How's y'r allotment these days Matt?" asked Jim with feigned interest.

A knowing chuckle spread through the cage.

"Fine, fine," came the cautious reply, "Why d'ye ask, like?" His tone was defensive.

"Ah'm interested, Matt, I heard about your *'tattie'* that's all."

Before Matt could reply, Jim turned to Tomas and with a smile on his face that was hidden in the shadowy gloom said,

"Did ye kna Thomas, Matt grew a tattie that big they had chips off it for a fortnight!"

As the laughter subsided, Jim added wickedly,

"And they gave the other half to the people next door!"

Guffaws greeted the outrageous remark, but Matt's spluttering retort was lost as the cage started its fast plunge downwards, and the roar of the updraft drowned out his remarks.

The shift was only half over when the roof came down. Big Jim was *backbye* at the time, a short distance from the work place, helping a young putter lift his supply tub back on the *'way'*. It had run away from him, back down the slight incline that lead into the face before he could get the *'keps in'* - short metal bars used as crude brakes which they jammed into the wheels. The tub had accelerated rapidly before jumping the track and knocking out two heavy support timbers at the roadside amid clouds of stifling dust.

"Pillock!" said Jim, as they turned to see the turmoil.

"Leave it. I'll help him!" He went back to do so, and Tomas resumed his work

Minutes later, as Jim and the young putter sweated at their task, the roof above them began to creak, and dirt and debris started to rain down onto the young lad's head who stood gasping and blowing in panic, as dust choked his nose and throat. In a flash Jim threw himself at the lad and knocked him backwards away from the impending danger. But then he tripped and crashed to the ground , banging his head against the hard steel edge of the track. He lay unconscious and still, as the falling debris landed on him, while the young putter made only wailing noises, as he stared at him in terror safe from the danger himself. Tomas, turned sharply at the new commotion to see his companion, face down on the ground, disappearing rapidly beneath a shower of small stones, which cascaded down with increasing rapidity. He was being buried alive. Racing back Tomas threw himself across Jim's body, and arching his back to protect his friend's head, screamed at the petrified youth to get help. The young putter startled into alertness ran to the face, shouting to raise the alarm. The repairmen on the face came scurrying out to the scene. By the time they got to them, Tomas and Jim were barely visible under the rising mound of stone, which threatened to bury them completely. It took several frantic minutes to drag them free, and hardly had they done so when the roof above groaned, then with an angry roar crashed down onto the spot where they had lain. When the clouds of dust had passed they looked in silent horror at the large boulder that almost completely blocked the road. They had escaped death by a hair's breadth!

Tomas's back was a mess of blood and dirt where the rocks had cut deeply into him. His rescuers rubbed in fine coal dust to staunch the bleeding. Miners commonly used it as temporary first aid on open wounds, which when healed would remain as permanent blue scars. The Deputy arrived at the scene soon afterwards and deeming it unsafe to carry on working, ordered everyone out of the work place; the shift was abandoned.

He then cleaned and bandaged Tomas's wounds more appropriately, with antiseptic salves and unguents from his medical kit, but by then the blue scars were already Tomas's for life, and all the cleansing in the world would never remove them. Amongst his peers, he would carry them as a badge of honour for the rest of his life. Jim had suffered concussion in his fall, and was unable to stand or walk. However due to Tomas's timely intervention , he had suffered relatively minor cuts and abrasions and these were quickly cleaned and dressed.. . four men carried him out, still semi-conscious and strapped to a stretcher, while Tomas walked out leaning heavily on the Deputy for support. By the time they got out to the shaft, Jim had regained consciousness, and as realisation of his position dawned on him, he hotly gave vent to his 'spleen'. He began protesting vehemently that he could walk perfectly well.

"Ah'm not a stretcher case Matt! Ah can walk! Let me gerrup! Ah look really daft on here!"

"You always look daft, but you'll stay on that stretcher till the doctor sees you," ordered Matt.

"Come on Matt, it's embarrassin'! Give us a break!" Jim pleaded, but Brownlie was unrepentant.

"That'll teach you to take the piss out of my tatties!" he said with a wicked grin. "Stop where you are!"

Tomas smiled through his pain, and the others laughed loudly.

As Tomas convalesced at home, his companions visited him regularly, calling to applaud his courage and bravery, and he knew his reputation was entrenched when the colliery manager sent a letter of congratulations - with an accompanying bottle of whisky. From then forward it would be only a matter of time before his mining career progressed first to Deputy and then to District Overman. Tomas Mulholland had arrived in Eastinglea. He felt deeply satisfied with life, and as he contemplated his status within this close community, he sipped at the scotch and drew on his briar. The radio played quietly behind him and he smiled. It was time. He could start making his plans now!

❦

They sat around the oaken table; six each side with Tomas at the head and Michael facing him from the opposite end, between George and Padraig. As he stood up to address them, the quiet chatter faded away as they turned their attention to him.

"Gentlemen," he started stiffly, then relaxed with a thin smile,

"Friends," he corrected himself,

"Thanks for being here tonight. It's cold out there and I know that like me some of you would have been much happier at home by the fireside listening to the radio with your wives and children, so I say again thanks for making the effort and coming here. I hope once you have heard what I have to say you'll think it was worth your while."

His smile faded and his mood became serious once more.

"All of you have an inkling what this meeting is about, some of you may already know the details. I'm sure none of you believe it's about organizing yet another charity dance, or another pie and pea supper for the old age pensioners."

He allowed himself a slight grin and his listeners chuckled politely.

"When we founded the *Christian Men's Charitable Society,* here in this club those few years ago, it was created as an organization for the promotion of good works and charitable functions within the Eastinglea society, an organisation that would front our underlying purpose. We have achieved that objective; we have established ourselves very well within this community. In the eyes of our neighbours we are a respected institution that can be relied on, even to repair the ravages of the Luftwaffe's nightly rages. We shall continue to promote that image to the full, for that is our front, the public face that has helped us to permeate into local society as trusted citizens, and we have enhanced this image by joining in the Defence of the Home Front in the Home Guard and the Territorial Army.

"As you know, Michael here is already established in the T.A. with the rank of sergeant. I cannot emphasise enough that his military status and position is essential if we are to pursue the course we now have in mind.

"For now and for the future, we shall remain paragons in this society; we will render our services whenever and wherever asked. We have done this in the past and we will continue to do it for the present. Nothing we do must cause any concern; no one must distrust us. Let caution be our watchword. We shall practice it, we shall sustain it, till all our targets have been met."

He paused and looking around searched each face for dissent or dismay. He saw none, and so he carried on.

"As I said, the *C.M.C.S.* is a front, and you all know that. It has been a front since its creation, for fund raising activities, and you have all participated in those activities. You have all been involved, and you have raised considerable monies over these past few years, monies that we have sent to Ireland, to the freedom fighters of the IRA. Your monies have helped to provide guns, ammunition, explosives, ordnance of all kinds, which has been used to promote the fight against the British, and sadly against some at home who would stand against unification of all Ireland under a single flag.

"We are Irishmen everyone, are we not? Then we must prove it! We must go the extra mile."

He stopped again as he saw confused glances pass between his listeners.

"I know some of you are British by birth, but all of you are Irish in your heritage, for you come from Irish stock, from families who have suffered before you. Your parents and guardians, some of whom are now unable to bear the banner of freedom because they are too old, or sadly in some cases, no longer with us, expect this of you. You are their representatives and the fact that you are in this organisation and have stood with us since the start makes you as Irish as anyone before you, who through ill fortune and circumstance were driven to settle in this alien land. I put it to you all here and now, is there anyone among us who doesn't look to Ireland for his origins, for his roots?"

A murmur of 'nays' followed, but as he looked around them, he was not sure that he could carry them further with him.

They were a fine group of enthusiastic young men, he had no doubt, and he knew them all personally. Each was handpicked and they all had an ingrained Irish heritage, and they had travelled with him so far.

James Kennedy was there, so typical of the rest. Tomas liked him a lot. His presence was not entirely chance however, due in no small measure to the fact that he was an eager admirer of Tomas's daughter Bridgett. James hoped that in achieving Tomas's approval, he might make comfortable progress with his more personal priorities. Tomas was happy enough with this 'ulterior' motivation, since it ensured that James was ready to carry out everything that Tomas might ask of him without question.

James's parents too had become victims in the Easter Uprising. They had been forced to leave him, as a child, in the care of relatives with whom he had travelled to England when just a boy. When his uncle Bob Wallace, another suspected activist, with his loyal wife Annie had evaded their pursuers and escaped to England, they had been only a few steps ahead of the police and the "*forces of occupation*" as Bob Wallace contemptuously described the British Army. They had brought James with them. They had made him their responsibility when he was passed to them, literally at the dock gates in the port of Dublin. James's father had handed him over, with a desperate plea to his brother-in-law to take James with him as his own.

"They're after us Bob, some bloody traitor has grassed us up! They won't let us on the boat! We'll have to go into hiding; we're on the run now! "

So the Wallaces had taken James in that instant, and if truth be told, he had helped their image, when, as a family they had made their way past the scrutiny of the vigilant security guards onto the boat to England. Like Tomas, they had then been forced to assume new identities and forge a new existence for themselves and their 'son James'.

James's real parents had returned to Dublin, and their fates became a mystery after the military authorities detained them both on unspecified charges. Later, not even contacts in the movement had been able to discover what had happened to them. They were never seen or heard of again.

So while James was genuinely of Irish birth, others amongst his listeners were not, and Tomas wondered if they were ready to commit that bit further, to sacrifice a little more.

Could he call them to the *Cause,* would they be willing to step over the line between law and outlaw! He pondered these thoughts before he continued.

"However, while all of you have consented to, and participated in past activities, not all of you are aware of the further ambitions that we nurse to move our organisation forward, to go beyond the fund-raising exercises we have so far engaged in, and to become a proactive force in the pursuit of war against the British, for only by fighting them can Ireland ever become a united and independent republic. It is to make you aware that I have called you all here tonight."

His listeners looked tense, but they remained silent.

"Those nearest me are conscious that I have intense personal motivation in promoting this organisation. Those of you who don't know of my motivation, should listen carefully now.

"I openly admit to a desire for retribution. I admit to seeking justice against the one man who is responsible for the death of my father and my mother. A man, dear friends, who now lives his life in good health and luxurious wealth not too far from where we are now. This man is guilty of murder, but he will never be brought to justice in the courts of this land, and will have long ago forgotten the deaths of two inconsequential Irish individuals who crossed his path during the years of his corrupt crimes in Ireland. I have not forgotten dear friends and I intend to see that justice be served! This man's name must for now remain a secret, but I promise you that come the hour I will reveal it to each and every one of you. I will not ask you to act against him without you know who he is and why he must see justice. Furthermore, I will seek that justice within the laws of our *Organisation,* within the military codes of the IRA unit that we shall institute.

"For that, gentlemen, is why I have brought you here tonight, to establish an Active Service Unit of the IRA in Eastinglea, with you as its core, its soldiers, its heroes. And in it, we shall fulfil our purpose and rise to glory, *to a greater glory* than you could have ever thought possible"

The was an instant buzz around the room and the air grew thick with excitement, visible in the assortment of the tentative smiles, the worried glances, and the sharp expletives that immediately spread through the room.

Tomas seizing the moment raised the mood further, as he continued in a loud and commanding voice.

"None of you can be surprised by this announcement, for you have been alerted to the possibility for the past two years. Michael has assiduously brought you to a state of military preparedness, fashioning you all, from raw recruits to skilled soldiers of the Territorial Army, and all by the courtesy of his noble majesty, King George VI! If you believed you were doing this because you were good and loyal citizens, then you have deluded yourselves. For no one can actively participate in the real objectives of the C.M.C.S., whose function you all know, and yet be a committed loyalist of this King and this country as well.

"Listen carefully to what I have to say, and then you must make some decisions!" His tone demanded their full attention.

"First we all need to remember- to be reminded even - why are we here! Why do we live here in England? Why are we Irishmen in exile? Why are we not back in Ireland, with our families and kinsfolk? That small and beautiful island, made even smaller by its division, a division imposed by the wealth of the Protestant landowners and their industrial allies in the North, who with only their own interests in mind have determined that Ulster shall prosper as an integral part of the United Kingdom, while the rest of the Republic wallows in what it defines as self imposed deprivation and poverty.

"The British contempt for our nation goes back a long way. For while our histories have been inexorably linked for centuries, the contempt in which we are held goes back just as far.

"Did you now, my friends, that Elizabeth I, the Virgin Queen herself, recognized today as perhaps the greatest figurehead of England's imperialist past, once said *"Let the Irish go hang themselves!"*" His audience looked surprised, but guffawed loudly as he continued,

"And you know something boys, we have been doing our best to oblige the lady ever since."

Tomas resumed,

"Not much of an insult you might think, but such contempt from 'Good Queen Bess' set a yardstick of disregard that has prevailed ever since. We find ourselves here today my friends because down the centuries such people have continued to refuse us the right to self-determination, and to crush by force all those who were bold enough to seek it!

"The British became the landlords, they taxed us into penury, and then confiscated our holdings to pay these unsustainable taxes. They drove us out to foreign fields like the one in which we find ourselves today, for England is a foreign field my friends, make no mistake about that!

"And what has happened since, to the *Cause* that our fathers died for? Our own politicians, at home in Ireland, fight among themselves even as I speak, and incredibly many betray the very cause for which they fought just a few short years ago.

"They have forgotten already, and they have compromised themselves in the eyes of the people by making concessions to the old enemy on the divisions of our land.

"It's the same land, it's our land, and it's the same enemy, the same British enemy!

"These people have betrayed the very reason why we fought in the first place; and now they will have us as outlaws! They have declared the Organisation illegal, just the same way as the British did! They are conspiring to placate the enemy!!

"They have pillaged our heritage just as surely as if they were British themselves. They have made *The Army* a criminal group in our own land, and imprisoned those who still stand for the declaration of 1916."

"But let me not digress, I haven't finished with the Brits yet!" A few smiled as he took a drink form the glass before him.

"So where could we go then, and where can we go now, us "criminals"? To America – some did! To Australia – some did! But for most of us the easy route was the only route, and so we came to England, to the very country, which had ejected us from our homeland in the first place. This was a bitter pill to swallow, but we have had to swallow it. And now my dear friends we are subject to their laws, their customs, their aristocracy, and even *their war*! And this is the for the second time in only twenty years!"

The silence in the room was unbroken, as they contemplated his words with unwavering attention.

"Gentlemen! Friends!" he spoke quietly again, encouragingly,

"It's time to fight back. It's time to reclaim what's rightfully ours. It's time to reclaim our country. All of it! North and South! And we are going to do just that!

The air was heavy with expectation. Tomas felt he was winning them over as he continued,

"I will tell you where we go from here. How we are going to advance our activities to a proactive level of involvement, but before I can do that I want to offer you, each of you, the chance to walk away, because once you have heard what I propose there can be no walking away afterwards.

"Each man that commits to me tonight stays committed to me for keeps. Allegiance - total and absolute is essential - loyalty is mandatory."

The mood stayed sombre but still no one spoke. A few shuffled feet were the only sounds as he looked around them. He continued,

"I know you all. I trust you all. You are all honest men. Your loyalty has been proven time and time again. Our position in this community is established on the foundations of the personal integrity of each one of you. Yet I fear you! I fear the very integrity that has proven your trustworthiness; I fear the consciences of such honest men. I fear the confusion of conscience that comes upon people of integrity when the limits of right and wrong are challenged. That is my worry, my concern. To take this organisation forward to the next phase, that of direct action, I must be sure that clarity of mind will *justify* and not *inhibit* the projects in which we shall become involved."

Again he scrutinised the faces before him, looking for doubt, for fear, for resistance to his words.

"If any of you are disturbed by what you hear right now, then I urge you to leave. Do not commit to what you doubt, for such doubt constitutes a threat to the structure of our organisation that may jeopardise our activities in the future. We cannot have such threats among us."

There was an edge to this final remark, which was not lost on his listeners.

"I shall go to the bar now for half an hour. I have some monies to pay over to Gilpin from recent activities of ours. You may wish to take this opportunity to discuss all that I have said, to assess your feelings and your reactions. Some of you may wish to take this opportunity to leave, and I will respect your decision.

"I shall remain confident in your continuing silence as to the secret activities of the C.M.C.S. I must emphasise that those who go, cannot return! They are out, just as permanently as they who stay are in! Regrettably gentlemen, I must also add this rider.

"If I should be proved wrong in judging the loyalties of any who leave, and someone who is now a friend should later become a betrayer, then appropriate reckoning will be exacted against that person.

"I don't need to remind you that activities against the state in times of war are judged treasonous by the British government, for which the penalty is death. Gentlemen, we must protect ourselves in similar fashion."

There were audible intakes of breath before a tactile silence descended on the room, as they each contemplated the implications of his words.

Then Tomas, in more relaxed mode, said,

"I'll have the steward send some beer in." Then turning he left the room closing the door quietly behind him.

Behind him, they emitted a collective sigh of relief.

Tomas went to the bar feeling very exhausted. He wasn't sure that he had achieved his purpose. But he believed that most would stay with him, and he was satisfied that should any in conscience be unable to do so, they would not betray the comrades with whom they had worked so loyally over these recent years. Of the twelve he felt sure of eight, and eight would be enough to complete his self-appointed task. He leaned on the counter as he contemplated these things.

"Penny for them Tommy!" Tomas was shaken out of his reverie by the sharp voice of the steward who stood before him grinning broadly. Tomas gave a startled laugh.

"Sorry Martin I was miles away."

"I gathered that, what can I get you?"

"Nothing really Martin, I've just come to pay you some money." He handed over an envelope that rattled with cash.

"I never refuse money, Tommy", Gilpin was the only man who ever called Tomas by the diminutive 'Tommy'.

"It's payment for the grub you supplied at the last social evening in the hall."

"Fine I'll take it if you have it, but I haven't put the bailiff on you yet, you know, I can wait. I don't believe you are about to flee the country, are you?" he beamed.

"Not for a while just yet" was Tomas's guarded reply.

The steward laughed loudly,

"I'll take a pint now Martin, and the boys in the committee room would appreciate a dozen pints of your best bitter if you can organise that for them. Michael will have his usual brown ale. There are a few dry whistles that need wetting in there. They are thinking of renaming it the 'Desert Lounge'."

"Consider it done Tommy," said Gilpin as he placed an overflowing glass on the bar before Tomas.

"Take the money for the beers out of the cash in the envelope, I think there's enough," he added as he raised the cold beer to his lips.

"Aren't you going back in there?" said Gilpin curiously.

Tomas was momentarily caught off guard but he replied quite plausibly to the unexpected question.

"They are discussing electing a new chairman for the C.M.C.S. It's hard to believe but we have never got round to making it official after all this time. Can you believe it?" he added, with a less than convincing smile.

"I think it could be me – since they asked me to leave! Don't forget to knock before you enter, it's like a secret society in there. They'll have the door locked probably!"

The steward nodded and reached for a large tray on which he placed the glasses to be filled. Tomas turned from the bar to seek a quiet spot in which to sit alone. He acknowledged each of the members present but he did so only briefly, with a pleasant but non-committal nod that implied he did not wish to engage in social chitchat with anyone. He made his way to an empty table in the corner by the dartboard. As he sat down to contemplate his future, Gilpin's words came rushing back to him.

"...I don't suppose you are about to leave the country!" They sounded almost prophetic, and a sudden shiver ran through him. For a moment he felt scared.

"Get hold of yourself," he reprimanded himself, but he could not shake off a growing feeling of apprehension. He took a long draught from his beer, and as he put down the glass Michael appeared in the bar, and made his way over to where Tomas was sitting.

"We need to talk Tomas, before you go back in there, there are things you need to know before you commit yourself to statements you might afterwards regret."

"What the hell does that mean, Michael?" said Tomas slightly irritated and nervous.

"Just end the meeting now, Tomas; tell them that's enough for the first meeting and we'll have more to say next week about where we go from here. Send them home happy – and curious. You won't regret it I promise you. I have information you need to know, about our ongoing operations..."

At that moment Gilpin reappeared, casually swinging the now empty tray. He walked across to where Tomas and Michael were deeply engrossed and his arrival stopped Michael from continuing.

"They're ready for you up there, Tommy; looks like you've got the job"

Tomas's apprehension disappeared and feeling relieved and elated, he downed the rest of his pint in one. Michael tried to restrain him, but Tomas was already on his feet.

"Right Martin thanks, I'll go up then."

As he entered the room, there was an air of friendly geniality. Michael followed behind, looking serious and concerned.

"Three cheers for the Commander! Hip hip...!" cried a voice at the back,

"Hooray!" was the unanimous response.

Tomas tried to hush them, fearing to draw attention to their activities, but they would not be stilled, and continued their cheers with gusto. Michael stepped back, smiling stiffly, but his smile faded to an apprehensive frown as he studied the eagerness and enthusiasm in the admiring young faces around Tomas.

A muffled voice from an anonymous person entering and passing down the hallway was heard to shout,

"Can I have a pint of what they're drinking please?" and laughing at his own cliché moved onwards to the bar.

The incident sobered the mood enough to get them to resume their seats, chatting lightly as they did so. Tomas moved ceremoniously to the head of the table again, and Michael retreated to his place at the opposite end. Tomas stood for a while quietly enjoying his confirmed authority, and he felt satisfied that his purpose had been vindicated by their support. He spoke in quiet voice, carefully choosing his words.

"I want to thank you all for your vote of confidence in me, and in what we plan to do. Before I go any further I want to take some time to convince you of my personal sincerity in our right to fight, our right to seek to unite our homeland and to free it of the last vestiges of British dependency.

"The leaders of the 1916 Easter revolution were murdered, for fighting for this cause and for spitting in the face of the of the world's biggest Empire. They were murdered because they dared to demand freedom in the land that was their own. We must never forget those men; we must remember their names. We must teach our children to recite them just as they so easily recite the catechism of the church, with which they are indoctrinated daily in the classrooms just across the road from here. Who takes time in those classrooms to teach them their Irish heritage, may I ask, no one. Who teaches them about the martyrs of our past I ask, no one. Well brothers we must fill those gaps in their education, we must be teachers as well as soldiers. Turning to Padraig, his eldest son he nodded an unspoken command. Padraig stood up, and with his arms reverentially straight down at his sides began to recite

"The men who proclaimed the first Republic of Ireland on the steps of the General Post Office in Dublin's fair city were: Thomas J Clarke, Sean

MacDiamada, Thomas MacDonagh, Padraig H. Pearse, Eamonn Ceannt, James Connelly, and Joseph Plunkett." Then he sat down again to a round of applause from the group, and an approving nod from Tomas, who paused briefly before continuing,

"When they crushed the Uprising so brutally, and executed these patriots in such haste, within only days of arrest and without fair trial, the British stirred in the good citizens of Dublin a surge of sympathetic reaction that had hitherto been absent. This grew into bitter resentment, which flooded like a tidal wave into the provinces and beyond into the other towns and cities across the land. It carried a demand for retribution that has not, and will not be stilled. It cries out yet for fulfilment. It has survived the civil strife of the twenties, and remains an enduring mandate for freedom, unity, and justice for *all* Ireland.

"I tell you men, this flickering flame will not be extinguished!"

There was a chorus of approval as the passion in Tomas spread like a virus to infect them all.

"Here in this insignificant corner of northern England we are charged with fanning this flame back into life. We are the wind that shall re-ignite it. We shall create confusion in this backwater, and our actions shall generate shock waves that will be felt at the heart of government, in London itself. Gentlemen we shall be the enemy within!"

He tried to hush them but could not, and the noise of their celebrations was heard loudly down the corridor in the bar where heads were turned and voices raised in question, before Gilpin took it upon himself to offer explanation.

"Tommy's just been made Chairman of the C.M.C S. I know we all thought he was already but now it's official, it seems."

They accepted the explanation with a few wry comments and returned to their usual pre-occupations with their beers and their arguments.

In the committee room order was restored and Tomas proceeded in quiet voice,

"First, we need training. Our soldiers must all receive specialist training and you are those soldiers now. I shall send some of you to Ireland. There are camps in the hills of County Wicklow for just this purpose. Four of you will go there, ostensibly by invitation to attend a retreat for Catholic Charities. I don't know how they did it, but the Army Council has contrived to convince the authorities of the validity of the Catholic Charities as an organisation and travel papers are available whenever we want them. The selected four will be our specialists in bomb making." A murmur of excitement rippled from his engrossed listeners.

"Those of you who stay will extend your local training beyond the basics in the TA and the Home Guard, and Michael will ensure you come directly under his personal command. The British have challenged us all to do our duties, so we will, those among you who are young and fit enough will that is. As you know Michael is a sergeant - in the local DLI battery. His position serves our purpose admirably. Once assigned to his group, you must behave as all his other soldiers behave. When spoken to by him or given an order by him, you will respond in an appropriately disciplined manner, just like all the others. You must not draw attention to yourselves by over familiarity with Michael. Take your situations seriously, we shall put you all to good use believe me, when we go operational in a couple of months time. We have already identified specific targets around the county, none of which will be traceable back to us here in Eastinglea." He smiled as he added laconically,

"As for me, I shall not be joining you in this enterprise. I disqualify myself as a candidate on counts of both age and fitness." They laughed politely, as he continued,

"Michael will brief you on what weapons we have, and where they are stored. He will also instruct you as to how more can be appropriated. I see no need to transport arms from Ireland if we can acquire them on our doorstep" He smiled lightly, and they responded similarly.

"We who are left – the unfit lot – will develop the administration, and the lines of communication, particularly with other Active Units throughout the UK. For a while we will be totally dependent on them. We will need their help in establishing depots and stocking them. We will have to establish safe houses in the community for visitors and friends from "abroad".

"Other Active Units?" James Kennedy looked surprised as he interrupted.

"Yes James, other units, cells like ours. You didn't think we were alone in this enterprise now surely! There are many units already established, some of which have been on active service for years now, and have survived despite the joint efforts of the British over here, and even the Government back home. They have been very active in London, the Midlands and the North West. in particular. There are a lot of them, but common sense security demands that only two of us here can know the details of their structures, locations, and the likes, as indeed only two in each of those cells will know ours. I can give you some background if you wish." It was a rhetorical question and he continued without pause.

"The Army has been engaged in UK operations for several years now, even before the current conflict with our German friends got started. 'Targeting Britain' is a current operation you will not have heard of, but it is an established campaign. Its activities have been reported in the press, but always been underplayed. In the current climate of news censorship you may have missed it. The British don't like to publicise the bad news too much, but I can give you some of the recent history.

"In 1939, the Army engaged in successful bombing attacks in Manchester, Birmingham, Liverpool and even not too far from our doorstep here, in Alnwick just up the coast into Northumberland. Further bombings were carried out in the London tube stations, and as a result police activities around the capital were heavily intensified. Apparently you couldn't walk down Whitehall without being confronted by policemen on the look out for our soldiers, who the newspapers of course described as terrorists.

"This pre-occupation with chasing our boys distracted their attention from the pressing problem of the oncoming war with Germany. And it gave prominence to the question of a united Ireland by lifting its profile. We made sure we weren't forgotten in the panic about Germany. However back home things were not going to well.

"It was about this time that De Valera began to show his true colours, and condemned the IRA movement for what he termed its 'physical force' politics. He was shit-scared of anything that might compromise what he regarded as "Ireland's neutrality". So much so that when Winston Churchill tried to court him, thinking that this might be a good time to persuade him to let British ships use Irish ports, De Valera wasn't having anything to do with it, even after Churchill promised to commit the British government to the principle of a united Irish State. He didn't trust them to keep their word, once the war was over. He was bloody well wise not to! At least he got that right! However he was so bloody hung up on the neutrality thing, and so scared the Army's activities might give the British an excuse to invade Ireland, that he then went to war on the *Organisation* himself, introducing his "Offences against the State Act" and creating military tribunals to deal with the IRA in our own backyard at home in Ireland!

"All he accomplished with that was to increase the contempt and hatred with which he was viewed by the Army. They treated him with total disregard and the military operations in London actually increased. All in all, during 1939 there were 242 operations carried out against the British in their own backyard, and all they could do was to throw more police at the problem, introduce the "Prevention of Terrorism Bill" and as you all know, compulsory registration of Irish citizens in Britain. What they never understood was that only the so-called 'law-abiding Irish' ever registered, while the boys from the Army stayed very much under cover.

"On the down side, De Valera's campaign in the Republic right now is being intensified in an all out attempt to wipe out the IRA, and because of it many good patriots have been imprisoned and some even murdered in that hell hole of a camp at the Curragh. The irony of this is that because of this persecution in the South, the centre of operational activities has been moved North to the six counties which is the focal point of the whole dispute! It seems to be absurdly ironic that it is now actually safer to be there - among the Unionists!"

He paused to take a drink, looked around his listeners and in a voice filled with bitterness and contempt said "There is another paradox in this affair, which some of you know and which some of you don't. I will tell you about it now.

"When this man - Eamon De Valera – now President of the so-called Irish Free State fought in the 1916 Uprising at Bolands Mill, he had at his side his most loyal supporter, Seamus Mulholland, my father!"

A murmur of surprise emanated from his listeners. Tomas paused again before he continued.

"This same man attended my father's funeral, unidentified and incognito, as the Army Council's official representative."

Another murmur drowned him out for a second. Tomas waited and then continued, "He spoke of my father's heroism, and he made my mother feel very proud. He made me proud too, just to be my father's son, and I felt honoured, just to meet the man. There were arguments about his identity, and he never did reveal his name. Some people said it wasn't De Valera at all. They said at the time De Valera was in jail, and they said that the man who came to the funeral was just someone who looked like him, a double in fact. At that time, common sense secrecy required that he remained anonymous, and so the confusion was all to the good. But I saw him, and I heard him speak. I spoke with him - one to one - and he talked with feeling and sensitivity about my father, and I tell you when I see pictures of him in the papers now, I recognize him! It was he all right! If there was a double anywhere, then it was the double who was in the jail, because Eamon De Valera was at my father's funeral, and that's a fact!"

He paused to control the emotion that had now possessed him. They waited intently.

"Now this man, this very same man, persecutes the movement he was part of; the very movement that gave him his power today! I hate him!" He was shaking with anger as he continued,

"I tell you, men, he is a traitor, to his country and to all our people! But we are steadfast; we are true! We will fight on! To victory – over him - over the British - even over God himself if He gets in the way!"

He was still trembling as he sat down, and a difficult silence followed as they contemplated his emotional words, which for the more devout of the Catholics among them had a tinge of blasphemy about them.

Tomas felt he had said enough for the night, maybe even too much, and he was tired. The evening had drained him, and he needed a drink. He brought the meeting to an abrupt end.

"I won't answer any more questions now. I want you to take time to consider all that has been said here. Take it home with you and ponder it all carefully. I don't need to tell you not to talk to anyone outside this group about any of what we have discussed, and if you discuss things amongst yourselves be careful. The British said it! We'll practice it! "CARELESS TALK COSTS LIVES!"

"Next week Michael will outline plans for our first major operation, which we intend to carry out in the early spring, so be here, all of you. Then he sat down.

❧

They came to him individually as they prepared to leave. James Kennedy came first and stood hesitantly at attention before Tomas.

"Permission to speak Sir, " he said tightly, in military fashion. Tomas suppressed a tired smile, slightly embarrassed at his new status before these men, so recently his friends and contemporaries.

"Relax James," he said kindly, "we are not on operations yet. What can I do for you?" The boy's demeanour eased slightly.

"I'm a little nervous about explaining our absences - like from work and from home! Especially if I'm selected to go to Ireland."

"It's all been prepared already. If you are chosen to go everything will be arranged through proper channels. It can be done and will be done above board and legitimately. You can talk about it as a charity trip to sponsor good relations between our two countries. Since you don't know the details, you can openly say you don't know."

James smiled his satisfaction and said goodnight.

Slowly they all came to him one by one and each in turn saluted before leaving, some hesitantly, some with exuberant enthusiasm. Eventually only he and Michael remained.

Tomas leaned his elbows on the polished table, and lowered his head as he ran his fingers through the curls of his thick black hair, which was showing increasing grey around the temples. Michael silently studied him for a while, noting the fatigue which was so obviously upon him. Then he spoke up, brightly with enthusiasm,

"Do you remember Tomas, when you and I were young men in Ireland, what happy ordinary simple folk we were. We lived for the moment, – like all the other young people of our age – and we laughed a lot. We chased girls, we drank beer, plenty of it too, and we didn't give a thought or a damn about politics. And for sure we didn't hate anybody. We were happy Tomas. Now look at us."

The tone had altered in his last sentence. Tomas raised his head heavily.

"What do you mean – now look at us?"

"You know well what I mean. You've been in this country some twenty years now, and I've been here even longer. We *live* here now. It's almost unbelievable. Neither of us could have conceived it as young men. You've taken on a new identity. You've escaped your past - raised a family here! You're an official at the pit, a respected man in this society, admired by all - and envied by many. Why, you've even got a son in the priesthood, and he and the rest of your offspring speak with an English accent."

Tomas raised his head and looked at Michael suspiciously, who continued,

"This is also true of all those young men in here tonight. They are British now, in everything but origin.

"And that Irish heritage that you wave like a banner before them all the time won't make them any less British. They all respect their origins Tomas, as all our children do, but in the end they live here in England and if you force them too fast, you'll find that's where their ultimate loyalties lie. You have lots of reasons to be grateful to this country Tomas, and even more to this community. Don't you think that maybe you should reflect on these things, and maybe review some of your prejudices? Isn't it time to leave your bigotry behind and start laughing again?"

Tomas began to bristle, but Michael stopped him before he could speak,

"It's a question Tomas, not an accusation. I'm not trying to change you personally, but before you commit these young admirers of yours to something that might end in tragedy or death, ask yourself this. Are you committed to this cause for Ireland, or for yourself? Are you sure you are not motivated only by your self-indulgent search for vengeance!"

They looked at each other across the long table in challenging silence before Tomas spoke,

"Why are you bringing up all these objections now Michael. I thought of all the people here I could depend on you. If you have doubts about me, about the cause, why are you here? Why have you waited to present them now, are you telling me you want out?" Michael laughed.

"Oh not me Tomas. I'm no deserter; you should not need to be told that. I'll not betray you. I'll be at your side every minute, come what may, you can be sure of that" He paused, then his tone changed as he added,

"But you can be sure of something else as well. If for a moment you loose sight of our purpose, our single objective to act for the cause under the aegis and direction of the Army council, I'll be there to re-focus your eyes for you. And as I've said before Tomas, I'll do nothing, and I'll allow nothing to be done, that makes me a party to murder for vengeance sake. Whether it is James Spencer-Lambert or anyone else. Do I make myself clear?"

"Eminently!" said Tomas tersely

"Neither will I endorse any actions that directly threaten the people of Eastinglea, Tomas. These are our friends, our neighbours; our comrades even. They cannot be threatened. All our activities must exclude civilian risk. Military depots, equipment and installations are legitimate targets. Citizens are not!" He paused as he gazed across at Tomas who had never flinched while Michael spoke.

"And one more thing, I need you to understand something. I am your Second-in-Command for all operational activities. The Army Council has decreed it. They have also decreed that all communications between us and Dublin come and go through me."

Tomas rose from his chair sharply and angrily.

"And what makes you think I will accept you as a Second-in-Command after that little speech you have just made, Michael? How do you suppose I could trust you to carry out my orders? How on earth could I confide in you about strategy and war plans? You are not fit to be a Second-in Command. I'm not even sure you are fit to serve at all." Michael interrupted him loudly.

"Tomas, you have confided in me since we were boys! Every cock-eyed prank you ever conceived as a lad – every scheme - every trick to get a girl – you had me vet them all before you dared put them into action. Even now, when you are running the C.M.C.S. you need me to look over everything beforehand. I've kept you right till now, and I'll keep you right in the future. You need me Tomas as you need the air you breathe!"

A moment of tense silence followed before Michael added,

"In any case you have no choice!"

Tomas turned white with anger, but Michael continued.

"Get used to it Tomas, It's too early in the day to have dissension in the ranks! I'm the new conscience you have to listen to, the sentinel at your shoulder. We'll be together as a team, with two voices of authority, not one, for this is a project that is much too vital to allow you to exercise unbridled control over it. There has to be checks and balances Tomas - I am yours!" He paused, then added in a quieter voice,

"There's fresh news from Dublin too Tomas, and it's not good. I tried to tell you earlier but you wouldn't listen."

"The organization in Ireland is pretty much in disarray right now. All that you said about De Valera's suppression is true, but what you should have added was that he has pretty much succeeded. The 'Target Britain' campaign has been abandoned. The Army itself is all but a spent force right now, and it has had to run for cover. And while it is re-grouping, it is essential that all units should keep a low profile. Any undue aggravation, whether here or back in Ireland, could result in disastrous repercussions for all. All bombing attacks are suspended. No training is possible at this time. The camps in Wicklow are closed indefinitely. The Council has sent out instructions to curtail all major activities. Minor operations deemed necessary to keep up morale may be completed, but with no IRA claims for responsibility. We have been instructed to disrupt rather than to destroy, to burn rather than to bomb, to irritate but not to fight. For the foreseeable future, we have been pretty well downgraded to a non-active division! We go underground, Tomas. In the meantime, we will continue with the T.A. training for the boys as you outlined, ready for the day when we get back in business. Everything else is on hold. You and I will make the announcement at the meeting next week.

Those are your orders Tomas, and they come from the top."

Chapter 11

Raging Seas and Contemplation

Tomas 'rode to bank' the next afternoon at three-thirty. He rode alone, an hour before his shift was due to end. He had arranged to meet with the Colliery Safety Officer, Mr Mitchell Birbeck. Formerly a district overman like Tomas, Birbeck had moved with his age into a job more appropriate to his years, and had been promoted to Safety Officer where he was now responsible for the all matters pertinent to security of the mine workings and related assets, the principle asset being the colliers themselves. Birbeck was a man fully qualified for such a responsibility.

Ostensibly, Tomas's reason for asking for a meeting was to discuss the refurbishment of the overhead *roadway dust barriers*. These structures were flat wooden boards, set loosely on high supporting frameworks and filled to overflowing with finely divided stone-dust powder. Thus loaded, the boards were straddled across the roadways at pre-determined intervals, as dictated by the Colliery's safe working practice codes.

Coal miners, through the experience of many generations, had developed an inbred respect and understanding of the lethal hazards of coal dust, and were instinctively aware of its potential to ignite and explode in an accelerating flash over great distances in very quick time. However, Mine Operators and Mining Engineers were just as quick to recognise that non-combustible stone-dust could be used as a very effective damping agent to this fearsome danger.

The principle was simplicity itself. In the event of a spontaneous ignition precipitating a flash, the initial blast would blow the loose boards off their supports, spewing clouds of the powdery stone-dust into the air, thus creating an impassable cloud of non-combustible matter to snuff out the following flame. This sequence of events depended on one important fact. The ratio of coal dust to stone dust in the airborne mix must always be below the defined explosive limits.

Tomas considered that in many of the return airways in his district this ratio was being compromised due to the overlay of coal fines, which inevitably accumulates on top of the stonedust, as 'drop out' from the ventilating winds that blow through the warren of roadways throughout the pit. The time had arrived to reload the barriers with fresh clean dust. He would ask for the '*Stonedusters*' to move in.

In truth, he was using this as an excuse to leave the pit early. He could have arranged it all by telephone or left a note at the office, but he felt he had to get out of the 'hole'. He was suffocating down there.

All shift he had found himself pre-occupied with the previous night's conversation with Michael. Watching his men ripping out the earth's black entrails, he had been totally detached and his presence there was more an encumbrance than a help. His supervisory skills were noticeably prominent by their absence. His mind was elsewhere.

He was unable to come to terms with what Michael had said, words which to Tomas's way of thinking sounded increasingly like betrayal. How could he talk to the *Army Council* behind Tomas's back?

Tomas knew that Michael was in frequent touch with HQ. As *Communications Officer* that was his job. What he had not realised was that he was in such personal and confidential contact, and on such a routine basis. He should have been aware, but he not been, and cursed himself for this omission; he had lost personal contact with the 'grey' faces in Dublin.

It came back to him now as he made his way *'out-bye'* - how Michael had been able to relate the circumstances of his mother's death, down to the smallest detail. It occurred to him that if HQ were issuing "back off" instructions about their future activities it may well have been at Michael's instigation. Things weren't that bad in Ireland surely, he asked himself. Michael had to be exaggerating. Maybe he had made them think Tomas was unreliable!

"What a fool I've been," he thought.

He had always been so sure of Michael, never for a moment doubting his loyalty. Even now, in the aftermath of their conversation he found it hard to accept such doubts. Michael was the brother he had never had. Margaret had said so as well, many times. He was the uncle their children loved most. For God's sake he was family! He was blood! Why would he want to challenge Tomas's authority right now? Tomas felt the mission he had so carefully planned, and was now ready to execute, was under threat, and not from some enforcement agency of the British establishment, but from within; from within his own family!

He could not let that happen. He had devised his purpose, and he had the means to execute it. Michael himself had created the opportunity. He had developed and embarked on a strategy to acquire the arms and explosives. And his plan was a good one. They had discussed it all in detail, so recently.

Explosives were straightforward. Tomas was able to get them from the colliery. Supervising 'shot-firing operations' was a particular responsibility of the colliery official, and acquiring powder and detonators was not too difficult a task.

Michael had outlined how they would obtain the arms, and their stocks were already growing.

"Guns, bullets, even hand grenades, guns won't be easy, but we can borrow them when necessary" he had explained.

"During extended combat training exercises, all ranks, which include our men, keep their guns with them. These exercises can last up to a week, and in some cases more. Therefore we can coordinate our operations so that they will coincide with exercises that are already tabled, and that just means we have to be a little flexible. We have to set both our plans and our targets to meet the timetables that are already laid out.

"As for the ammo, that's a much simpler task. We take it little by little, just enough for each operation - no more - no less. *'Combat exposure to war zones'* simulations are an essential training feature of all troops, and there are plenty of target practice drills in the field, and on the rifle range, where we use live ammo. We can always justify a few missing rounds, and the unused ammo is of course returned to the ammunition store where it must be routinely accounted for.

"As the Sergeant in charge of the magazine, I will select the men responsible for that particular task, and since it is I who carries out the stock checks when required, I am always in a position to control these things."

They had been collecting for some time already, and the ammunition chest was filling up. An accumulation of boxes was stored under the floor of the padlocked Anderson air raid shelter in the garden, which protruded from the ground bedecked with burgeoning flora. Neglected and unused, like so many of the other households' half-buried refuges, it was seen but unobserved by the neighbours.

"Come the spring" some admiring gardening buffs had commented innocently, "those plants will really shoot up!"

The cage stopped with a clatter at the surface, and Tomas stepped out as if in a dream. He hardly acknowledged the cheerful greeting of old Tully the 'onsetter' who held up the heavy griddle door for him. He made his way down the iron stairs to the lamp cabin, his boots clattering on the metal steps. He checked in his cap lamp and his official's Davy lamp, and walked out into the cool air blowing from the sea across the open yard. He started towards the red brick office building, but at the last minute he changed his mind and walked past the entrance. He wasn't in a mood for talking dust barriers today. He headed straight on, without so much as a glance into the lighted office windows, which would soon be hidden behind the wartime blackout curtains, a mandatory requirement once the day had faded to dusk. He strode directly out of the yard, and crossed the road to the cliff tops that overlooked the wintry shore below.

For a while he stood as near to the cliff edge as the barbed wire barrier would allow, then he sat down on a nearby wooden bench, and leaning forward with his forearms resting on his knees, gazed blankly out to sea. He sighed deeply, oblivious to all that was around him, totally immersed in his thoughts, thoughts that deeply depressed him. Eventually a squawking seagull broke his reverie, and he straightened up and looked around.

"Get a grip, Tomas," he scolded himself, "You're losing it - again!"

He looked down, at the huge concrete blocks on the beach, dumped there in random disarray, stretching northwards and southwards as far as the eye could see. A constant reminder of possible invasion, this man-made obstacle seemed an unimpressive barrier to an enemy as formidable as the mighty and powerful Third Reich, who might yet arrive on these shores over the heaving waters of the bleak North Sea.

The sea itself seemed to mock the obstruction, as it swelled in majestic waves and came racing in, swamping the static blocks before crashing in a burst of foaming fury against the high ramparts of the limestone cliffs, which stood impassive against the onslaught. Then it retreated back over the beach with a frustrated hiss, to re-muster and attack the cliffs again; impervious it seemed to the cement barricade that lay uselessly in its path. The concrete blocks put there with considerable effort over considerable time and with extensive toil, were already showing signs of wear and tear from the unrelenting tides. The edges were visibly rounded, battered by the erosive power of the pounding seas, and there were conspicuous cracks in the sides, damage caused by the corrosive properties of the saline waters. In the brief spell since their construction and emplacement the blocks had also acquired long tresses of green seaweed, and glistening wet diadems of clinging black mussels could be seen shining through as the ebbing waves dragged the straggling weeds in their wake.

As Tomas watched, the futile confrontation was repeated with continuing ferocity, but with little point or purpose other than perhaps to distract him briefly from his own unease. The sea may pass, but the invader - and his craft - will founder, he thought.

Some chance, he concluded!

Behind him, the retiring sun was fading, a vivid red ball slipping behind a blanket of thin cloud and the shrouded streetlights flickered into life, glimmering dimly through slitted cowls, which, it was believed, would render them invisible to hostile aircraft passing overhead. On a distant hilltop a frenetic radar dish revolved frantically, stark and conspicuous against the evening skyline, seeking through its radioscopic eye early evidence of incoming bombers returning to resume their nightly campaign of terror against the defenceless civilians below. The raids were now less frequent than in the earlier years, and the worst seemed to be over, but the radar dish, unaware of this improving state of affairs, continued to spin relentlessly. Tomas dismissed further thought on these matters, as he re-focussed on his earlier reflections.

Had Michael forgotten so much, so easily! Has living half a lifetime in England caused an Irish-born patriot such as he to become a latter day anglophile? His accent was certainly no longer Irish - Tomas had retained his and was proud that he had! His cousin's thinking is no longer focused on Ireland, as it should be - like it used to be! Tomas was confounded, confused. He could not believe the thoughts in his head. Was Michael a turncoat? He couldn't accept that! He wouldn't accept that! Michael would never betray his trust; it simply was not possible!

He began to feel the chill of the cool night air, and shuddered. He stood up somewhat stiffly, and turned up his collar against the wind. Then with his tin lunchbox tucked firmly under his arm, and his hands thrust deep in the pockets of his jacket, he set off for home.

Behind him the sea continued its relentless attack on the unmoving cliffs.

Chapter 12

To the Manor Drawn

The Manor in its vast acres, stood on the banks of the river Wear, which on this cold winter's evening ran like a broad black ribbon through the white and frosted countryside around it. Built in the 16th century by his forbears, from monies generated from vast estates in Ireland and sustained more recently by mining profits from Durham County's rich coalfields, it was the proud possession of the 14th Earl Lambert, as were the historic old buildings accompanying it, some of which dated back several centuries. References in the Doomsday Book added credence to their history.

It was a large house with a magnificent Corinthian portico supported on huge marble pillars. The entrance hall reached upwards to a high domed roof with an ornately gilded ceiling. Two heavy oaken panelled doors with oakleaf and acorn designs embossed in the surrounds led into The Grand Hall which was panelled in mirror glass on all four walls, as was the Ballroom beyond, where a gathering of some fifty-five distinguished couples assembled as guests, chatting, smiling, and sipping sherries while exchanging shallow compliments with people they mostly did not know.

They were dressed for dinner. The men wore traditional black jacket and tie, although some were in the dress uniform of the nation's armed services. The ladies, for their part, ignoring for the evening the parsimony of a nation at war, were dressed in elegant gowns, exquisitely adorned with expensive jewellery, which glittered in the glow of the logs blazing in the large central fireplace from where they emitted an aroma of pine that wafted comfortingly throughout the room. Household staff moved amongst them, serving drinks from silver platters, as they skilfully navigated a course in and out of the small clutches of people waiting to be called to table in the Grand Hall nearby. It was a birthday celebration, given by Lady Margaret Spencer-Lambert, for her husband James Spencer-Lambert, Lord of the Lambert Estates who had inherited his title some ten years earlier on the death of his elderly father.

Lady Spencer-Lambert, a gregarious lady, was celebrated throughout northern society for her appetite for social entertainment, and had instituted this now traditional party for his Lordship's birthdays, decreeing that the numbers of the attendant guests - with their ladies – should be matched to the numerical advance of his Lordship's accumulated years. Thus each year, the numbers were increased by two, and this year there were fifty-five couples gathered in the quite crowded room, the latest additions to join the select group being the honourable Jasper Haslett, heir to the Haslett fortune with his recently acquired French bride. The Hasletts were descendants of a family of former shipbuilders on the river Tyne, who having accumulated a vast fortune over the previous one hundred years, sold their considerable assets to the major cartel that now controlled the capital which funded ship-building on both Tyne and Wear.

In accordance with Lady Lambert's traditional decree, the new couple would lead the party in to dinner, to the accompaniment of a fanfare of trumpets provided as always by two formally uniformed soldiers, graciously made available for the occasion by the garrison C.O. of the Durham Light Infantry barracks, just a few miles down the road from the manor.

Bridgett was now among the household staff, and would be serving at table for the first time. She was nervous, and butterflies churned her stomach, but her nerves were completely outweighed by the sense of elation she felt, as the glitter and glamour of the occasion unfolded before her. She carried her tray with focused attention, and as she mastered her task, her confidence grew. She smiled across at James who was watching her anxiously, concern etched on his face as with practiced ease he himself moved smoothly amongst the guests.

Bridgett had been quite content in the kitchen with the downstairs staff, before Marianne her roommate had taken ill, and Mr Henry, the butler, had asked the housekeeper Mrs Butterworth to find a temporary replacement. Mrs Dobson had suggested Bridgett to Mrs Butterworth, and so she had been moved 'upstairs', where she and James, 'going out' together long before Bridgett had arrived at the manor, were thrown closer together by dint of circumstance, and their already meaningful relationship flourished yet even further. Now six months down the road, Bridgett was still in service upstairs since Marianne had not returned, and in that time she had matured into the job to everyone's satisfaction. Tonight's dinner was her first such grand event, and she was really enjoying it.

When Tomas realised that James Kennedy had developed a young man's passion for his daughter, he had been at first inclined to put obstacles in the way, discouraging all contact except that which their mutual social circles made inevitable. It wasn't that he disliked the lad, far from it. In fact James had all the attributes of an acceptable suitor for his daughter. He was a strong hard working young man and he had a good pedigree, being from Irish Catholic farming stock whose family had lived in County Cork. James had travelled to England on his own as a child, for his safety and security after the failure of the Uprising. His father, James Senior, a man whom Tomas knew well, was an Irish patriot who prior to the Uprising had had his farm confiscated for tax duties, and this event had caused him to become directly involved in the Easter Uprising, where he came very close to being among those arrested afterwards. He had avoided capture, and inevitable prison, only because the authorities could not prove he had carried arms. By the time the final surrender came and the ringleaders were in custody, he had already left the city and hidden himself away in the country villages far from Dublin itself. When the heat died down, and it seemed safe to return, he had come back, but found it impossible to find work in the city, and he was soon under constant suspicion again by the British. Under these restrictions and constant observation, he had been forced to abandon all association with the Republican movement and to move out of the public eye once again, as far away as possible, but when he attempted to leave for Britain in search of work he had been stopped at the dockside and turned back. It was there on the dockside that he and his wife parted with their son, never to see him again. James just a small boy, with tearful reluctance, and persuaded by his agonized parents, had travelled alone to England, entrusted to the care of the aunt and uncle who would, to all intents and purposes become parents to him from thereon, once they had settled in Eastinglea in the County of Durham. There he had grown up, going to school with Tomas's own children. And it was there that he had first become conscious of Bridgett, and she of him, although nothing between them at that stage gave any hint as to how their knowledge of each other would later develop into a deep and close relationship.

As a boy, then later as a young man, James grew taller and sturdier than most of his contemporaries, but remained of a quiet and constant disposition. At school he rarely got into trouble, save for the occasional schoolyard fight when some of the more aggressive of his classmates saw his size as a challenge in itself. They invariably found to their cost that it was in fact an asset that James, when forced to do so, was happy to exploit to advantage.

While not seeking to hide himself or his talents under any kind of a bushel, James was not particularly extrovert, but often found himself thrust into positions of minor office, simply because he stood out physically. This characteristic started in his schooldays, where he was invariably selected as *Class Monitor* by the nuns who taught him, who needing someone to help with the lifting and carrying tasks of a classroom environment, found him to be very well suited to such duties. This attribute continued into his youth and manhood, particularly in sporting activities where his size proved largely advantageous, particularly on the football field. Though not a particularly handsome young man, and of only average academic proficiency, his sporting prowess made him popular with boys and girls alike.

James was just one year older than Bridgett.

Bridgett first became aware of the young James, when she attended her first St Patrick's Day dance in the school hall, which traditionally was attended by final year students and post-school teenagers, accompanied more often than not by watchful parents, particularly those with daughters. The *Ceilidh Mor* was a popular event in the parish calendar, anticipated with unbridled delight by all. An evening of Irish song and dance was invariably accompanied by a lot of 'tall-story' telling from the elders of the community, who – once in their cups – would inevitably hark back with emotional tales of the hardships endured in the bad old days in the '*Old Country*'. For the young however it was a night of gaiety and fun!

When James asked her to dance, Bridgett mumbled stuttering apologies that she could not dance. Two reels, a St Bernard's waltz, and two lemonades later, she began to think she was in love. After he kissed her in a shop doorway four hours later, she ran home on a cloud, convinced of it!

James had left school a year earlier and had been given a start at Eastinglea Colliery, and after a brief spell 'on the screens' at bank, had graduated to underground work where he was employed, under Tomas, as a 'putter', moving coal tubs in and out for the hewers to load at the working face. An accident to his leg when a runaway tub hit him forced him to settle for work 'back-bye' and ruined all expectations of working at the coalface, where the "big money" was to be earned. Disappointed at the early curtailment of his career as a collier, he felt compensated to some extent when they gave him a job in the stables. James was an avid lover of horses, and it was his affection for his ponies that eventually afforded him the opportunity to move out of the pits altogether.

One day, he had just finished the grooming of his charges, and was amusing himself with them, when a party of sightseeing guests, including two young ladies wearing white coveralls and safety helmets that shone incongruously against the inherent blackness of their surroundings, came through the stable area accompanied by the manager. They were just in time to catch James taking *Jasper* through his paces, performing his latest trick, whereby he removed the pit helmet from James's head and deposited it on the head of *Blackie,* his docile stable-mate who was standing meekly by. Both animals were customarily rewarded for such performances, when they nosed into James's pockets for the fresh carrots that he invariably carried there for them.

The colliery manager spoke up.

"Is this all you have to do, Kennedy?" He said with some irritation.

James turned in surprise, flustered.

"Sorry Mr Armbrage" he stammered, "I didn't know you were there."

"Obviously, young man. Come to my office when you finish your shift. I'll have things to say to you that are best said in private! Maybe a more fulfilling task is in order for you. Keep you a bit busier in future."

"Yes sir, of course sir," stammered James apologetically.

"Now show us round these stables. Tell these guests what you do here! How many horses you have etc. and be quick about it!" James hurried to oblige, and as he warmed to his task, his earlier embarrassment was soon forgotten.

He explained about the life of a pit pony. They were Shetlands for the most part he said, each with its own name, and its own distinctive personality. They worked every day, like the miners themselves, pulling coal-laden tubs to and from the pit shaft. He explained how, once they were underground they rarely saw daylight again, and how when they did get to '*bank*', - twice per year - they would race with delight round the fields they were released into, ecstatic in the sunshine, gorging themselves on the fresh grass they were denied when underground. He talked of grooming and feeding them; of 'mucking out', and his enthusiasm for his work impressed his listeners. They asked questions too, which for the most part he was able to give good credible answers, in particular to the taller of the two young ladies, whose probing inquiries demonstrated that she herself had a considerable knowledge of equine husbandry. Even the manager listened intently, impressed by the content of their exchanges and conversation. Before they left however, he reminded James of his appointment in the office later, and James felt a renewed anxiety as he watched them go. His fears were allayed a little when the young lady turned and smiled as she departed. He was wondering who she might be, when Jasper bumped him from the back, and snorted as he nudged into his pockets. James's worries changed to laughter as he turned to rebuke the precocious pony.

When he knocked on the manager's door some six hours later, it was Mr Chatsworth, the Colliery Clerk who called for him to enter. James opened the door full of trepidation, and entered into a spacious anteroom to find Mr Chatsworth seated behind a large mahogany desk, in front of a tall Victorian bookcase. As he stood waiting, he cast his eyes in awe over the bookcase shelves, stacked with official looking documents and imposing lexicons of mining engineering practices and procedures. He had never before seen such a collection of heavy tomes, each of which was embossed with impressive gold-lettered titles. They served only to add to his discomfort in these surroundings. He looked elsewhere around the office, seeking to soothe his jangling nerves.

Two junior clerks seated at tables adjacent to Mr Chatsworth's, pored over heavily bound ledgers, making entries into the large pages with their scratching pens, which periodically they cleaned on large ink-spotted blotting pads before recharging them at the inkwells set in one corner of each of their respective desks. They paid him scant attention as he stood waiting hesitantly.

Eventually Mr Chatsworth looked up, and with a silent nod indicated that James should take a seat on the leather couch resting against the wall facing his desk. James sat down stiffly, subdued by the silent authority around him. Behind and to the right of the Colliery Clerk, an oaken door bore a sign, which spelled out in bold black letters *R.B. ARMBRAGE, COLLIERY MANAGER.*

A buzzer sounded loudly on the Clerk's desk causing James to jump nervously. Mr Chatsworth rose and tapped lightly on the manager's door, then without waiting further opened it and entered. The juniors continued to work impassively. A few minutes later, the door re-opened and Mr Chatsworth emerged. He looked at James,

"Mr Armbrage will see you now; you may go in." James's anxiety showed in his face as he stood up slowly. He moved to the door, stopped, and seeking re-assurance from the Clerk turned and glanced at him. He received none. Mr Chatsworth had already resumed his work, his head bent low over his desk. James knocked nervously.

"Come in!" The heavy door muffled the manager's voice, but in James's ears it resounded like a gong. He opened the door and entered.

Mr Armbrage was seated behind a desk even larger than Mr Chatsworth's, in an even larger room surrounded by more bookcases and more shelves, and set centrally before his desk at right angles to it was a long mahogany conference table, down each side of which were placed eight chairs all ornately carved with matching sculpted legs. Fully draped curtains, hanging to the floor and tied back with tasselled cords, adorned the bay windows behind the manager's desk. At both sides of the desk were two large leather armchairs, and in one of them the young lady visitor who had smiled at him in the stables was seated, to the left of the manager as James looked at them.

"Sit down young man, up here at my desk."

Mr Armbrage's invitation was friendly enough and a comforted James relaxed somewhat, as he took the chair indicated near the manager's desk. Glancing sideways at the young woman, he took further comfort in the fact that she was smiling at him once more.

The manager spoke again.

"I have decided to overlook your tom-foolery in the pit today, because on reflection I can see that a job like that will sometimes lead to idle moments, and undoubtedly you care for the animals in a right and proper manner."

James breathed a quiet sigh of relief.

"However, you may still be required to consider changing your employment." His heart sank again.

"Let me introduce you to the lady on my right here. This is the Honourable Miss Jane Spencer - Lambert, and she is the daughter of his Lordship, Earl Spencer – Lambert, the owner of this – and several other collieries in this area. Miss Jane has a proposition to put to you, which you will be wise to listen to."

He turned to her, "Miss Jane, would you explain please?"

Jane Spencer-Lambert's smile broadened even further as she spoke,

"Thank you Mr Ambrage" she said, and then she addressed herself to James directly,

"Mr Kennedy, - may I call you James". He nodded instinctively, and stammered a reply,

"Yes, Ma'am."

"You don't have to address me as Ma'am, James, I'm not married just yet. Please call me Miss Jane."

"Yes Ma'am, - er – Miss - sorry" stammered James. The young lady ignored his discomfort and continued,

" I want you to come and look after my horses for me, at the manor house. I want you to come and live there, in the servants quarters, with the other staff," she added.

James looked perplexed.

"I watched you with the ponies most carefully today, and while Mr Armbrage here, thought you were indulging in what he amusingly described as horse-play," she smiled before continuing,

"I saw it as a measure of the confidence and trust the animals had in you. I liked that, and I want you to come and instil the same degree of confidence and trust in two of my horses.

"I have recently rescued two beasts from a local farm rented from our estate, where they were being cruelly abused. I can't stand to see animals suffering, and the farm has since been confiscated and the abusers evicted."

James felt a surge of resentment at the mention of eviction. The word was an abomination to mining folk, and more so to those who had memories of it in their Irish origins. He had thought the practice had long since ceased.

" I see some indignation in you face Mr Kennedy." He noticed the formality of surnames. "I take it you object to the eviction process."

"I certainly don't like to hear of people losing their homes Miss Jane, even if guilty of maltreating animals. I hardly think the punishment fits the crime." He spoke nervously, but with feeling.

"Crime is the correct word in this case James, but not only did these people abuse the horses, they abused the community as well. The farmer was a thief who stole stock from his neighbours; his son is a convicted felon with a record for grievously wounding a neighbour who had accused him - quite correctly - of stealing a valuable pocket watch, while enjoying hospitality as a guest in this same neighbour's house.

"The farmer's wife was forced out of the household by her husband's cruelty, and the farm was falling into a sorry state of disrepair. Incidentally the rent hadn't been paid for over a year before the bailiffs moved in! Now both the son and father are in jail, for a variety of misdemeanours, and ultimately eviction was the only option to bring the farm and its animals back into care.

"It was totally legal, applied for and granted through the courts. I really don't think this case qualifies as a return to the bad old days of eviction of mining folk from their tied houses by the autocratic mine owner; I sincerely believe those days are well behind us!"

James felt foolish. He felt he should have contained his indignation.

"I apologise Miss Jane, it's just that - well you are right. Mining folk do get a bit over-sensitive when we hear about evictions."

"Apology accepted, James." She spoke lightly and he felt at ease again.

"Well what about it? Are you interested, do you want to know more? Does the prospect of getting out of the pit not appeal to you?"

She went on to explain that he would not loose financially by leaving the colliery, in fact he would earn somewhat more working in the stables at the manor than he currently earned down the pit. His main duties would be to the two horses, and general stable work, but he would be expected to help out at the house if and when the need should arise. He would receive the necessary training for this latter job, and if he showed himself to be satisfactory in this capacity he would be invited to move onto the household staff once the two horses had been fully re-habilitated. If he were found unsuitable for employment in the household, he would have the option of staying on as a stable lad, or returning to the pit. He had really nothing to lose."

At this point Mr Armbrage interjected to say he could not guarantee re-hiring James underground again in his current capacity, but he would always find him work at bank, albeit at the wages appropriate to surface work of course.

James sat for a while considering these unexpected circumstances and wondering what to do. He felt doubt that bordered on fear about working for what he conceived as the upper classes, at the invitation of the daughter of a man, whose forbears in past generations had wielded power like a club over families such as his own, particularly in Ireland, their mother country. His instinct was to say no, but fearing the wrath of the manager over the incident in the pit earlier that day he found himself accepting the offer and agreeing to move his life to the unknown territory of Westerside, County Durham, and the home of the Spencer-Lamberts.

"Right" said Miss Jane with a degree of satisfaction, "That's that then. Mr Armbrage will arrange for you to be paid your outstanding wages before you leave today. From tomorrow you work for me. You can find your way to Westerside quite easily. There's a bus to Durham City, and there are frequent connections from there. Anyone in the village will direct you to the manor, and you must report to Mr Ryder at the stables when you arrive; I shall make sure he knows you are coming."

She turned to Armbrage and smiled.

"Thank you letting me steal your stable boy, Mr Armbrage, I hope you will be able to find a ready replacement."

They stood together as she prepared to leave. James was still a little hesitant, but Armbrage was beaming with satisfaction.

"My pleasure Miss Jane" he said, "If I can do anything further for you please let me know."

After she had left, Armbrage dismissed James, but not before he instructed Chatsworth to pay him his dues.

James walked out into the evening air in a state of exhilarated confusion, his money clutched tightly in his hand.

All that had happened three years ago, and in the interim Tomas had allowed James to associate with Bridgett more openly. He even encouraged it, recognizing that having an ally at the Manor might one day prove to be an advantage he could make use of. When Bridgett went there as well, Tomas felt the fates were smoothing his path to Spencer-Lambert.

James flourished in his new position to such an extent that eventually he was moved full time onto the household staff, where he was junior only to Mr Henry the butler, Mrs Butterworth the housekeeper, and Walter the footman. Mrs Dobson the cook was probably senior to him as well, but he quickly wormed his ways deep into her affections, and he could get her to do virtually anything for him that he wanted, and in many ways he had become an 'adopted son' for the second time in his life.

It was through her intercession with Mrs Butterworth that James was able to get Bridgett into service as a kitchen maid.

The horses it must be said had prospered under James's care, and looked for him each day to receive their regular ration of carrots and sugar, a habit he continued even after moving onto the household staff. Mr Ryder, the Stable Manager frowned on this practice, but with Miss Jane as his sponsor, was disinclined to chastise James for his behaviour.

❧

By two a.m. the guests had gone, most to their homes throughout the county, but some who had travelled far, retired only as far as the sumptuous comfort of the manor's guest bedrooms upstairs.

The on-duty staff cleared away the tables and removed the detritus of the evening's entertainment. It was accepted practice that the morning staff would complete the job, and restore the place to its accustomed condition of pristine regularity.

Later, they sat around the table in the servants' hall, resting their weary bones. It had been a long night, but all in all a successful one. The guests had enjoyed themselves, and most had retired smiling happily, many of them well 'under the influence', as Mr Henry had remarked.

Now the household staff could relax at last, and they did so, kicking off patent leather shoes and button up boots, and putting their feet up on the scrubbed wooden chairs. They helped themselves to the tea and the fresh sandwiches, which Mrs Dobson had prepared. Mr Henry, James, and Walter preferring something stronger than tea, served themselves with glasses of the evening's red wine from the several bottles stacked among the remnants of the upstairs feast.

Lady Spencer Lambert, "Her Ladyship" as they would respectfully address her when speaking among themselves, had been effusive in her praise, and had insisted that, should they wish, they could help themselves to anything that was left over from the celebrations.

"I hate good food to go to waste, Andrew" she had said, addressing Mr Henry informally – a sure sign of her pleasure and satisfaction.

"Thank you your Ladyship" Henry had replied courteously, "Perhaps we can send it to the orphanage in the village."

"Excellent idea Andrew," she beamed with even more thanks, before bidding him a peaceful night as she started up the broad staircase to her rooms.

"Everything but the wine, that is" he muttered to himself.

At the landing, she turned to find him still watching her.

"That's all, Mr. Henry, you may go now," she said. The informality of the moment had passed, and she waited while he bowed slightly and left. Then she too turned, and passed down the long corridor to her chambers.

ℭℑ

The wine had run out, the teapot was empty, and the sandwiches had all been eaten. So as fatigue overtook them one by one, they too drifted off contentedly to their beds. Finally only James, Bridgett, Mrs Dobson and Alice were left. Mrs Dobson was adamant that the last of the dishwashing had to be completed before Alice could go off as well, but the young kitchen maid was clearly so far out on her feet that James felt persuaded to plead for her with the kindly cook, and to offer that he and Bridgett would happily relieve her of the late night task. Bridgett nodded her agreement.

A careful study of their faces told Mrs Dobson they were anxious to be alone, so Alice was allowed to go to bed and they made their way to the

139

kitchen to complete their chores. A while later, with the glassware and the crockery, the cutlery and the pots and the pans, all cleaned and stored away, she herself made a diplomatic withdrawal, but not before she admonished them gently that they should not be too late themselves or "she would be back in to them with a big stick!"

They giggled somewhat guiltily at her maternal concern as she left, muttering incoherently about "the young folks of today".

James looked at Bridgett with wonderment; this girl is mine he thought. No, he corrected himself this woman for whom I have developed such powerful feelings - is mine. And what he saw filled him with deep joy and pride. She returned his gaze, smiling back through bright blue eyes, which glistened expectantly in the soft light of the partially darkened room. He moved towards her and she met him half way. He took her in his arms and kissed her intently. She returned his embrace with a ready abandonment and intensity that far exceeded anything she had ever felt before in her whole life. She stopped, shocked at herself, and broke away panting. James feared for a moment he had offended her, but he was soon reassured. Bridgett looked at him with a deep and passionate longing, and in that moment she knew that she loved him and wanted him. As if reading her thoughts he spoke softly to her.

"I love you Bridgett, and I want us to be together, both now and for the rest of our lives."

"And I you, James. I want nothing more than to be with you always. I love you with all my heart."

He reached for her again, but she held him off, and taking his hand lead him out of the kitchen.

"We mustn't be caught down here by Mrs Dobson now must we" she said, " She's got a big stick!" she added in a voice heavy with desire, but tinged with happy mischief. Then she guided him up the backstairs, through the maids' quarters, and into her room.

When true to her word, Mrs Dobson returned, her failing hearing did not pick up the sound of the door quietly closing above her head as she peeped into the kitchen to find them gone. Nodding her satisfaction, she sighed contentedly, and made her way back to her quarters in the cottages outside, pleased that they had heeded her wise counsel and retired, each to their rooms for the night.

Later, in the large bed she had previously shared only with Marianne, Bridgett smiled in the darkness as she lay snuggled up with her back to James, as close to him as she could get. Locked in his arms, with the warm caress of his breath upon her neck, she felt safe and secure. She was so deliriously content that she fought to stay awake; fearful her joy would slip away while she slept. Eventually the night took its toll, and she dissolved into the deep and peaceful slumber that James had already surrendered to. She could not know it then, but the happiness that she felt was to be short lived.

Over the next few weeks the realisation that she was pregnant came to her loudly and clearly, as on successive mornings she arose from her bed and headed straight to the bathroom to be sick. Mrs Dobson was the first to notice, and the suspicious frown on her face left Bridgett in no doubt of what she thought. Finally she could contain her disapproval no longer.

"I think you should visit a doctor, young lady," she scolded, "preferably one out of town, where no one knows you. It looks like you may have picked up a bug, or maybe you've had one planted in you!" she said with thinly disguised disdain.

"If you are due a day off, I think you might want to take it now."

Some days later Bridgett's fears were confirmed as the doctor she had visited in Durham verified what she already knew. Then followed panic, and a desperate need to confide in someone. As she made her way back to the Manor, she decided she had to tell James, after all he was the father; he had a right to know, and she felt so certain of his love she was confident he would do the 'right thing' and marry her. Carrying her secret alone was too much for her, and she feared it was only a matter of time before Mrs Dobson made it public news. She dreaded the thought of that; James must never find out from anyone but her.

141

She found him at the main entrance, busily polishing the brass and the glass of the elaborately designed front doors, which opened onto the main hallway.

"I must talk to you – urgently," she blurted out, ignoring the smiling welcome he gave her.

"Me too," he replied, and his eyes glistened with excitement "I have something very important to tell you. Meet me in my room at lunchtime, this is the most exciting thing that's ever happened in my whole life, and I have your father to thank for it. See you later, don't be late."

Without another word, he picked up his cleaning box and walked off to continue his chores on the several intermediate doors along the length of the high corridor. Bridgett stood looking after him, feeling ignored and irritated, and baffled by the reference to her father.

೬೨

At one o'clock, she made her way with some trepidation to James's room, concerned to hear what he had to say and fearful of telling him what she must. His news was apparently exciting; hers meant only trouble. At the door she glanced in both directions, and satisfied she was not being observed, opened it and entered quickly.

He was waiting for her and met her with a smile and a kiss. Then taking her gently by the shoulders he sat her down on the tall straight-backed chair, that was standard furnishing for each servant's quarters. Before she could say a word, he spoke up excitedly,

"Bridgett my love, your father has accepted me as one of his men. I am to be among his field operatives. We shall be going into action together."

Bridgett looked at him in total confusion, and an instant feeling of apprehension gripped her already sensitive stomach.

"What do you mean, James - going into action – with my father? Are you joining up together?"

It sounded ridiculous, even to her ears, and she was relieved when she saw him laugh at her questions.

"Of course not, silly girl" he said with irksome patronisation.

"Your Father would never join the war to fight with the British. Good Lord he'd rather fight with the Germans! You of all people should know that. Quite the opposite in fact! We are going to fight *against* the British. We are forming an operational unit of the IRA, here in Eastinglea, and your father is the Commander. I am to be one of his soldiers! It was all decided at our meeting last Tuesday night."

He waited for her reaction, but she remained nonplussed.

"Surely you knew something like that was in his plans. After all, George and Padraig are in it too!"

A cold chill of realisation seized her. All her life she had been brought up to see "the English" as Tomas referred to them as the enemy, the hated overlords of all Ireland and all Irish people. When they were children Tomas managed to make "the English" sound like the Devil himself, and English soldiers were his legions of dark angels. He instilled them with fear for the very sight of a British uniform. His belief in the justice of "the fight" was unwavering, and he took every opportunity to preach his anti-English rhetoric into each of his four children.

George and Padraig had succumbed to his dogma, but for herself, being the girl of the family, she had been largely excluded from the expansive propaganda of her father's anti-British indoctrination.

"Girls are not expected to fight", he would say, and even in the current conflict with Hitler, he would repeat this firmly held maxim with total disregard for the enlisted women he could see all around him. So Bridgett grew up, unaware of the full depths of her father's prejudice and intent.

Dermot too, she thought. His tardy arrival had come as such a severe shock to Tomas, that he never quite came to terms with this youngest son, and his subsequent removal to Corshaw at the age of eleven ensured his absolute exclusion from all the plans and confidences that his father already shared with the elder siblings.

In short, thought Bridgett, neither Dermot nor I were ever likely to be considered as confidantes in our father's bellicose ambitions. The true shock for her was in realising that James, - her beloved James - now was!

James was still talking, but she heard little of what he was saying, lost as she was in her own contemplation She saw with absolute clarity that within her family, whether by accident or design - she could not decide which - there existed a division, a schism in fact, which aligned Tomas with George and Padraig, and Margaret with Bridgett and Dermot. It was a divide that had crept insidiously between them, and had caused them to become a completely dysfunctional unit. Until this moment, Bridgett had never considered that her father's misguided ideals had any real part in her life, but now they posed a direct threat to them, and to both her and to James. And on top of all this, there was now a baby.

"Bridgett, Bridgett, you're not listening to me! You haven't heard a single word I've said!" James was annoyed, and it showed. Bridgett gathered herself and spoke nervously,

"I'm sorry James, it was the shock. I don't know what you are talking about – IRA – you - Dadda! You scare me! You can't be serious!"

"Never more serious in my life, Bridgett", he spoke proudly. "Your father is a great man, a great patriot. And he is like a father to me as well."

He glanced at Bridgett as he said this, and a look of concern crossed his face as he saw she was not reacting well to his news. He wondered if confiding in her had been a mistake.

"I was told not to say anything - about the new active unit – under your Dadda, but I know I can trust you not to repeat it, can't I? And I wanted to tell you Bridgett. I don't want any secrets between us." Still she looked distressed. He tried a fresh approach.

"You are as Irish as the rest of us, aren't you? You do approve don't you?" He waited anxiously for a reply, but when she spoke her words were sombre and without enthusiasm.

"I am his daughter, James, and yet I knew nothing of what you have told me. Did you not think if my father wanted me to know of this, he would have told me himself?

"I cannot say I approve, nor can I say I don't approve. I am at a complete loss to know what to think. The two most important men in my life are involved. All I know is that it sounds dangerous and foolhardy. I would say stupid if I did not know what drives it all. My father wants revenge, James! It's not patriotism that drives him; it's vengeance!

"And James, '*Vengeance is mine saith the Lord!*' James don't you see, this can only end in tears."

A sudden surge of fear grabbed at her again, but this time it was for James not herself.

"James if you love me you will not be a part of this, it's too dangerous! Give it up now before it is too late."

James was bewildered. Bridgett was pleading with him to desert her own father, and to break his word. To him it was unthinkable. He couldn't do it, and moreover he didn't want to do it.

"You can't be serious Bridgett, you are asking me to break an oath I have taken to a cause. A cause that is lead by your own father no less. Even if I wanted to I can't, for the oath I've taken binds me under penalty of death. But I don't want to anyway, and I won't. It's unreasonable of you to ask me." His tone hardened as he snapped at her,

"There is nothing more I wish to say, there will be no further discussion on the matter!"

A warning bell rang in Bridgett's mind. He sounded so much like her father. '*There would be no further discussion!*' How many times had she heard him speak like that to her mother, when short of valid argument. She felt that James and she had reached a crossroad, and the road they chose would shape their future forever. If she gave way to this kind of verbal bullying now, she would regret it for the rest of her life with him. She was filled with a sense of foreboding. She could not sacrifice her right to independent thought. She chose her words carefully,

"You are *not* my husband James, and even if you were I would not have you talk to me like some serving girl. I will say what I have to say whenever I want to say it, as long as I feel justified in doing so. I have hopes that one day you and I will be wedded, that you *will* be my husband, for I love you deeply, but if you persist in this folly, then I cannot marry you, for you may believe that your oath is binding unto death, but as an IRA agent your actions are much more likely to take you there.

"Whatever my father has planned for you and the others whoever they may be......"

"I never said there were others!" snapped James, whose exasperation had changed to anger. Bridgett ignored him.

"Whoever they may be," she repeated, " will be treasonous and punishable by death. This country is at war for god's sake!

"So you are between the devil and the deep blue sea, it seems. The only plus is that if you give up this foolishness now you will still have me, and even my father is unlikely to order the execution of a future son-in- law, especially one who is clearly such an ardent admirer.

"I suggest if you are wise, you will risk the lesser of the two evils."

She had angered him and it showed.

"You are right Bridgett, I am not your husband, and nor are you my wife! I have not promised to honour you till death us do part, - but I have made such a promise to your father!   In these circumstances I have no choice but to keep my pledge to him, and as to the option for you to become my wife - or not - as the case may be, the choice will be yours to make only when you have been asked!" He fixed her with an angry stare.

"As I recall, to date you have not!" Then turning on his heel he stormed from the room, slamming the door behind him.

For a moment Bridgett sat immobile, paralysed with shock. Then she folded up on the chair in anguish. Weeping bitterly, she rocked to and fro in despair, hugging the new life within her.

❧

Bridgett had already left by the time James came downstairs the following morning. Mrs Dobson had not noticed her leaving, and would have missed her altogether had Alice not spotted her through the kitchen window as she busied herself preparing the staff breakfasts. Together they watched the heavily clad figure disappear down the frosted driveway. At the gate Bridgett turned left towards the village and vanished from their sight.

"I don't think we'll be seeing her again," said Mrs Dobson with disapproval. "Good riddance too if you ask me," she said with finality as she returned to her household tasks.

"She should be ashamed of herself, sneaking away like that, with not so much as a word. She's obviously got something to hide she has, and I think I can guess what it is. Wonder what his lordship will think about it when he finds her gone!"

"His Lordship! What is it Mrs. D.? What's Miss Bridgett gone an' done?" asked Alice with naïve curiosity. "Upset the Master 'as she?"

"No Alice not *The Master*, just young Mr. James. He is her master these days, isn't he?"

"Is he really, Mrs. D.? I never knew that." Alice's face was an image of confusion.

"That's the trouble with you girl, you never see what's right under your nose, do you?"

"Sorry Mrs. D., I didn't mean to annoy you."

"You haven't Alice, you haven't."

Mrs Dobson sighed with resignation, before resuming her authoritative manner,

"Enough of this chatter anyway. Let's get on. It's after six now. Have you buttered the bread yet?"

She glance at the empty bread-plate.

"Apparently not! Get on with it, girl!"

"Yes Mrs. D.," said Alice timidly.

"I wonder what Miss Bridgett's gone and done," she thought to herself, as she liberally smeared the meagre butter ration thickly over the sweet smelling bread, freshly baked and still warm from the oven.

The morning air was bitingly cold, and the people waiting for the bus were pleased to see the six-thirty to Durham appear on time and stop for them to board. Bridgett took a seat near the front where the chrome-plated fan heater wafted warm air from the engine down the aisle into the interior. She was not feeling too well, her resistance was low, and the morning air had chilled her somewhat more than it might normally have done. The stress and strain of recent days was exacting a heavy toll.

After her confrontation with James, when eventually she had been able to calm down, she had tried to assess her situation rationally. She was devastated still that James had let her down so badly, but she could not bring herself to approach him again with news that she felt he was not of a mind to accept. Now was not the right time to tell him about the baby, and as a consequence she knew she could no longer stay at the manor.

She could not go home either. Her father would be scandalised and feel humiliated before his peers, and his anger would know no limits for both her and her mother, and while she was confident her mother would not desert her in this her time of need, she also would be hugely distressed. She felt she could not bring down such disgrace upon either of them. There seemed no alternative; she must go away. She would leave and take her problem with her.

She would try to get into a home - a place for unmarried mothers. She knew that such places existed, because during her school days with the Sisters of Mercy, Sister Alphonsus had told them all about such institutions. At the time it had little impact on the lives of the carefree young girls in her charge, but being the judicious old nun that she was, the good sister had spelt out very carefully that if at any time anyone of them ever needed help in such circumstances, then she would be always be there for them.

"I'm always here to listen to anything. I will never presume to judge but I will help if you ever need me. You need never feel alone."

The girls had giggled amongst themselves at the underlying message, but in the happy optimism of youth soon forgot what their teacher had said. Now her words came back to Bridgett as an echo from the past, and she felt that appealing to the elderly nun was her only course of action.

Two hours later she was seated in the convent of St Mary the Virgin, unburdening herself to the ageing mentor, taking comfort in the smile of compassion on the kind face before her. Later when she left, she posted a letter from Sister Alphonsus addressed to Margaret, explaining everything and seeking her understanding for her daughter's indiscretion.

Margaret received the letter two days later, and as she read it, her face turned ashen, then her eyes flooded to overflowing. After a while she calmed herself, and folding the letter carefully, placed it in her handbag. Putting on her coat and hat she left the house and headed for the convent to see Sister Alphonsus. She would find out where her daughter was, and bring her home.

James looked for Bridgett at breakfast and when he did not see her, asked around as to where she might be. No one among the 'upstairs' staff knew, and it wasn't till he spoke to Mrs. Dobson that he discovered that she had left early that morning. His shock verged on alarm as he fired impatient questions at the cook and her assistant, but the answer was always the same. She had gone before six, and had left no messages for anyone.

Eventually in despair he gave up asking, and spent the day lost in a daydream, hoping with each passing hour that Bridgett would return with a simple explanation for her baffling behaviour. Unauthorized absence was frowned upon deeply at the manor, and the housekeeper was known to have dismissed staff before on several occasions for such 'misdemeanours'. Marianne, whose job Bridgett had been given originally was a case in point, having herself been dismissed for unexplained and extended absence. Eventually she had been re-instated, but only as a cleaner, and in the servants' quarters at that. Apart from the loss of face she had sustained, she also suffered a significant loss of income in this lower capacity. Marianne would jump at the chance to re-establish herself in her former position should Bridgett fail to appear. James's concern included the very real possibility that Marianne might succeed in this expectation.

By evening, when there was still no sign of her, his depression deepened, and by bedtime, he was on the point of despair. As he lay awake gazing at the ceiling he made up his mind. If Bridgett had not returned by the following day, he would go to Eastinglea to look for her. If he did not find her, he would speak privately with the Commander. Her father would advise him. He would tell him where she was, and what he must do.

Chapter 13

Confinement

Bridgett walked slowly up a narrow path, bordered on both sides by low wrought iron fences in front of neatly trimmed hedgerows cut equally low. The journey to Dublin had tired her, and now at low ebb, she felt very apprehensive about the unknown world into which she was soon to step. At the entrance she stopped, and tentatively studied the door before her. The frosted glass was etched with a representation of Lourdes, with the Blessed Virgin Mary looking down on the young Bernadette kneeling before her at the famous grotto, and the French words *"Je Suis L'Immaculee Concepcion"* engraved in a ribboned banner below. Beneath this elaborate iconography, a large brass knocker shone brightly around the letterbox, making superfluous the doorbell in the saucer-shaped mounting on the wall at the side. This was also made of brass, with the word *PRESS* inlaid into the white marble button at its centre.

"What else would you do with it?" muttered Bridgett to herself, and in an irrational act of childlike defiance rattled the doorknocker instead.

After a few moments she heard footsteps approaching softly from the other side, which opened to reveal a little nun with florid features and a sharp nose, upon which was perched a pair of rimless spectacles.

"Yes?" she asked, "May I help you?", and the kindly voice and smiling blue eyes belied the austere image that Bridgett had at first perceived, causing her to stammer a little as she replied,

"Er - yes – please" she managed, "I have a letter from Sister Alphonsus – in England – for the Mother Superior."

"Come in" said the nun still smiling, and standing to the side indicated that Bridgett should take a seat in the nearby reception room.

"I'm Sister Lucy, may I know your name, my dear?" she continued pleasantly.

Bridgett gave her name and handed over the letter, and as Sister Lucy went off to find the Mother Superior, sat down in the chair that had been proffered. Then looking around, she weighed up her surroundings. A large statue of the Sacred Heart, occupied the corner near the window, and gazing down from a high stone pedestal, dominated the room. There was an all-pervading smell of incense and candle wax in the air, which aggravated Bridgett's nervous tummy, and she concluded that she had arrived shortly after morning mass or some other sacramental ceremony. Whatever the case, the convent chapel was obviously nearby, and her sensitive feelings were heightened by the cloying smell in her nostrils. She was suddenly possessed by the fear that she was making a dreadful mistake and panic gripped her insides. She stood up to leave, just as the large and commanding figure of an elderly nun appeared in the doorway, blocking her exit. Exuding an air of absolute authority, the big nun scrutinised Bridgett silently for a few moments. Bridgett, for her part waited anxiously, wiping her hands nervously down her coat.

She supposed, correctly, that this person must be the Mother Superior, and the sight of her intensified her already burgeoning fears.

"Follow me please" was all that was said, as the nun turned and walked ahead down the corridor.

It was an order not a request, and Bridgett felt obliged to follow the retreating figure down the carpeted hallway into the office at the end. As she followed behind obediently, the swish of the voluminous skirts and the accompanying rattle of the long rosary dangling from the nun's belt, gave the Mother Superior a defining air of religious authority that made Bridgett feel tense and nervous. As the woman took her place behind a large desk, she pointed to a nearby chair, into which Bridgett obediently sank. Not a word was uttered as she regarded the letter, already open, that Bridgett had brought with her.

Sister Mary Theresa, Mother Superior of the Sisters of Mercy in the *Convent of St Bernadette* in a small parish on the west side of Dublin, was not a person to be meddled with. She did not tolerate fools gladly, and she managed the convent with the iron hand of one who expects to be obeyed without question. A stickler for rules, she had no compunction about metering out punishments for offences that others would regard merely as shortcomings. She cared little for what these others thought, and not even the priests of the parish in which the convent was placed, and as such her appointed superiors, would consider challenging her on matters that took place within her "domain". Her domain included not just to the convent of St Bernadette with its twenty resident nuns, but the associated nursing home, to which unmarried pregnant girls, from across all Ireland retreated, desperate in their time of trouble.

Sister Mary Theresa folded the letter and returned it to its envelope before looking up and inspecting Bridgett with eyes that seemed to pierce her very soul. When she spoke she did so in a voice that was firm and assured,

"Sister Alphonsus has sent you here with what is a very good reference," she said. "She asks me to take you in because she believes, that despite your unfortunate condition, you are a good honest Catholic girl. Is she right?"

Bridgett considered her response carefully before replying,

"I cannot judge myself; that is for others to do," she said quietly. "That I have made a mistake is - or soon will be - obvious. I know that I am not unique in this, and others like myself have had to accept that they have erred, then pick up the pieces of their lives and get on with them. One way or another that's what I intend to do. If you choose to help me, I will be grateful. If you do not, then I must go elsewhere, although at this moment I have no idea where that might be. I only know I cannot go home to England before this baby is born."

"Do you regret getting yourself pregnant?" asked the Mother Superior bluntly. Bridgett took a deep breath before answering,

"In these circumstances, yes I do. In a different set of circumstances I most certainly would not. I still believe that the father of my baby will marry me willingly, because he wants to. In such a case I would have no regrets about getting pregnant, quite the contrary, in fact, I would be very, very, happy."

"So the welfare of the child is not your primary consideration, then?"

Bridgett felt she had fallen into a trap, and she reacted defensively.

"Of course the welfare of my baby is important, above all other consideration. My baby will come first no matter what happens to me!"

"If you do not get to marry the man who made you pregnant, will you be happy to bring up your child alone then - as an unmarried mother with a bastard?"

Bridgett flinched at the Mother Superior's blunt language. She found it offensive and it made her angry, but she could not readily respond. Though confused and stunned by the dilemma with which she had been presented, she recognised it was a reality that she might well have to face, and it filled her with deep concern.

"I know some married couples that are childless; they would jump at the opportunity to have my baby."

It was a desperate thing to say, and she struggled to come to terms with the thought.

"Do you really think that would work, Bridgett? People you know, and who know your family, bringing up your baby?" The Mother Superior's tone was softer now, but her question was no less challenging.

"Maybe it would," said Bridgett defensively, but she could hear the doubt in her own voice. Then more forcefully she continued,

"Anyhow I don't have to think about that now. I know it won't come to that. James will marry me because he loves me, and when he finds out he has a child he'll be delighted."

She regretted mentioning James by name, feeling that she should have kept him anonymous.

"But I won't tell him before he has proposed to me. I will not use my baby as a lever to force him." She was rambling and she knew it.

The Mother Superior stood up and came round the desk to face Bridgett. Perching on the front edge, she said,

"I'm going to let you stay Bridgett. We have never taken in a girl before who wasn't from this country, but I'm making an exception in your case, because of the letter from my friend Sister Alphonsus. I hope your young man does the right thing by you in the end, so that your faith in him is rewarded, and you can leave here with him and your baby together, with your heads held high. My experience tells me otherwise, but we shall see how it all works out over the next few months.

"I shall pass you on to Sister Agnes now. She will complete the formalities with you; there are forms to sign, and then she will show you to your quarters. You will be allocated a bed in a dormitory with the other girls, and you will be issued with suitable clothing. Your will store your own clothes in your locker until you leave. While you are with us you will respond to the name *Catherine*, after *St Catherine*, a most holy martyr of the Church, for whom you might do well to establish some devotion."

Bridgett's expression reflected her concerns at the suggestion of uniform and the imposition of another name. Seeing her face the Mother Superior quickly added,

"It's not a prison, Bridgett," said the Mother Superior, "but conformity adds to discipline in institutions like this, and discipline is essential here. You must, like the other girls, comply with what are necessary regulations." She then added,

"The given name is for your protection after you leave here." Her authoritarian approach was firmly back in place as she led Bridgett away to meet Sister Agnes.

❧

As the weeks went by, Bridgett developed a loathing for the home that bordered on revulsion. She became convinced that she had made a great mistake in coming here. She found herself confined in a life that she believed bordered on workhouse conditions. Forced to scrub floors, wash windows, and launder for all the inmates her morale became lower and lower, while conversely her belly became bigger and bigger. Eventually, as she became quite heftily pregnant, she was taken off 'heavy duties' and spent her days in the knitting circle with all the other expectant mothers whose babies were within three months of being born. With more than enough time to think, it was at this point that she decided to leave the home. Taking her chances, and making her own way on the outside seemed to become a more attractive proposition each day. She would go home to James and tell him everything. She was convinced that even in her present condition, he loved her more than enough to want to marry her. They would be a family together. One evening, she decided to broach the question with the only girl she had hitherto befriended - given name Anne - as they sat together in the workroom, clacking away with their needles on cardigans and booties.

"Have you ever considered leaving here Anne?" she asked casually. The response from her companion was instant laughter.

"Where have you been hiding these last few months my dear?" and as her laughter persisted, Bridgett felt foolish and irritated by her reaction.

"Have I said something funny?" she said, her annoyance conspicuous. Her friend's amusement receded, to be replaced by serious concern. She took hold of Bridgett's hand,

"They won't let you leave here, Cathy dear. Not before they've got your baby anyway!"

The significance of Anne's words did not register. Bridgett was at a loss to understand what she was saying.

"What do you mean? Before they've got my baby?"

Anne's facial expression deepened as she explained further,

"You are not married and have no prospects of marriage, at least not before your baby is born. You won't walk out of here as a single mum with your baby in your arms. No chance love!" Bridgett looked horrified.

"Surely you knew that my lovely. They gave you the forms when you came in here, didn't they? That's the deal. You get somewhere to have your child - without anyone knowing - they get the kid for adoption to a suitably vetted Catholic family. Can't have little Catholics going to Protestant homes now, can we?", she added scornfully.

"As soon as it's weaned they take your baby away from you! It goes to the nursery, you see it less and less – to make it easier for you when it goes, - they say, - and then as soon as a suitable Catholic couple can be found to take it, it goes out with its new parents. Most of them go to America. But the longer you feed your baby yourself, the longer you get to keep it with you, so you've got to keep on nursing as long as possible."

Bridgett sat motionless, too staggered to respond. Anne put a comforting arm around her, as she broke down in shock,

"They can't take my baby, - not just like that. Nobody told me that!" she wailed.

"I thought you knew, love", her friend said kindly. That's what you signed up to. Did you not read the papers?" Anne pulled the distraught Bridgett to her, and held her tenderly, but her words of comfort failed to bring any consolation.

❦

That night Bridgett slept only in fits and starts. She rose silently while it was still dark and all was quiet. Clutching her few belongings she crept out of the dormitory and on out of the building without being discovered. She got to the main gate unseen, but found it was heavily padlocked. She went round to the side gate, hoping it would be bolted from the inside only, but it was chained up and locked too. She looked at the walls, but they were too high to scale in her current condition, and besides there was no obvious way up. Feeling frustrated and powerless as to what she should do, she crouched in the bushes close to tears. It would be light soon, and it wouldn't take long for them to realise that the bolster under her blankets wasn't her. She felt trapped and close to despair. Suddenly she heard a noise at the gate itself. There was a rattle of keys, followed by the noise of chains being slipped, as someone prepared to enter. A moment later the door swung open, and Mr Cunningham the caretaker, whose many tasks included firing up the central heating boilers in the early morning, entered. Bridgett knew Mr Cunningham as a kindly man, who always had a ready smile and a pleasant word for her.

Deciding in an instant that this was her chance, she came out from behind the bushes and confronted him.

"Please Mr Cunningham, I want to go out. Don't lock it yet," she whispered.

The elderly man was startled, but managed to contain his surprise, "Goodness me, what are you doing here?", he asked.

Bridgett shushed him, and in rapid-fire whispers explained that she wanted to leave the home and why.

Mr Cunningham, with disarming kindness and a sympathetic manner that encouraged Bridgett, responded positively.

"You need time to think this out a little, my girl," he said in a quiet and soothing tone. "You must rest a little and gather your thoughts, my dear.

"If, after some thought, you are still of the same mind, my wife knows someone who will help you. Right now you need to stay out of sight. Go to my house; tell my wife I've sent you. Wait there till I come home.

"Don't worry, she is out of bed right now," adding, "she always sees me off to work with a cup of tea and something to eat; then she goes back to bed, but not before she's tidied away the breakfast dishes and had a cuppa for herself. She will be busying around right now, so you won't disturb her."

He gave her directions and said, "It's not more than ten minutes from here. Now off you go, quickly."

Bridgett couldn't believe her luck. On an impulse she reached up and kissed him on the cheek and hugged him, then she hurried off in the direction he had indicated.

Mrs Cunningham behaved as kindly as her husband, and Bridgett listened to her sound advice.

"The Sisters will ask the police to search for you as soon as they find you have gone, and if you are spotted on the streets they will take you straight back. Others have tried to run away before my dear, and failed. So like Bernard says, - he's my husband - you must stay hidden for a while. The nuns are very diligent when it comes to catching girls who want away."

"Have you had to do this for other girls then?" asked Bridgett. Mrs Cunningham pondered before she answered then conceded,

"We have helped others, yes, but not too often. Bernard says we should only help those who have the welfare of their babies at heart. Some girls leave because they only want to escape the restrictions of the home, and can't wait to get back to their old ways, which got them into trouble in the first place. They are usually girls whose morals are as low as the gutter, and who don't give tuppence for what happens to their child afterwards. We don't help people like that."

Then she added quizzically, " Who told you to go to the gate my dear, one of the other girls? "

The question surprised Bridgett, for it had not occurred to her that her chance meeting with Mr Cunningham might be viewed as anything more than that – a chance meeting.

"No one told me, " she said " I just happened to be there. I was looking for a way out. Mr Cunningham came to the gate while I was looking."

Mrs Cunningham smiled, but her look betrayed the fact that she did not believe Bridgett.

"You were very lucky then, but anyway, it doesn't matter now. The fact is you are here, and that's all there is to it. We must make some plans my dear. Right now we both need to catch up on our sleep. Bernard comes home for lunch; he rests in the afternoons, because of this early start each morning. He doesn't have to be back in the home till four o'clock, but you and I might be busy at that time, so we had better take the opportunity to catch up on our sleep right now while we can.

"We have a spare room. The bed's made up, so you can just jump straight into it."

The thought of a few hours sleep after her restless night, in the comparative freedom of the Cunningham's home appealed to Bridgett immensely, and it was with a relieved sigh that minutes later she snuggled down into the sweet comfort of the fresh clean linen and surrendered herself to peaceful slumber.

The bedroom door burst open noisily and Bridgett woke with a start from a deep sleep. Initially confused as to her whereabouts, it was a few moments before her befuddled brain cleared, and her eyes focussed on her surroundings. Sister Agnes's voice swiftly brought her to full consciousness, and dismay instantly filled her heart. The realisation that she had been betrayed hit her like a hammer.

"Get up Catherine," said the Sister sharply, "You are coming back to the home immediately."

Bridgett moaned in dismay, and tears rolled down her cheeks once more.

"Lord Jesus Christ!" she cried out, "Will you not free me from these damnable people?" It was a prayer of desperation pleading for divine intervention.

"The Lord does not respond to blasphemy, Catherine," was the only answer she heard, and it came, not from the Lord, but one of his avowed servants.

Sister Agnes indicated to her two colleagues to get Bridgett dressed. She did not resist, and in a few minutes was being ushered from the house between her two escorts, as Sister Agnes handed over an envelope to Mrs Cunningham, which the housewife accepted with a look of greedy pleasure.

Bridgett stopped before the woman and remarked contemptuously,

"Forty pieces of silver, no doubt." Her guardians moved her on firmly, while Mrs Cunningham just continued to smile.

Back in the home, Bridgett found herself the butt of many caustic comments from her fellow inmates. Her attempt to run away was ridiculed as naïve and stupid. Most of the girls, it turned out, were very aware that Mr Cunningham and his wife were unreliable allies in escaping from the home. The pair were held in common contempt, and the man Bridgett had considered kindly and friendly, was known for his duplicitous smile, and renowned to the other girls as a mercenary, a spy in their midst, who would report any and every occurrence that might disturb the smooth running of the home, for his own financial gain. His kindly attitude was recognised as no more than a facade, which encouraged the girls, new ones in particular, to talk to him in trust and confidence. Worthy of nothing but their scorn, he was generally avoided by all who knew him for what he really was.

Bridgett wondered how she could not have known this, how she had not been made aware of him by the others, and she realised that it was because that apart from Anne, she spent little time talking to any of the other occupants. Had she been more open to them, they might well have warned her of the folly of her amateur escapade. Anne shook her head sadly as she admitted that she herself did not know of the Cunninghams' notorious reputations.

Her interview with Sister Mary Theresa was, as she expected, sharp and punitive.

"I took you in because you came here desperate and homeless, with no defined future for yourself or your child, and at the request of my dear friend Sister Alphonsus, who trusted you, as indeed I did," she said. "You have repaid that trust with ingratitude and betrayal."

She gazed at Bridgett with a look that bordered on contempt.

"Where on earth did you think you were going to go in your condition and with no money? How far did you think you could get, before some rogue or other found you, and dragged you and your child down into poverty and deprivation? You spoke of the father; - he would marry you, you said, - but he hasn't turned up, has he? They never do you know!"

She was angry and her anger was unforgiving.

"There are no circumstances that might allow me to treat you leniently. You have offered no reason for us to let you leave here. From now until your baby is born, you will be kept in isolation in a room by yourself. If you think this is an easy penance, you might view it differently after a while. Even the company of the girls in this place is preferable to the loneliness that you will experience for the remainder of your stay with us. You will take your meals separately in the dining hall, and your only contact with any person outside your room will be at daily mass and prayers, where you will be escorted to and fro by a sister of my choosing. Your work will be limited to handicrafts such as knitting and sewing, and you will be expected to meet quotas that I will set for you.

"Once you have been delivered of your child, you will be required to leave as soon as you have been deemed fit to travel by the doctors. Normally mother and child are allowed more time together. You have forfeited that privilege."

The remaining months passed as slowly and as lonely as Sister Mary Theresa had predicated, and Bridgett's morale reached a new low each day. She saw Anne, her erstwhile friend only rarely, at meal times, when they would exchange furtive hand signals from a distance, as she was forced to take her meals at a separate table accompanied only by her own personal keeper, usually the Sister on duty in the dining hall. Bridgett's mealtime custodians rarely spoke to her during these encounters other than to utter a restrictive command or similar instruction, except of course for the good Sister Lucy, whose attitude remained as compassionate as ever. One day when acting as her escort, Sister Lucy pressed a beautiful rosary into Bridgett's hand, and whispered to her,

"Our Lady will always help those who seek her intercession my child, pray each day to her and you will see."

Bridgett believed the good sister to be the nearest thing to a saint she had ever known, and thereafter regularly recited at least one decade of the devotion each night at bedtime.

It was after this that she began to find some peace with herself, and to turn her solitude to positive purpose. During the long periods of quiet reflection she began to rationalise her situation for both herself and her baby. She learnt to accept the tortuous reality that her child was lost to her, and she finally recognised she was unable to change that fact. It was then that she determined to do all she could do to ensure that whatever future was in store for her baby, and whichever parents were chosen, she, Bridgett, would do all that was possible to ensure that her child would know who its real mother was, and where to look, should it ever want to find her.

Over the remaining weeks she carefully composed a letter to her baby. As she wrote, she spoke aloud as if her child could hear her. She explained who she was, and who James was, and she expanded her explanations with details of both their family histories. She included home addresses in England, where 'God willing' she said, one day they might meet. She told how cousin Elizabeth lived in Ireland, and avowed that even though, through time and circumstance, these details must surely change, she would pray daily that they would find each other somewhere in their unknown futures. She affirmed her dedication to her unborn in the purest and simplest terms she could set out, and assured the child that it was conceived in love, and only the cruelty of time and bad circumstance had imposed a separation from her beloved James. She stated solemnly that God would vouch for her sincerity in all that she had written, and begged her child to pray for her each day. Then she finished with the words,

"As I write this letter to you, we are together, and you grow within me daily. My words to you are from my heart, and come what may, I shall treasure the reality of this precious time with you for the rest of my life. As you read this, know that I am hugging you to me."

When Bridgett asked her, Sister Lucy agreed to visit Bridgett in her room, and listen to her secret request. As she did so, she could see the heartache and the fear of rejection, as Bridgett begged for her help. When she replied she did so with deep compassion.

"To do what you ask, my child, to conspire for you to be present when the selected parents come to collect your baby would be to flout the authority of my Mother Superior, to who I am bound by a vow of obedience; also to supply you with names and addresses would contravene the rules of adoption, as communication between the mother and the adoption parties is forbidden. But it is irrelevant anyway, as I am not privy to such information."

Bridgett sagged visibly at her words, but Sister Lucy continued.

"However, I will try to help you another way. I promise you this; I will make every attempt to hand your letter to the adopting couple when they come to collect your child. I will make a point of seeing them. I will ask them to take your message and in conscience keep it safe till the child is adult enough to read and appreciate its contents. I cannot do more than this, and should they not want to accept your letter, there is nothing I can do to make them, my dear. I can only promise to try, and I will do that."

Bridgett's gratitude was effusive.

"God bless you, Sister. Thank you, thank you, thank you so very much!"

Three weeks after her baby boy was born, Bridgett left the nursing home, and moved into a local boarding house. She had not been allowed to see her son again, and the trauma that overwhelmed her at her loss was only slightly eased when her mother turned up to take her home.

Margaret had been in Ireland throughout the duration of Bridgett's confinement, and had searched its institutions in vain. Battling ceaselessly against the sectarian bureaucracy and secrecy that surrounded the activities of the churches' nursing homes, she was finally given details of her daughter's whereabouts, but not before her grandchild's future had been irrevocably decided, and he had been entrusted to parents whose identities would remain protected by the system. Thus for all practical purposes, he was untraceable.

Chapter 14

Wings for Victory

In the early month's of 1943, an air of optimism pervaded the national psyche in Britain, and the "feel good" factor was high. The forces of the Wehrmacht had been defeated at Stalingrad, and daily news bulletins from the BBC's Home Service indicated that the Russian advance was set fair to steady, and unrelentingly westwards. The battle for supremacy in the Atlantic was almost won, and the U-boats of the German fleet were scuttling like foxes to their holes, seeking refuge in the bunkers and pens along the coastal seaboards of France and Germany and in the intricate channels of the Norwegian fjords. In North Africa, the German and Italian forces were on the point of surrender, and plans for the invasion of Sicily had already been formulated.

On the Home Front, bolstered by the news from the war zones, and anticipating the arrival of spring, with the prospect of summer's warm pleasure to follow, the nation was nurturing a growing conviction in the inevitability of victory. All this was producing an exuberant expectation that had not been seen on the public face of Britain for many years. Enhanced by its deep-rooted conviction in the justice of the cause, the nation's assurance of the predestined outcome was further compounded by the latest of the government's propaganda promotions, the *Wings for Victory* campaign.

"This effort," said an anonymous government source, *"is designed to generate more war bonds and more national savings to provide the essential cash with which to support our valiant airmen, whose courage in the defense of our*

land represents the very essence of the fight over evil in which we are so fiercely engaged."

In truth, the Royal Air Force was at this time engaged in an actively *offensive* programme against the enemy, unleashing vengeance of an horrific kind, in the form of twenty- four hour bombing on the defenceless citizens of Germany's inner cities, in what was acknowledged in the halls of power as a clear and ruthless reprisal for what Goering and the Luftwaffe had done to Britain some two years earlier.

Air Marshall Sir Arthur Travers (Bomber) Harris, C. in C. Bomber Command, was at the pinnacle of his power, which for many was an evil in itself.

Nevertheless, back home in March that year, the nation took the spirit of the campaign to their hearts, and it quickly gathered momentum. Across the country, people of all ages, in the cites, in the towns, in the villages and the hamlets, competed energetically to create the most imaginative exhibitions; to put on the best of brassy parades; and to entertain with spectacular and glittering theatrical presentations; all in the cause of national savings, and they did it with a cavalier disregard for the frugal circumstances of wartime austerity.

In Eastinglea the 'Wings for Victory' frenzy was as spirited as it was elsewhere in the country. Even the town's schools stood united, in an uneasy liaison which replaced the religious and social differences which so frequently divided them, and which, though not normally apparent between the schools' governing hierarchies, were demonstrably evident between the pupils themselves, whose extra-curricula behaviour invariably included inter-school warring conducted outside and beyond the restraining influence of the schools' perimeters. These rivalries, amongst boys in particular, were invariably characterised by a feudal and belligerent vehemence that verged on tribalism! The ostrich-like school authorities however chose not to acknowledge their activities, and on such occasions as they became unavoidably embarrassed by them, chose to refer the problems to the local police. They in turn preferred, at least for the most part, to pay little attention to them, arguing that deploying resources to keep a vigilant eye out for German spies and downed German aircrew was a more necessary expedient, and took absolute precedence over 'petty school squabbles'. For the present however, in the euphoria of the nation's celebrations, all such academic confrontations were suspended, bringing a heartfelt sigh of relief from all authorities concerned.

The local welfare groups and the voluntary societies joined the general celebratory activities as well, getting caught up in the hectic commotion of assembling floats and tableaux that represented their diverse functions. These turned out to be vivid, imaginative, and often humorous.

The Boy Scout troops, The Girl Guides, and The Boys' Brigade were equally involved, building up displays and 'mobiles', which they guarded jealously, screening them from public view, fearing that their novel ideas might be stolen or copied by rival groups, before they themselves could exhibit them to an approving and admiring public on the day of the grand parade. The well entrenched lack of geniality and trust that marked relations between these competing organisations regrettably remained unappeased by the wave of popular goodwill and 'bonhomie' which prevailed elsewhere.

The local ice-cream vendors exercised their creative ingenuity producing frivolous confections of red white and blue, in wafers and cones that were themselves similarly decorative. Bunting appeared on houses, offices, and across streets, and cardboard shields embossed with silvery "V"s replicating Churchill's renowned victory symbol were hung everywhere.

At the local Drill Hall, where the Army Cadets, the Home Guard, and the TA battalions of the Durham Light Infantry and the Royal Artillery gathered in mixed assembly for regular drills and gunnery practice, an impressive assortment of field guns, anti-aircraft guns, and armoured vehicles were on show. In pride of place two Churchill tanks, borrowed for the occasion from the army battalion at Brancepeth stood imposingly in the outside yard. These fearsome weapons of war were being afforded the tenderest care and attention by men in khaki fatigues, who cleaned, polished, and caressed them with a regard that the casual observer might have thought verged on youthful passion. That this was more than just a labour of love was evident from the barking orders of the men's' attendant taskmasters, the NCO's, whose authority was personified in loud demands for even greater efforts by their "spit and polish" minions.

Among these martinets strode Michael, immaculate in a uniform, that had razor-sharp creases on the battledress sleeves, with a marksman's badge displayed conspicuously above his sergeant's stripes, while below his knife edged trousers were gathered neatly at the ankles into carefully blancoed khaki spats. The DLI badge glittered brightly in his khaki cap, which was angled precisely on his head, and his highly polished black boots glistened brilliantly on his feet. He was the epitome of a serving British soldier. With him in his squad, also working in denims and pre-occupied with their chores were those cell members who had "joined up" specifically to receive the military training essential to an active IRA operative. Six of them had enlisted, three in the infantry and three in the artillery. The British were providing the training that the Army Council in Dublin could no longer undertake. The smell of lubricating oil and Brasso was everywhere. Preparations for the forthcoming grand parade were well underway. The scene was set for a spectacular show, and a final curtain that no one could anticipate.

Tomas stood at the small entry portal set in the huge wooden concertina door, through which all heavy ordnance entered and exited the Drill Hall and watched Michael efficiently discharging his duties as a 'non-com' in the T.A. He felt confused by what he saw. Michael was an Irishman, an IRA executive appointed by the Army Council in Dublin, and he was standing there before him at ease in the uniform of their enemy, comfortable with himself as he ordered about the English subordinates around him. Tomas found it hard to believe that he was only playing a part.

He knew the justification. He accepted that acquiring explosives and the guns would have been impossible without the access that Michael had provided. The crates of 'SPARE ORDNANCE, EMERGENCY USE ONLY' that were now in fact no more than boxes filled with sand bags, and which Michael had stowed away from prying eyes at the back of the magazine house were becoming increasingly less likely to be discovered, as the threat of invasion became an ever diminishing possibility. He had done an excellent job for the unit and had covered his tracks so well.

As QM Sergeant, Michael was able to appropriate supplies quite easily, little by little, bit by bit, and had done so. In doing so he had fulfilled his function, as he had said he would. Yet Tomas remained uneasy. He wasn't sure that, come Saturday week, Michael would be at his side in what he was planning. He doubted that he should tell him the exact details. He decided not to. He would meet later that day with James Kennedy. He felt certain of him at least.

For a moment their eyes met across the expanse of the Drill Hall. They gazed at each other, but made no sign of recognition, and in that moment Tomas felt Michael was a stranger to him. There was no trust any more.

Chapter 15

Confession

At St Leonard's Dermot was busy with the schools. As Easter approached, the children being prepared for their First Confessions and their First Communions needed to be examined to measure the catechistic understanding of their undertakings. As the curate, the task fell to him, rather than his aging superior Father Petrie, who's failing health grossly and adversely affected his active participation in the affairs of the parish. Dermot didn't mind the increasing workload, and he particularly enjoyed the friendly exchanges with the young communicants in the classrooms, where his easy relationship with the young children made him extremely popular. It even rubbed off with some of the older ones. In fact Dermot's status in the parish was never better.

He actively participated in the parish football team, which competed in the local football league. Dressed anonymously in the team colours, his physical approach to the game often exposed him to profanities, abuse, and robust retribution from opposing team players. Later when the game was over, their startled recognition of his vocational status - loudly announced by his clerical cloth and accompanying dog collar - led inevitably to awkward discomfort, shamefaced embarrassment, and an inevitable profusion of apologies. This created an air of unwarranted superiority among his teammates that served to alleviate the humiliation of the frequent defeats St Leonard's untalented team sustained. Nevertheless, Dermot's gracious dismissal of the apologies, and his insistence that he was just another footballer when on the field, impressed opponents and team-mates alike, who admired him increasingly more as a man than a priest. Nonetheless within the team his fellow players acknowledged that his pastoral standing allowed them no license to use disrespectful language in his presence, and they never did, reserving their cussing habits for the bar later once he had left them.

His initiative in establishing an active youth club for the teenagers of the parish also added to his reputation with the youth of the parish, once his political allegiances, initially disputed, were correctly established.

A "really good egg" was a description foisted on him by a distinguished and conspicuously Tory diocesan guest at the official opening of the St Leonard's Youth Club. The remark later gave rise to a barrage of sarcastic badinage from the new club's die-hard young socialists, who labelled him as an upper class snob, more fitting to the Young Conservatives Association than theirs. It took considerable effort on Dermot's part to explain that he had never been, and was not now, a Tory, and even less so were his parents or his paternal or maternal grandparents! Even then, it was only later, after extensive enquiries while they 'checked him out' as a genuine Durham miner's son that he was able to laugh with them about the matter. Snobbery he thought afterwards, inverted though it may be, was clearly not the prerogative of the upper classes.

Dermot was happy in this vocation, and he felt his purpose in life was fulfilled. It was with some trepidation therefore that as he emerged from the old hut that was used as a dressing room - following St Leonard's latest defeat - he spotted his Uncle Michael waiting for him on the touchline. Trouble at home was his immediate thought. He was right.

"Uncle Michael," he greeted him smiling, " What do I owe for this unexpected pleasure? What are you doing in this neighbourhood? I didn't see you during the game."

"Just got here Dermot," said Michael taking Dermot's hand and shaking it firmly in his own. "It's good to see you again. How are you, my boy, you certainly look fit enough. Did you win?"

Dermot smiled "We rarely win, Michael, if we only played to win, we wouldn't play at all." Then he asked quickly " There's something wrong at home isn't there?" Michael's smile faded at the question.

"I just wish I was here under different circumstances, Dermot. I have come to see you about your father, and it's not good news, I'm afraid."

Dermot felt nervous.

"Is he sick?"

"No, he's not sick, at least not physically, but I can't vouch for his mental state!

"We need to talk, Dermot. He needs your help. Can we go somewhere private?"

Later in the presbytery, they sat facing each other over tea and cakes provided by Bridgett, recently appointed housekeeper following her return from Ireland, where she had been for the past year. Dermot spoke anxiously.

"What's going on, Uncle Michael?"

"Dermot, you are probably totally unaware of what your father has been up to these past few years, and before I can tell you what the current problem is you have to understand the background. How much time have you got right now?"

"Enough" replied Dermot, "if it concerns my father's health and welfare, I've got all the time in the world!"

Michael nodded before he continued,

"It began a long time ago Dermot, with your grandfather's death during the Uprising in Dublin in 1916............................."

Michael related the whole story, the history with which Dermot was for the most part familiar, having heard it so often during his childhood. He knew the tragic circumstances around the murders of his grandfather and grandmother. He knew the circumstances surrounding the death of Father O'Malley and his father's enforced flight from Ireland. He knew of his father's bitterness against the English and the Church in which he himself was now a priest. He knew of the conflict this caused between his father and his beloved mother, and he felt the pain of it all in his father's rejection of himself. He hurt deeply inside more and more, as days turned to weeks and weeks to years and his father's rejection of him and his vocation continued inexorably. What he didn't know and what came to him with profound shock was his father's involvement in the IRA and the creation of a local cell in Eastinglea.

He instantly recognized the dangers and the potential consequences arising from this fact. Treason was the word, for which the penalty in wartime was certain death. There could never be any extenuating circumstances.

Michael watched as the impact of his words showed on Dermot's face, and waited.

Dermot spoke tremulously,

"You were - you are - part of this as well, Uncle Michael, and all those so called 'soldiers' you have recruited. Are you not? You are all at risk!"

"Yes, I am! And yes, we are! You are quite right! I have told Tomas that we can't go on, and it's got to stop now. The Army Council itself has gone underground due to political pressures in Ireland, and they have ordered everybody else to do the same, including us."

Dermot looked aghast. Michael continued, slightly apologetically,

"What we have done so far consists of relatively small and none to serious operations. We've blown up a few unmanned lookout posts, a couple of pillboxes, most of them during exercises within the T.A. We've started a few fires in some out of town factories. These activities were judged necessary as field exposure manoeuvres; all carefully contained and swiftly executed - to get the boys used to being on active service and to let them 'feel the pressure' as it were. We have claimed responsibility for nothing. As a policy the IRA has not been mentioned so far. For what it's worth the boys have come back elated from these exercises, and as for the authorities, they are half inclined to take the easy and obvious route and blame the German saboteurs without offering any evidence to support such claims, I might add - and what they can't blame Jerry for they put down to legitimate T.A. exercises or vandals.

"We have stolen ammunition and guns of course; but these haven't even been missed yet. So far no one has been killed or injured. If we stop now, no one need be, and I'm confident they'll forget about us. They have much more important digressions to occupy their minds right now. After all there's a war going on."

"So stop then, for goodness sake! What are you waiting for?"

"I want to, but your father wants one more operation! He wants to do something big - during the 'Wings for Victory' celebrations. He wants to mobilise the cell for his own reasons. He's planning to get to The Lord Lieutenant of the County, Dermot. He plans to kill him! You see Dermot, the Lord Lieutenant is James Spencer-Lambert, the man who murdered your grandfather!"

Dermot gasped and in total shock sat stunned silently gazing into space. A thousand confused thoughts were racing through his head. His emotions were in turmoil. He felt very afraid.

"What do you want me to do, Uncle Michael? What can I do that you can't do better?"

"I believe that only you can stop him now, Dermot. Despite everything that's gone before, you are still his son, and you are a priest. That combination is strong enough to prevent him committing murder. Your father is still your grandfather's son, a man of honour and a man who honoured God. You represent God in your father's eyes, and you are the living image of your grandfather."

"Why haven't you tried to stop him? You have been his lifelong friend. If he will listen to anyone surely he will listen to you"

"Believe me Dermot I have tried, but your father doesn't trust me any more. He sees me as one who betrayed him with the Army Council; he thinks I have gone over to the British, that I would betray him further. He will not tell me what his plans are, he even denies that he has any."

"How can you be sure that he has?" Dermot felt an irrational surge of resentment towards his Uncle Michael. " How can I be sure that you would not betray him – or that you have not done so already?"

Michael looked hurt. "If I wanted to harm your father, do you seriously think I would be here talking to you now?"

A strained silence between them followed, with Dermot confused and engrossed in his thoughts. Finally Michael sighed and stood up as if to go, but he paused to say,

"I thought about asking your mother to speak to him Dermot, but I couldn't burden her with the knowledge of your father's intentions. They're already estranged, and have been for a long time now. They hardly speak to each other, as you already know. It started when you went to Corshaw and their relationship has gone progressively downhill ever since. He'll not listen to her any more, so I decided to come here instead. I beg you Dermot at least talk to him; give it a try, before it's too late. Because if ever a man was set on a path of self-destruction, that man is Tomas, and only God can stop him. And you're the nearest thing to God we've got Dermot!"

After he had gone, Dermot sat alone contemplating their conversation for a long time. Eventually as the evening shadows began to creep in, Bridgett looked in on him.

"You have 'Confessions' in half an hour Dermot. You've just got time for a hot bath and a cup of tea before then. Hurry up; get that football muck washed off you."

❧

The fading light of the early evening cast its long shadows into the dim corners of the church as Dermot made his way to the confessional at the back. In the benches nearby, people were already waiting patiently for him, deep in prayer and contrite contemplation. He always made a point of looking down to the floor as he walked past the early penitents because he felt the anonymity of the confessional was best served if he did not see the faces of those who were about to bare their souls before him. Dermot wasn't great as a confessor. It was a weakness in his vocation which he acknowledged, but no matter how hard he tried he could not rid himself of the feeling that he was nothing more than a prying inquisitor, to whom devout people must expose their innermost secrets, as a contractual requirement they must meet in order to qualify for the ultimate reward, as a sin-free soul aspiring to eternal happiness. He wished that people could simply be allowed to make their peace with God, sincerely in their own private way, and he could not understand why the infallible Church refused to agree that this was all that was needed. However until it did, he and his fellow pastors must continue to listen to their good peoples' 'sins' and administer absolution for what, for the most part, were nothing more than minor human misdemeanours. The real sinners, he had always maintained, rarely go to Confession anyway.

Thus, head bent as usual, Dermot failed to notice little Jeanette Pardew in a warm pink coat and hat, with her mother Mrs. Anne Pardew, in a powder blue equivalent. Neither did he see the two pensioners, who he would later recognise from their voices, as the delightful old couple Mr and Mrs Burns, unfailing attendants at monthly confession in all of the time he had so far spent at St Leonard's. Nor did he notice the tall man in the corner of the last bench who with head bent low, carefully hid his face in the shadows.

Dermot was lucky this Saturday evening. The local sports paper, *The Football Echo,* had arrived early, and as he settled into his chair inside the confessional box, he pulled it out to sneak a peek at the day's results. He had just time to glance at the headlines before the door on the other side of the curtain opened, and the first penitent entered. There was a creaking noise as someone knelt down, then Dermot heard a young voice speak. It was little Jeanette, who instantly invoked his blessing as she recited the prayer of intercession she had been taught at school, then without pausing, proudly followed up with a list of sinful trivia that Dermot listened to with an amused smile. When she had finished, he congratulated her on a good confession, and invited her to say a fervent *'Act of Contrition'* as he administered absolution. Then, ceremony over, Dermot told her how pleased God was with her, and instructing her to say one Our Father and One Hail Mary as her penance, sent her off happily with his blessing. With a contented 'Thank you Father' the little girl left the confessional, secure in the knowledge that 'her soul was again free from sin, and as white as an angel's'. That's what happened in confession, just as Sister Mary told them in catechism class at school, she reflected. Dermot sighed at the unnecessary ritual he had just conducted with the innocent child. Then as he reached for his newspaper, the door opened again and in came her mother. And so it went on. For the next two hours Dermot listened patiently to the transgressions of his parishioners, snatching occasional glances at his sports paper during the intervals when there was a pause in the flow of the self- denunciations. Generally the last hour of his "spiritual surgery" hung heavily on his hands. Each week the most devout and regular of his penitents had been forgiven in the first hour. Unburdened of their routine sinful excesses – overeating – drunkenness - gambling - and even minor sexual aberrations - acted out in a futile attempt to relieve the boredom and tedium of their repetitive lives, they had all departed by seven p.m. The remaining hour was then interrupted only occasionally by those who skulked in late, reluctant supplicants, who to his discredit, Dermot knew would confess to more sinful ways, and thus be much more interesting.

Eventually, as the in and out traffic slowed to a halt, Dermot glanced at his watch. It was approaching eight o'clock and his 'confession-session' was almost over, and he sighed his contentment at the thought. He relaxed and opened the paper to read the *'Minor Soccer Roundup'*, where sadly, and often scathingly, the details of St Leonard's weekly footballing fiascos were frequently reported. It was a masochistic habit, but one he could never resist. Finding no such report on this occasion, scathing or otherwise, he contented himself with the front and back page reports of Sunderland's match that day, absorbing the expert critique that always accompanied it, being ready to dispute within himself its usually uncomplimentary conclusions.

It came as a surprise therefore when he heard the door open yet again and another person entered. He put the paper down once more, and waited with impatient curiosity.

A man's voice, instantly recognizable, spoke out to him.

"Dermot, it's me, your father!"

Dermot gasped his disbelief. He could only sit in stunned silence as his father spoke again.

"What's wrong son, cat got your tongue?"

Dermot forced himself to speak.

"Why are you here, father?" he said, and his voice trembled with the effort.

"Well I'm here to confess of course. Why else would I be here?", he asked, with some derision.

Dermot's anxiety was very pronounced as he appealed to his father.

"Father, I cannot hear your confession! I don't want to hear your confession, please don't do this to me!"

" Oh don't worry Dermot, I'm not here to embarrass you. I'm only here to gag you. Seal of confession and all that" His easy tone consoled Dermot no more than slightly, and he remained tense and puzzled.

"I need to tell you that I intend to commit a grievous mortal sin. I'm going to kill someone, and since I think you might be approached to try and stop me, or even talk about it in public - with the authorities for instance - or even within the family, I decided to come to you and tell you all about it myself, under the Seal of Confession. I'm invoking your priestly vow of silence my boy. I can't risk my son being persuaded to interfere with my plans now, can I?"

"Oh God, father, what are you saying?" The reality of Michael's earlier warning came rushing back to him.

"I'm saying to you that I intend to murder the Honourable Lord Lambert Earl of Lumfield, James Spencer-Lambert himself, Lord Lieutenant of the County, the man who murdered your grandparents, and who by now probably doesn't even remember doing it. And now that I have informed you here in this confessional of this impending sin, I can rest assured you are helpless to speak on the matter or interfere. So no matter what your Uncle Michael asked of you today, you are powerless to get in the way now."

Dermot's gasped his surprise again.

"Oh yes, I know he's been here Dermot, I saw him at the bus station this morning, he got on the bus to Satsworth, and there's only one place he could be going to in Satsworth now isn't there. So I followed on a later bus, and here I am, - here we are - all together like the folks of Shields, as they say around here. God alone knows why they say it, but they do."

"I would never do anything to endanger or threaten you father, surely you know that," said Dermot in dismay.

"I don't believe you would, not deliberately or consciously, but misguidedly you might. Now you can't even talk about it, and that's why I'm here."

"Father you have not confessed properly; there is no seal of confession, and I'm not bound by my vow of silence where there is no contrition or intention of change for the future."

"Well now Dermot, I'm here on my knees in front of you, and I have confessed - to what I'm about to do - and when I have done it I'll be as contrite as I can. What's more I promise never to murder anyone again as long as I live! Will that not do for now? I would advise you to talk to your Bishop about this, but you might compromise your vows if you disclose the details of a man's confession under these circumstances, might you not? What a dilemma I've put you in son; you'd do better just to stay silent about it, I'd say!" Without another word he got up and left the confessional.

Dermot sat motionless in a daze, for how long he did not know; then he also stood up and left, bewildered. Behind him his crumpled newspaper slid to the floor.

Chapter 16

"Noblesse Oblige"

When, some two weeks before the fact, James Spencer Lambert was invited to be guest of honour during Eastinglea's WINGS FOR VICTORY WEEK celebrations and take the salute in the Grand Parade, he responded positively and enthusiastically. As Lord Lieutenant of the County, he believed implicitly in the pomp and ceremony of such occasions, and revelled in the esteem and respect afforded him because of his high rank and social standing. He took particular delight in the theatrics of dressing up in the distinctive uniform that it was his privilege to wear, and which set him above his peers clad in the routine attire that their lesser stations required of them. He was in truth an aristocratic snob, and it bothered him not one jot that all around him knew it.

When Mr Henry informed James that he would be included in the party to accompany his Lordship during these festivities, he was both delighted and flattered. His rising status within the household had thus far been noted by all, but not officially recognised, and in no way formerly acknowledged.

However this assignment as his Lordship's personal attendant rubber-stamped his standing in the administrative pecking order, placing him second to Mrs Butterworth the housekeeper and third behind Mr Henry himself. The ultimate confirmation of his new station was subsequently endorsed with notice of an increase in his annual salary, which came to him in a letter signed by his Lordship in person. James felt rightly proud that he had succeeded thus far in the Spencer-Lambert establishment, yet his overall sense of fulfilment was greatly diminished due to the continued absence of Bridgett, whose love and presence he yearned for beyond all other considerations.

His enquiries as to her whereabouts had been met with non-committal disinterest by her father, who referred vaguely to a holiday in Ireland, for both Bridgett and her mother. James's dismay at this strange turn of events was exacerbated when he realised she had chosen not to tell him of these plans at all.

That evening, at the special meeting called by Mr Henry to co-ordinate the timetable of events and define each individual's responsibilities, it was made clear that James would be at his Lordship's side during all the planned occasions, serving his needs personally and responding to any and every eventuality that might arise. Once the ancillary duties had been defined and finalised for the remaining attending staff, a copy of the agenda was despatched for printing to the local stationers. The prints were returned promptly the following day. They were set on fine quality card, with the Spencer-Lambert family crest embossed in gold on the front cover of each. James thought they looked splendid as he examined his copy, taken from those laid out on the table in the servants' hall. Then, having proudly inspected his name inside it, he took another one, 'for luck'.

Chapter 17

Disillusion, Dissension and Opportunity

Following repeated confirmation of orders from Dublin to freeze all operations until further notice, attendance at the Tuesday evening meetings of the "C.M.C.S." diminished progressively, as the enthusiasm of the original recruits - my very own 'Twelve Apostles' - Tomas had irreverently named them once, began to wane.

Once the last training exercise, yet another 'attack and destroy' raid on a recently constructed unmanned guardhouse, had been completed, again plausibly explained to the irritated constabulary by Michael as *essential Territorial training*, there seemed little reason to continue the drills. Now interest had all but ended; his 'apostles' had lost their faith.

"What's the point!" was the common chorus, and slowly but surely they disavowed themselves of their oaths and shrugged off their predicated purpose. Consequently attendance at the C.M.C.S. Tuesday evening meetings in the "Demi" now consisted of only five people, Tomas, his two sons, Michael and the ever attendant James Kennedy.

As all this was happening about him, Tomas watched with an increasing sense of frustration, knowing that as long as Michael stood at his shoulder and remained as his contact with Dublin, there was nothing he could do to reverse the collapse of the Unit and with it the disintegration of his campaign. Thus, as they gathered in the committee room at what was in effect their final meeting, Tomas was compelled to announce the suspension of activities and the indefinite closure of the cell. There were to be no more meetings, no further operations, and hence no further need for the C.M.C.S.

It was a curt address made in an atmosphere of deep depression, with Michael finding himself somewhat cold - shouldered by the others. The impasse between himself and Tomas was now absolute; there was no way back. The profound silence that followed Tomas's declaration hung heavily in the air, till eventually Padraig spoke up.

"I'll be off then father, if that's it," he said unenthusiastically. He stood up, pulled his cap down onto his head and as he turned to leave he smiled sardonically,

"Constance will think I'm ill – getting home this early on a Tuesday – and not a whiff of beer on my breath."

Tomas looked at him " Yes son, she will that, but be away to your house now. Surprise her."

"I'll see you tomorrow," he added resignedly.

Padraig nodded and with a curt glance at the others left the room. They listened as the front door closed behind him.

Tomas looked to his other son.

"A pint George - before you go?"

"No thanks father. I'd just as soon be off too. There's little pleasure in drinking here now." He glanced at Michael coldly, and then he too left.

Michael looked at Tomas, who stared back at him, lantern-jawed and resentful. James glanced anxiously between them.

"What?" said Michael finally, a challenge in his voice.

"You are accusing me, Tomas! With your eyes! Of what may I ask?"

Tomas's reply was full of resentment.

"You know what you have done Michael. You have taken away my last chance for justice. You have undermined me at every step!" He spoke quietly but his voice was hard.

Michael's tone was equal to it.

"That's not true Tomas. I have helped you all the way. I used my position in the Territorials to further the cause at every step. Your "recruits" were trained professionally, under my supervision, and now they are soldiers. They are familiar with firearms and dynamite. They are capable of doing anything that this Unit needs them to do, - whenever we are ordered to do it.

"I've even sweet-talked the local constabulary for you. Why else do you think the police have taken no more than passing interest in the things we have done?

"It's just the *'Terras'* getting in their training, they thought. Nobody has even vaguely suspected that The IRA was in their midst, and even less that the British Army was training them!

"What has been achieved could never have been done without me, and you know it. I have fulfilled my role right up to the time that we were ordered to stop. And may I remind you Tomas, that order came from Dublin from the Army Council itself!" Tomas shook his head in frustration.

"For god's sake Michael, do you not hear yourself? Can't you see how you have changed?" He glared at him in fury.

"You could have helped me just one more time. The old Michael would not have hesitated. We would have succeeded! Together – like we used to be – back in the old country! The Army Council didn't need to know anything about it. But no, you worked against me, I believe you used your position to get this Unit closed down Michael!"

He paused to examine Michael's face looking for a reaction. He saw none and his desperation persisted.

"Just one more operation Michael. That's all I want! We can still do it! No one else need know!" He was pleading now.

Michael leaned across the table and spoke with calm inflexibility,

"I have never agreed with your obsessive plans for murder Tomas, and I have told you that since the first day you arrived in this country. Your commitment to *'The Cause'* has always been secondary to your personal plans, and you would have used this unit and risked the lives of everyone in it to achieve them. But now you can't do that anymore, and I believe firmly that it is a good thing that you can't. Murder, Tomas, is a cowardly crime, and your vendetta is a futile aspiration. I will not help you further it!"

Tomas ignored him and remained stubbornly silent. For a moment they examined each other with hostility. Finally Michael stood up,

"I don't think we have anything more to discuss Tomas, so goodnight to you." With a nod to James he also left the room.

Tomas hung his head dejectedly after he had gone, then remembering James he looked up. James was waiting and watching him keenly.

"You had better go too, James there's no reason for you to stay now."

The reaction was as surprising as it was sudden. James stood up, and standing smartly at attention spoke out fiercely,

"Oh no Commander, not me, I made an oath! I'm still with you, all the way wherever you go!

"Maybe this will help you with your plans, Commander" He pushed the programme of events across the table.

The gold embossed Spencer-Lambert crest glistened under the overhead lights.

Chapter 18

"Of Mushrooms"

Gilpin had found them for him. He had laughed at the reasons Tomas had proffered for wanting to hire a couple of boys with a working knowledge of explosives.

"Mushrooms! You want to make a mushroom bed in your cellar, but the floor is solid concrete?"

His laughter attracted the attention of the other members, and Tomas had been forced to hush him up. Gilpin's laughter faded as he realised Tomas had something more serious in mind. He leaned across the bar to speak in a quieter tone.

"You need a couple of guys who can handle powder?"

"Yes!"

"Up front Tommy, is this all legit?"

"Of course it is, Mickey! Just trust me," snapped Tomas." I just have to keep it secret for now. You won't get into any trouble I promise you!" Gilpin looked unconvinced, but after some thought, assented.

"Well you obviously don't want locals do you - you could get them yourself from the pit!" He paused again frowning, as he looked Tomas over thinking deeply. Eventually the frown cleared and he said,

"Two questions Tommy, how much is it worth, and when do you want them?"

"I need them next week, and I'll pay one hundred pounds, fifty up front and fifty on completion!" Tomas spoke quickly and his anxiety was conspicuous. "There's fifty in it for you too if you help me."

Gilpin whistled in surprise, and a few members looked up curiously.

"I'd better get busy then!" he said, and for a moment concern flitted across his face again. "Must be really urgent this one, Tommy."

"I need them to complete the job by a week on Saturday," Tomas blurted out impatiently.

"OK. I'll be in touch Tommy," said Gilpin, still looking pensive as he turned away to tend a waiting customer.

The following afternoon he called Tomas to the club, where two strangers were waiting for him. Tomas, who had brought the faithful James along, invited them to talk privately in the Committee Room.

Chapter 19

The Mushroom Plot

As they took their seats he viewed his companions with considerable disquiet. This unpalatable pair, appraising him with undisguised suspicion were a couple of convicted safecrackers, recently released from Durham jail. Former miners, they had developed their skills with explosives during their days as shot-firers in the thin seams of West Durham's coalfields, driving high roadways through the rock barriers that remained once the sparse coal of the shallow faces ahead had been extracted. However access roads were expensive, and cut ever more deeply into marginal profits as the thin workings progressed and the seams narrowed even more. Such costs eventually became unacceptable to the hardheaded coal owners for whom return on investment was the single parameter used to justify continuing capital outlay. As a consequence pit closures in West Durham were not uncommon, and as a result men with no talents other than their underground skills frequently found themselves dumped onto the unemployment scrap heap. Disillusioned by circumstance, many of these men turned to crime as an easy way to relieve their privation. Such was the case with 'Bill and Ernie'.

Declining to offer detailed identification, Tomas recognised instantly that the names they gave were bogus, and that since their motives were purely mercenary, some hard bargaining might prove inevitable. He accepted this probability, and it mattered little, as money itself was not a problem. Tomas would take it from the Unit funds, plentiful enough and now dormant in an account for which, as Commander, he alone was responsible. With such cash at hand, and the detailed knowledge he now had of Spencer-Lambert's imminent movements, outlined in the programme James had provided, he could yet see his plans fulfilled, and this time Michael would not be around to frustrate him.

Uplifted by these thoughts, he spoke up confidently to his new 'partners'.

"I'm sure Mickey Gilpin has already outlined the details, but so there is no confusion I'll repeat the terms now. It's fifty pounds up front and fifty pounds on successful completion." They instantly nodded their agreement and acceptance.

Tomas had expected to haggle, and was ready enough to go higher. Their immediate and easy concurrence caused him to hesitate, triggering a misgiving that quickly became a conviction that they were ready to abscond, never to be seen again, as soon as their initial fifty pounds was safely stashed in their back pockets. In an instant he realised new arrangements were necessary.

He spoke up firmly, as they listened cautiously.

"There are some changes in my conditions for payment that I wish to stipulate before we go any further."

Their suspicions instantly returned, but Tomas continued before they could intervene,

" It is with no disrespect to either of you that I say this, but quite simply I don't know you men, and before you get paid, I need to be assured that you will not go running back to where you came from as soon as you have collected your first payment. Fifty pounds is a considerable sum in itself – especially if you need do nothing to earn it."

They looked at each other uncomfortably, and Tomas felt he had touched a nerve. He lied as he went on, inventing as quickly as his mind would let him.

" So I have made an agreement with Mickey Gilpin, who we all know and trust - you wouldn't be here if you didn't - I have made him trustee for all exchanges of monies. I have handed him your first payments to hold. He will pay them to you at three o'clock on Saturday afternoon, after your task has been completed.

"Whatever happens you are each guaranteed fifty pounds, *but not before Saturday*. If the operation is successful he will pay you the additional fifty at the same time. I will authorise payment by telephone once I'm satisfied you have completed your part of the job. He will pay you immediately.

"In the meantime you get ten pounds to cover your immediate expenses – to be deducted from the final total of course. If you agree these terms, we will proceed. If not this meeting ends now."

They looked across the table at each other and their irritation was conspicuous.

"We was not told about these new terms" said Bill gruffly, "if we had been we might not be here now."

"But you are here now" said Tomas flatly, "It would be a pity to go away empty handed now wouldn't it?"

"We was told fifty down and fifty on completion, that's all," complained his partner. Tomas stayed resolute.

"This is the deal. Take it or leave it. There's still one hundred pounds each on the table."

Tomas felt sure they were not ready to walk away from such money. After a moment he got his reply.

"OK, we'll do it," said Bill "Now what's the job. And don't pussyfoot around, we know it's got fuck all to do with mushrooms!"

They waited for an explanation, while he stared back trying to anticipate their reactions.

"I want you to carry out a controlled explosion in the service yard behind the Lambert offices on the seafront at Eastinglea during the Wings for Victory parade on Saturday afternoon." He watched them carefully as they considered his statement.

"And then?" said Bill expectantly.

"And then nothing. That's it. You do your job and go. You see Gilpin, collect your money, and leave. You don't need to know more than that," said Tomas.

Bill and Ernie looked at each other quiet and pensive, then without so much as a word nodded their mutual agreement. They stood up and prepared to leave.

"Stop" Tomas spoke up sharply.

They halted smiling together, and then turned back to him. Tomas hesitated.

"And then?" repeated Bill and waited.

Tomas had to tell them and he knew it. He took a deep breath,

"During the confusion your handiwork creates, I intend to shoot James Spencer-Lambert, Lord Lieutenant of the County, as he takes the salute on the podium at the front of the office building. "

He scanned their faces surveying their reactions. Bill was expressionless, but Ernie was transfixed, his mouth wide open.

"This will take place at about 2.30 p.m. Your explosion will be timed to coincide with the first group of military marchers as they pass by – the focus of everyone's attention."

"I intend to kill him."

Tomas did not know why he had added his last remark, but it gave him a deep feeling of satisfaction to have done so. He felt committed more than ever now.

"Jesus H. Christ!" Ernie exclaimed.

Bill hardly flickered, as he sat down again facing Tomas, then a smile of triumph spread across his face.

"The price has just gone up, mister. It's £1000 - or nothing doing! Except of course to make a concerned citizen's telephone call to the authorities, warning of the threat within their midst." He smiled menacingly.

Tomas was inwardly triumphant. He had expected to pay a large amount and there were ample funds to meet this demand. He knew if he agreed they would never run out on a £1000 payday.

" I thought this might happen," he said with apparent reluctance. "OK. You've got yourselves a deal. £1000 - but only on successful completion". Bill and Ernie smiled their pleasure at each other.

"One last thing" Tomas said slowly, "once that bang goes off, Gilpin will pay you – here in this bar – brown envelopes etc – then you leave immediately, and I never want to see either of you again!" He paused as they looked at him.

"Do I make myself clear?"

"Yea, clear enough," said Bill with a sneer. "And if the bang doesn't go off?"

"Then maybe you had better *hope* that I never see either of you again!" said Tomas with a telling smile.

Throughout the whole discussion James had said nothing, but as he listened to all that was being said, the implications became clearer in his mind, and filled him with an increasing sense of misgiving, realising that the programme of events he had provided, had helped Tomas to formulate a plan for murder.

Chapter 20

Explosion and Frustration

The explosion in the storehouse threw bricks, masonry, and debris into the air in a plume of flames and smoke, and an instant later the fuel tank ruptured in a fireball that rose high above the rear of the building. At the front, the assembled crowds watched in horror. Windows in the yard were shattered and as shock waves raced through the empty offices, the windows at the front exploded as well. The parade came to an undisciplined halt as confusion spread among the marching ranks. For a while there was little reaction, but as panic and mayhem broke out screams and shouts raged through the startled spectators. Police and soldiers raced to the rear of the building. His Lordship's personal guard protecting the visitors on the platform rushed to form a defensive ring around them, and scanned the surrounding area in all directions in search of potential attackers. A tall Scotsman in Black Watch uniform ran forward to stand, with his arms spread out in a protective gesture, in front of the only lady present. She was Jane Spencer-Lambert, his lordship's only daughter.

Across the street, Tomas crouched on the hotel balcony enraged at what had happened – his plan wrecked by circumstance; Spencer-Lambert had not shown up! In a fury he made his way down the back stairs into the streets and away to safety, unseen by the searching guards.

Michael maintained his position at the front of the saluting platform. He too scanned the crowd. He was searching for Tomas, convinced that he was the instigator of the chaos around him, but at a loss to understand why. An explosion at the rear of an empty building, on a weekend, when no one was working made no sense at all. It had no purpose, unless turmoil was purpose in itself. He watched as Lady Jane, surrounded by her entourage, was ushered into her car and driven away. The parade had disintegrated and the assorted groups of its participants stood around in confusion, wondering what to do. Only the parading firemen reacted positively, responding to their ingrained instincts. A fire was a fire! They had automatically assumed control, and engines and tenders with bells clanging moved up to the scene, easing their way through the melee. In what seemed no time at all, the blaze was under control and a semblance of order restored

"It's a cock-up!!" Michael heard himself saying aloud. Spencer Lambert was the target, but he hadn't shown up!

Whatever had been planned was doomed as soon as Lady Jane had appeared as his deputy! He scanned the crowd looking only for Tomas. A sudden movement on the balcony of the Castledene Hotel opposite caught his eye. He glimpsed sight of the crouching figure of a man as he turned to leave the balcony. He couldn't see his face, but he knew it was Tomas, departing the scene.

౭౩

Dermot read the story in the evening paper. It was featured on the front page, in banner headlines. The official statement concluded,

'........*that the explosion had been a freak accident in which, fortunately, no one had been hurt. Seepage from a valve on a line from the underground petrol tank, used to refuel the company vehicles, was blamed. It had somehow ignited. The tank had been serviced only the previous day. It was regrettable that the two men who had carried out the work, had in fact clearly bungled the task, yet had stated quite categorically before leaving that all was well, and necessary repairs had been satisfactorily completed.*

The caretaker, who had seen them as they were leaving on the Friday evening, had been assured that the system was quite safe to use.

193

"They were wearing their company overalls," he told our reporter," so naturally I thought they were competent engineers".

"I would have asked them for a proper job report if they'd been on their own, but they was with someone, an official from the pit I think. Don't know his name though."

The article concluded,

'Ongoing investigations were being pursued and discussions would be held with the service contractor to clarify the circumstances that led to the incident, and to seek an explanation for the seemingly unprofessional behaviour of its employees. The possibility of a prosecution could not be ruled out against both men and employer.'

The article refrained from naming the contractor, but went on to add an apology from Lord Spencer Lambert for his absence at the parade. He had been forced to rest at home inconvenienced by a cold, which was now much better, and he was looking forward to attending the Sunday evening concert, given by the local schoolchildren at the Empire Royal Theatre.

Dermot frowned at the peculiar turn of events, and wondered if all was as straightforward as was being reported. The reference to a colliery official made him nervous and renewed his present fears for his father. He suppressed his concerns arguing logically with himself that Tomas wasn't the only overman in town, but the strange circumstances of the day's events left him deeply worried and the odd business of his father's confession was never far from his mind. He decided he must go to Eastinglea immediately. After mass tomorrow would be the best time. Perhaps Michael would be able to explain things in better detail.

Bridgett, he decided, must be persuaded to come too. The trip would be a break for her, and they both needed to see their mother; for it was quite some time since they had visited her. Bridgett tended not to go out at all these days since returning from Ireland, and he wondered about that as well. She had been effusive in her thanks to Father Petrie, when he had willingly acceded to Dermot's request that she could work as housekeeper for them at St Leonard's. The two priests had been forced to manage for themselves after

Mrs Johnson left to live with her family in Darlington. The elderly lady had been complaining for some time that the big house was now too much for her, and it took only a short while for the two men to agree she was right, as together they were forced to struggle unfamiliarly with the domestic chores. Bridgett's arrival came as a blessing from heaven.

Tomas also read the article, and smiled his pleasure at the news of his lordship's speedy recuperation from his cold! Maybe all was not lost after all, he thought. He rose from his chair, and with only a mumbled word to his wife, put on his coat and cap and left the house.

Margaret watched him go, and wondered what was going through his mind. We never talk now, she thought desperately.

Chapter 21

Resilience

He stood in the phone box with his finger poised over the silver button marked 'A'. His breath condensed to a white mist in the cold of the evening air, as he listened to the dial tone echoing through the receiver at his ear. He pushed the button firmly as the connection was made, and his two pennies dropped noisily into the cashbox.

"Hello" said a male voice that Tomas thought effeminate, and which caused him to grimace.

"I'd like to speak to James Kennedy please," he said, dispensing with introductory formalities.

"Who shall I say is calling?" asked the voice in high register.

"A friend," replied Tomas tersely.

"I see," snapped back the voice. " Then please wait, *friend*, and I'll see if I can locate him for you."

Tomas ignored the petulant 'tut' he heard, as he failed to acknowledge the latter comment. There followed a rattle as the phone was laid down, and the hollow sound of retreating footsteps across a marble floor as the voice walked off in search of James. He tapped his fingers impatiently on the cold metal of the telephone cabinet as he waited, and stamped his feet to warm his toes.

"Come on, come on" he muttered impatiently, "I haven't got all night."

Eventually he heard footsteps approaching, and there was a rattle again as the phone was lifted.

"Hello, this is James Kennedy, who is speaking please?" he asked, with distant curiosity.

"At last!" said Tomas, " It's me James. I have to see you, before that concert tomorrow night. We have plans to make."

There was a sudden intake of breath as James realised it was Tomas on the line; then his voice fell to a whisper.

"I can't get to Eastinglea tonight sir, and I'll be with his Lordship all day tomorrow, I....." Tomas interrupted him curtly.

"We must meet James. We have to act tomorrow night. We'll never get another opportunity like this so don't tell me *you can't*. We can get him in the theatre. He'll be in the 'royal box' and you'll be with him. You can get me in there. That's all I need you to do. After that I can do what's needed on my own. I repeat, we have plans to make!" His tone countenanced no arguments.

There was a pause and only the sound of James' anxious breathing interrupted the silence as he weighed up the proposal being put to him. For the first time since meeting up with Tomas, James felt his loyalty being pushed to a level he did not wish to aspire to.

"I'm not sure, sir" he said hesitantly, "Getting you into the box will not be easy. I can't see me doing it without being implicated. You may work alone afterwards, but eventually they will put it all together. They will know I'm an accomplice. I'll have to go on the run – and where can I run to?" He was sounding jumpy.

"Don't you get cold feet now, my lad," said Tomas with menace. Slight panic assailed him at James's reluctance. He had never questioned Tomas's authority before. He had to bring him in line.

"You are implicated already, and if you let me down I'll see to it your name is heard in the right places by all the right people, which will be all the wrong places and the wrong people as far as you are concerned. Your nice little career in service will be come to a sudden and disagreeable end. You'll find yourself swapping the banquet hall in the Manor for the mess hall in Durham gaol! And the clientele in there are definitely less than upper class, James. Worse still, if they charge you with treason, you could swing for it, my lad. Do I make myself clear?"

Tomas was reluctant to pressurise the young man, but he was desperate to have him involved. He simply couldn't succeed without him; he needed him to complete this task.

James was dismayed to hear Tomas threatening tone, but he felt trapped. He would have to go along with what Tomas wanted, and hope he might get out of it later.

"This will be the last time, Commander won't it. I don't think I want to be involved any more."

His reluctance was conspicuous and shrouded with fear.

"This will be the last time James, I promise you. There will be nothing more after tomorrow. " He needed to calm him.

"I get an hour off tomorrow afternoon, between four and five o'clock. I could meet you then sir," said James finally.

"Good lad. See you in the *Demi* at four. Don't worry James; my plan will leave you in the clear. You won't be blamed at all." There was silence at the other end of the line, which Tomas found disquieting.

"James I can rely on you in this can't I. Your word – no - your oath is your bond is it not?"

"Yes sir, of course sir." was the instant reply. Tomas had hit the nerve, and James capitulated to this demand on his loyalty and honour.

"Good, then I'll see you tomorrow."

Tomas put down the phone without further comment and walked home in the deepening shadows and as he walked his confidence in the outcome grew with every step. A satisfied smile played at the sides of his mouth.

That night, he sat alone in his sitting room, the radio playing quietly behind him, while upstairs his estranged wife slept alone, oblivious to all that her husband was planning. He carefully unwrapped the gun from the oily cloth in which he had stored it all those years ago, secreted away in the dark recesses of the now redundant motorbike shed, unused since the days before his sons George and Padraig had married and left home. He inspected it carefully, and the cold hostility he felt for its owner was as always rekindled at the sight. It was a classic British Army Service Revolver, a *.455 Webley Mk 5*. He weighed it in his hand - about two pounds he guessed. He gazed at the monogrammed handle with the initials *J. S-L.* etched into the design. Pretentious bastard he thought; then he eased back the hammer and squeezed the trigger. The hammer snapped forward, smacking crisply against the empty chamber. Still in good working order he mused. I wonder if he'll recognise it. I'll make sure he does! He smiled at the thought. After a while he re-wrapped it and returned it to its hiding place, next to the box of cartridges Michael had acquired for him. Then he went to bed.

In the manor James was filled with apprehension as he rested in his room and contemplated the following day.

℘

Tomas glanced anxiously at the large clock on the wall. It showed five past four and James had not shown up. He was alone, quietly caressing a pint, which he had helped himself to while he waited. The bar itself was closed, since afternoon licensing hours were long ago finished; Gilpin had thrown his towels over the pumps two hours earlier, and was now taking his customary Sunday nap, but before he had left, he had agreed to Tomas using the bar for his meeting. Earlier they had spoken guardedly about the events of the previous day, both feigning only casual interest in the affair, with Tomas carefully avoiding all reference to the details of the incident. Eventually Mickey quietly confirmed the handover of the monies.

"Your two friends came round and I gave them the letters you left. I hope that was satisfactory Tommy?"

"Fine, Mickey. You did what I asked you to do, Thanks." Shortly afterwards Mickey left, reminding Tomas as he went, to drop the latch on the way out.

Eventually at twelve minutes past four James walked in. He looked harassed as he sat at the table in front of Tomas.

"Sorry I'm late Commander" he said apologetically, " I couldn't get away as soon as I had hoped. We were late leaving the manor this morning."

Tomas breathed a mental sigh of relief, and took another drink from his glass, before speaking.

"That's alright James. Now let's get down to business. What I want you to do is quite simple, and it won't take long to explain so listen carefully. I will enter the theatre via the overhead fire escape, which runs up the back wall to the Upper Circle area where the 'royal' box is located. You can see it from the small window in the bar of the Golden Bear pub. All I want you to do is to make sure that door is open; once I'm inside your job's as good as done. Now listen carefully, here's what we do then………"

❦

The atmosphere inside the theatre that evening was animated and noisy. The children had gathered early, boisterous with rowdy expectation, as they waited for the show to start. Harassed parents struggled to control their enthusiastic charges, and teachers patrolled the aisles like sentinels, chastising the unaccompanied with firm but gentle authority. A number of uniformed soldiers had been posted in the shadows along the back of the theatre, hands crossed behind their backs in the 'stand easy' posture. The authorities had decided a display of readiness was necessary, following the strange events of the previous day. Among them was Michael, whose presence at the show was no accident. The presence of the Lord Lieutenant at this function had forced him to conclude that this might be an opportunity which Tomas might use, and the unease he felt had compelled him to make himself available - just in case he was needed.

Now, looking around, what he saw looked innocent enough. A profusion of colours were on display, representing the many schools partaking in the show, each with an act honed to perfection over weeks of rehearsal and each determined to win the attractive silver trophy, which had been donated by the Lord Lieutenant himself for the school adjudged to have produced the best performance and presentation. Michael was uneasy, yet had convinced himself that this was not a place Tomas would choose to bomb. Whatever he might be planning, he was sure that Tomas would do nothing to hurt these little ones. His fight had never been directed at children. But still a sense of unease persisted, so he watched from the back, with the others, alert and nervous.

The judges were already seated, aloof in the front rows of the circle above, two representatives from each school. In the interests of credible voting, each pair was prohibited from voting for the performance of their own representatives. All was ready, and as soon as the Lord Lieutenant and his guests were in their places, the show would commence. The party was expected soon, and no one doubted that they would arrive on time. Punctuality was a virtue for which his Lordship was frequently lauded, albeit by an obsequious press, and his regular group of sycophantic admirers, representatives of whom were already gathered in the foyer waiting to greet him on arrival. The special guests who would accompany him into the reserved box seats consisted of Eastinglea's Mayor and Mayoress, plus his Lordship's own personal invitees.

As the lead car came to a halt outside the entrance James was the first to alight. He moved swiftly to the rear to open the door for his Lordship, as the watching crowd cheered their approval and waved their paper Union Jacks in communal greeting. Tomas watched from the back of the crowd, awaiting the signal, the confirmation that no unexpected setbacks had so far occurred to confound their plans. Their eyes met for a second and James gave a nervous nod that all was well and they could proceed.

Tomas turned away immediately and made for the yard behind the Golden Bear, where he stood in the shadows and waited, his gaze firmly fixed on the doorway at the top of the theatre fire escape. After some fifteen minutes he saw it open slowly, and stay ajar. So far so good he thought and smiled; James had done his job. He waited a few minutes more to ensure that the door stayed ajar and no one else appeared, then satisfied, he swiftly ascended the external ladder and entered the building unseen. He stood for a while breathing heavily as he adjusted to the dimly lit corridor. He waited, listening tensely, assailed by the noise from the main arena, where the excitement of the exuberant children mixed incongruously with the cacophony of instruments that were being tuned in the orchestra pit. He heard no other sounds or movements to cause him concern, as he looked around and took his bearings.

The corridor sloped gently down towards two ornamental archways, each draped in a heavy velvet curtain on large brass rings, one of which had a stiff card hanging tenuously on the fabric with the words RESERVED printed on it in bold black type. It was clearly the entrance to the box, while the other shrouded the exit that led to the rear aisle at the back of the main dress circle. Satisfied that he was undetected, Tomas closed the fire door quietly behind him, and moved silently down the red-carpeted hallway. He tiptoed into the small cloakroom, where James had strategically arranged the guests' coats and cloaks. Hiding behind these clothes, Tomas smiled confidently at the prospect ahead, and looking around found the small courtesy bar, which was routinely opened for guests on occasions such as this. Well stocked too, he thought, and helping himself to a drink, he crouched down against the back wall and waited.

Inside the box, The Lord Lieutenant with his wife were accompanied by Lady Jane and her escort for the night - a young man from the village hunting fraternity, while The Mayor and Mayoress were between two anonymous people from Durham's County Council. Mr Perkins the colliery agent was also present but the look of polite restraint on his face showed that he was there only as an obligation to his employer and took little sense of pleasure in the event itself. The party was in celebratory mood as they chatted and sipped the drinks that James had served them, while they waited for the start of the show. The Scots bodyguard from yesterday was also there. He was seated behind the guests on his own, sombrely surveying the crowd around the theatre. Only Mr Perkins refrained from drinking, although the Scotsman had limited himself to a simple lemonade.

"Strong drink and duty don't mix, laddie," he had said pompously, when James had asked his preference. Then he preened himself proudly as his Lordship responded to his zeal.

"Hear, Hear, McRory! Well said!" was the approving commendation.

After a while the main curtains opened at the centre, and the Master of Ceremonies appeared in front of the house. In a plea for attention he was compelled to bellow in a loud and stentorian voice,

"My Lord and Ladies, ladies and gentlemen, - and CHILDREN!"

The clamour died away and a hush fell over the hitherto rowdy audience, whose rapt attention from then on was broken only by appreciative bursts of laughter at the M.C.'s warming up jokes. Eventually with the audience firmly attentive, he announced that the show was ready to commence, whereupon the house lights dimmed, the orchestra started up, and the first act, from the Eastinglea Primary and Junior School took to the stage.

Dermot and Bridgett watched also. They had arrived that morning; Dermot had persuaded Bridgett that she must accompany him, to talk to Michael and to visit their mother. Later, with Dermot feeling worried and nervous after their meeting with Michael, they had been persuaded to accept tickets from him for the show. They had taken them, hoping it might prove a relaxing distraction from the worries that assailed them that evening.

Now as the performance got under way, they were seated in the main auditorium, with Bridgett wholly unaware that above her, James stood at the back of the guest box in attendant capacity, nervously tapping a drinks tray against his leg.

⁊

The performances continued unabated, each greeted with unrestrained cheering and rowdy partiality from their own supporters, generating considerable amusement within the guest party, and it was not until the fourth act that James was required to wait upon His Lordship again, when laughing gleefully, he turned and holding up his empty glass indicated he would like another drink. James stepped forward to oblige, and at the same time enquired requirements of the other guests. They pleasantly acknowledged his offer to recharge their glasses, as they too joined in the general excitement of the evening's activity. The Colliery agent Mr Perkins however looked increasingly dour as he sternly refused again. Constrained by deep-rooted religious convictions in the evils of alcohol, his distaste for the evening's recreation was plain to see in the fierce scowl he proffered in reply to James's polite enquiry. He further rejected an offer of a non-alcoholic alternative with equal disdain, and so James, graciously conceding to his sour mannered response, withdrew to the cloakroom to pour the drinks requested by the less inhibited members of the party.

Tomas was waiting for him, hidden from view at the back of the dimly lit cloakroom, and impossible to see concealed as he was by the coats and cloaks. As James entered, it was an easy matter therefore for Tomas to get near enough to strike him hard on the back of the head with the butt of the gun he carried with him. As he slumped to the ground with a grunt, Tomas caught him and laid him gently on the heap of clothing that he had prepared beforehand. James never knew what had hit him.

"There we are m'boy," whispered Tomas, a sympathetic smile playing around the corners of his mouth.

"You'll have a sore head when you wake James, but you'll also have a cast-iron alibi. All your troubles are now over. Your part in this is finished. You are in the clear."

It was only then that he noticed a pool of blood oozing out beneath James's head, but after examining it further, assured himself that James would recover and no great harm was done.

"You'll be fine James! Sure you will hurt a bit, but it was only a tap on the head! "

His words were lost on the unconscious figure beneath him, as he proceeded to strip James's of his coat and trousers.

"Sorry about your dignity son, but I need this monkey suit to go in there. Can't have open panic as soon as I enter. Got to look the part now, haven't I."

Some minutes later he was ready, dressed in James's clothes; he tidied himself and picked up the small silver platter he had placed ready on the bar counter. The white Basildon envelope was rather dog-eared, but unsoiled. It was addressed faintly in hand written script to *Captain James Spencer Lambert.* In the top left hand corner were inscribed the words *Personal & Confidential.*

He checked his pocket and was assured by the hard metal feel of the gun; then he drew back the curtain and entered the box.

Spencer-Lambert was smiling as he turned, expecting to see James with fresh drinks, but instead found himself gazing into the steely stare of Tomas's cold eyes, as he held out the platter with the letter on it. Startled for a moment, Spencer-Lambert frowned and looked closer; feeling there was something threatening about the man, but his attention was instantly distracted by the gruff voice as the man spoke,

"A letter for you sir; you must read it now!"

"From whom?" Spencer Lambert's curiosity was tinged with concern, and an uneasy feeling stirred within him as he opened the letter. He extracted an old piece of crumpled paper upon which was writing that was faded and difficult to read in the theatre's dimmed lights. His concern heightened as he studied the contents.

SENTENCED IN ABSENTIA.

By

THE ARMY COUNCIL OF THE IRISH REPUBLICAN ARMY

JAMES SPENCER LAMBERT, YOU HAVE BEEN FOUND GUILTY OF THE MURDER OF SEAMUS MULHOLLAND, AN UNARMED SOLDIER OF THE I.R.A., WHOM YOU SHOT TO DEATH IN MILLERS BAKERY YARD IN DUBLIN ON THE 24TH APRIL 1916.

THE SENTENCE FOR THIS CRIME IS DEATH BY EXECUTION.

AUTHORITY FOR THE IMPLEMENTATION OF THIS ORDER IS HEREBY INVESTED IN TOMAS MULHOLLAND, SON OF SEAMUS, WHO SHALL DETERMINE THE TIME AND PLACE OF EXECUTION AND CARRY IT OUT IN A MANNER APPROPRIATE TO THE PREVAILING CIRCUMSTANCES.

ISSUED THIS DAY MAY 4TH, 1916

BY ORDER OF THE ARMY COUNCIL OF THE I.R.A., DUBLIN

Signed:

The signatures were impossible to make out, and Spencer-Lambert felt a surge of fear and anger rising within him.

"What the hell do you.........!" As he looked up to protest, he found himself gazing down the barrel of an army pistol.

"Is this a joke!" he snarled.

"No! No Joke! This is a gun! Your gun Lambert! The same gun you used to murder my father in Dublin. Well it's your turn now, and by the authority invested in me by The Army Council of the IRA I condemn you to die here and now."

It was then that McRory shouted out in recognition.

" Jesus, You're that murdering Irish bastard! The one who killed the priest! You are that dead Mick's son we were chasing. I know all about you!" Tomas looked at the kilt, the build of the man, the Scottish accent, and realisation dawned.

"McRory!" he snarled. The man lunged at Tomas grabbing for the gun.

Tomas fired, and the Scotsman was thrown back, dead in an instant.

The ladies screamed!. Lambert made to stand up, and Tomas fired again. With a gasp of shock and clutching his chest he fell backwards across the edge of the balcony, where he lay motionless. All the while the other guests stood by, helplessly shaking with horror, the ladies sobbing loudly in distress and turmoil. Tomas looked at his victims with cold contempt, then, pointing the gun at the terrified Simon Perkins, smiled malevolently and yelled,

"BANG!"

He laughed wildly as the man stumbled backwards with a terrified shout.

Almost instantly Tomas's mood hardened.

"It is done!" he said. Tossing the pistol to the ground, he turned abruptly, and vanished into the shadows beyond the curtain.

The screams spread to the watching auditorium, where attention had switched from the stage to the horror and commotion in the box. Pandemonium and chaos broke out with crying children and distraught parents, while on the stage the patriotic strains of the children's rendition of *"Lend to defend your Country"* a song specially written for the occasion, gave way to a discordant cacophony of crying and fear, as teachers and stagehands fought to restrain their panicked charges.

From his place below, Michael watched, aghast at the scene unfolding above him.

"My god Tomas, you've done it now!" and a thousand thoughts crowded his brain as he forced his way towards the exit in pursuit of his fleeing cousin.

"They'll catch him for sure - there'll be a trial - with all the publicity - Margaret - God knows - she's suffered enough!!
They'll hang him - he'll hang!"
His stomach churned at the thought! His mind was in a whirl.
"It can't happen - I can't let it happen!"

Dermot and Bridgett watched also, frozen in the moment and horror stricken. Both recognised their father; both were overcome with paralysing fear. Then as they searched around, they saw Michael rushing out of the theatre. Galvanised into action at the sight of him, they followed, Dermot forcing a way through the crowd that was now surging out of control towards the exits. Behind him he dragged his sister, distraught and in tears.

Tomas had thought little of where he could go, or how he might make his escape. His single consideration was to get away from the theatre as far and as quickly as possible. He was filled with an unexpected sense of elation, and the adrenalin rush pumping through his veins gave him a sense of exhilaration that he had never before experienced. He felt no fear. As he went past the cloakroom he grabbed an overcoat, and a quick glance at James confirmed he was still unconscious. Momentary concern for his welfare was outstripped by his other emotions and there was nothing he could do for him now anyway. He strode swiftly back to the door at the fire escape exit putting on the overcoat as he went.

Michael ran out of the front of the theatre and looked around. Mystified passers-by were gathering at the doors, startled by what was going on, their growing presence adding to the confusion.

"They've shot him! They've shot him!" was a cry ringing out, but no one knew who or where.

Some of the soldiers outside carried rifles, which they clutched tightly in the ready position, but with no idea of where to point them. Michael pulled rank.

"Soldier!" he shouted and the nearby private turned to him, rifle at the ready.

"Sarge?" he said as he recognised Michael's stripes.

"Don't point that gun at me man!" said Michael with authority. "Is it loaded?"

"Sorry Sarge" said the private, and lowered the weapon, then apologetically,

"Well yes, it is Sarge, but the safety catch is on!"

"What are you doing here with a loaded rifle?" Michael demanded accusingly

"We are his Lordship's bodyguards, Sarge," he explained nervously "Our Sergeant said we had to load our guns - after that fiasco yesterday, like." he said.

"But we never dreamed we'd have to protect him, or use them for real. We're really just a guard of honour. No shooting or anything like that. Sergeant McRory just told us to wait outside. Keep an eye out like. We've been in the café next-door, but only till the show was finished you understand."

"McRory! My God!" thought Michael. " *It gets worse!"*

The soldier interrupted his thoughts,

"Is it true Sarge, has someone really done for 'im? His Lordship Sarge?"

Michael seized on his deferential tone.

"Yes there's been a shooting, no thanks to you lot! Now get in there, and search with the rest of them. He's still there somewhere. Leave your rifle with me! We don't want any more gunshots in there."

"Right Sarge!" said the man, and handing over his rifle, he pushed his way into the exiting turmoil.

A woman screamed!

"There he is! On the fire escape! All eyes turned upwards to the side of the building, where a dark figure, barely visible in the shadowy light, was descending swiftly.

"It's Tomas!!" thought Michael as some of the armed soldiers forced their way forward making for the point at which he would reach the ground.

"We've got the bastard now!" said a burly man, his rifle held at the ready. For a moment Michael froze.

"I can't let them take him! They don't deserve that." His mind was in turmoil. Then instinct took over.

"Look out he's got a gun," he yelled, and the advancing soldiers stopped dead in their tracks.

Michael raised the rifle and aiming quickly, fired. People shrieked at the noise and instinctively ducked down, seeking cover.

His marksman's skills didn't fail him. Tomas was thrown back against the wall with the force of the shot, which took him in the middle of his chest. He crashed down the remaining steps and tumbled to the bottom where he lay in a heap, not moving. The soldiers ran forward as Michael slowly lowered the rifle.

"NO!" came a strangled cry from behind him.

Dermot forced his way past the cordon of restraining guards, already holding back the crowd.

I'm his son!" he cried, "Let me through! I'm a priest!" They broke to let him pass, as Dermot shouldered his way through pulling Bridgett with him. Together they rushed to their father's side.

Handing the rifle to a nearby soldier, Michael followed slowly after them, towards the crumpled figure on the ground.

Dermot was already at his side, pleading through his tears.

"Oh good Jesus, help him!" he sobbed; then he stammered in confusion through the prayers of the Church's Last Rites.

Tomas opened his eyes, looked at his son, and smiled at him triumphantly. Dermot pleaded with him,

"Make your peace father. Call on God's mercy, please!"

The smile on Tomas's face broadened mockingly. He was not afraid! Then he closed his eyes and died. Dermot prayed on in tortured desperation. Bridgett knelt beside him, numb with shock. Then as Michael drew nearer, she looked up at him through tears that accused him. Only her sobbing broke the silence between them before Michael spoke,

"I couldn't let them take him, Bridgett, They'd have hanged him," was all he could bring himself to say.

He reached for her, but she shied away from him.

"I don't understand!" she sobbed, "I don't understand! I don't understand!"

Dermot stood up and raised Bridgett to him. Clasping her tenderly, he looked at Michael and said tightly,

"You had better go now. God may forgive you for what you have done here today Michael, but I doubt that I will ever be able to."

Chapter 22

The Aftermath

The newspapers, local and national, reported the story in all its lurid detail, as they did the legal formalities that followed later.

The coroner at the first of two inquests on the case brought in a verdict of murder against *"One Thomas Holland, a collier at Eastinglea Colliery"* for the death of *His Lordship, The Honourable James Spencer-Lambert Earl of Lumfield*, coal owner, business entrepreneur, and landowner in the County of Durham, and that of his respected friend and protector *Sergeant Robert McRory* who had given his life in a vain attempt to arrest Holland. A verdict of premeditated murder was entered.

He made a passing reference to the crumpled letter discarded at the crime scene, in which his Lordship was accused of criminal behaviour during service in Dublin, at the time of the notorious Irish Uprising against the British Crown in 1916. He went on further to dismiss public speculation that an enquiry based on the evidence of this paper might be necessary to ascertain the facts surrounding Holland's assertion against his Lordship, describing it as an unsubstantiated fabrication concocted by the murderer to justify his crime.

Furthermore, he added, since The Irish Republic was no longer an intrinsic part of the United Kingdom of Britain and Ireland, cooperation in what would be a protracted in-depth investigation of a futile and unfounded allegation such as this could be of no benefit to either side. He then added the rider that since both countries were still at loggerheads politically, over refusal of the Irish State to provide harbour facilities for allied Atlantic shipping, this would most certainly render cooperation in such an investigation at best difficult, and in practice, totally impossible.

The gun was entered in evidence as the murder weapon, but the coroner made no reference to the monogram on the handle.

The coroner at a separate inquest found that death by misadventure was the cause of Tomas's demise. No charges were considered necessary against any person involved in the apprehension of the criminal, and *Sergeant Michael Railley,* a well respected member of the Eastinglea Territorial Army, was singled out for commendation in that his swift action in bringing the murderer down, had prevented his escape, and removed a very real threat to the surrounding public. It was deemed unfortunate that the assassin had been killed rather than apprehended in this incident, but in the turmoil prevailing at the time it was not surprising. Sergeant Railley's action was judged swift, timely, and fully justified. Moreover, although after careful search, no further weapon was ultimately found on the deceased's person or anywhere at the scene, several witnesses had testified that they too had seen what had appeared to be another gun. In such circumstances, said the coroner, Sergeant Railley was justified in shooting and thereby cleared of all blame. The community, he stated, should be forever grateful for his decisive intervention.

The coroner then expanded his statement to include a message of sympathy for the unfortunate circumstances that led up the injuries to *Mr James Kennedy,* his Lordship's personal manservant, who was yet to recover from the head injury he had sustained from the murderer during the lead up to the fatal attack on his Lordship. Mr Kennedy had suffered a brain haemorrhage, and while he was hopefully on the road to recovery, the medical consensus was that this process might prove to be long and tedious. He then added that the possibility of a permanent injury could not be ruled out at this stage.

On a more optimistic note, he added, *Lady Jane Spencer-Lambert* had given her personal assurance that Mr Kennedy would be afforded the very best of care that money and medical science could provide.

೮೨

Chapter 23

Restoration

Once the inquests were over, and after their father had been decently interred, Dermot and Bridgett returned to Satsworth, where they were subjected to the intrusive curiosity of many uncharitable neighbours, but their ungracious attention was more than offset by the polite sympathy of the parishioners of St Leonard's. Eventually, with the due passage of time, the tittle-tattle ceased, and their newsworthiness diminished, till they became no more than 'neighbourhood curios'.

The same could not be said for their brothers back in Eastinglea, to whose care they had entrusted their ailing mother.

Exaggerated rumours about their father's anti-British activities flourished in the aftermath of his actions, and George and Padraig, along with their wives, became increasingly ostracised within the community, while their children were derided and bullied at school.

Things came to a head when the colliery manager was forced to dismiss them both, due to what he described as 'an increasing threat to the harmonious working of the pit, created by their presence there'. Appeals to the union against unfair dismissal were halted at local Lodge by the Lodge Chairman himself, who informed them that, for once, the management was not at fault, and that it was their workmates, "*their marras*" in fact, who had tabled a motion that they should be removed from the workplace. In it they were defined as 'threats to their fellow miners and a danger to mine safety itself'.

"In truth, lads," said the Chairman firmly, "the only safety threat is to yourselves, and I strongly advise you to go quietly – without any fuss."

A few weeks later, George and Padraig travelled south to London, where they enlisted in the Auxiliary Fire Service that had served London so heroically during the recent blitz, and there they became members of the *Fire Brigades Union*. It was through the union that they met and befriended a man called *Jack Dash*, who helped them to get their families settled in the strange metropolis, which for them initially seemed so alien. Later Dash, a renowned left-wing radical of his day, persuaded them to think about becoming active in the socialist movement. They did so, and in time, they followed him into work in the dockyards at the Port of London. There they eventually joined Dash as members of the Communist Party, and went on to participate actively in the extremely militant and unofficial practices that abounded at that time, and which gave rise to conflicts which would ultimately divide the workers, not only from the docking management, but even from their own unions for several decades to come. While working in dockland, they joined a local Hibernian club, where their links to their heritage were rekindled. Ultimately they left London for Dublin and became active in the movement for the unification of all Ireland, ultimately joining the IRA. The wheel had gone full circle!

Dermot knew nothing of these things as, back home, his concerns for his mother accelerated enormously after his brothers had left. The circumstances of Tomas's death had dealt her a severe blow from which she seemed unable to recover. During the sporadic visits they were able to make to her, necessarily restricted because of their obligations at St Leonard's, Bridgett and he observed a steady deterioration in her health and mental welfare. The obvious solution was for Bridgett to move home to care for her, and this she did so immediately, but it proved an unsustainable solution to the problem, in that it resulted in nothing more than a location change for Bridgett, who, with mounting stress and weariness, struggled to fulfil the dual role of caring for her mother and maintaining a good house for her brother and his parish priest, Father Petrie. She was reluctant to give up her position as Dermot's housekeeper, but when her own health began to suffer it became ever more obvious to them that the situation would have to be resolved in a more practicable way.

In the end, Dermot appealed to the bishop for help. Aware of a new curate's appointment at St Hildreth's to assist the ageing Father Docherty, it seemed a reasonable idea that Dermot and he might change locations, until his mother's predicament could be resolved on a permanent basis, and so Dermot submitted this idea to his Lordship in Newcastle. The bishop however thought the proposal was totally unfeasible, seeing it as flying in the face of custom and practice for the allocation of priests to their vocational placements. It was a strict principle that priests should never be assigned to a home parish, where twin loyalties might create an unacceptable conflict of interest in which the Church could come off second best. His response to Dermot therefore was an uncompromising refusal, and Dermot and Bridgett were left to find another solution, exclusive of diocesan consideration.

Circumstance itself intervened however, when old Father Docherty at St Hildreth's died suddenly following a severe attack of pneumonia. An immediate replacement, in the form of someone experienced enough to take on the job was not instantly available, and the recently assigned curate was not considered mature enough for the task. It then became convenient for the Bishop to remember Dermot's earlier request.

Consequently he transferred him on 'temporary assignment' to St Hildreth's, where Dermot assumed authority as caretaker, pending the appointment of a permanent parish priest. At the same time, the young curate, Fr Bernard, was moved to Satsworth, to assist Father Petrie.

Dermot, for his part however, was left to carry on alone in his new situation.

So Bridgett was able to move back home, where she dedicated her time to providing the care and attention her mother needed, but was still able to keep Dermot and his new house in good order.

At Saint Leonard's meantime, a rota of lady parishioners, devoted members of the *Mothers' Union*, attended to her responsibilities - in what was seen initially only as a stop-gap arrangement.

Bridgett looked after her mother with the unstinting dedication that only a loving daughter could provide, making her days as comfortable as humanly possible. Sadly however her tender loving care turned out to be of only transitory value, as despite the close attention, Margaret continued to waste away both physically and mentally. A succession of puzzled doctors, unable to diagnose her condition, relieved their sense of inadequacy by prescribing ineffective palliatives and placebos, one after the other.

"How do you mend a broken heart?" challenged Bridgett one day, in reply to the clichéd enquiries of a visiting young locum. Embarrassed by her disconcerting answer, the young man hurriedly scribbled yet another order for yet more medication, and mumbling some incoherent instructions, left swiftly.

The doctors' visits became gradually less as the months passed by, and within the year, Margaret had died, and Dermot and Bridgett mourned her passing bitterly.

After his mother's death Dermot threw himself completely into his parochial duties at St Hildreth's, steadfastly supported by his ever-loyal sister. Together they bore the twofold wounds of the loss of both parents, and the added salt of their brothers' departures to distant lives elsewhere.

Throughout this difficult period, they were undisturbed by the bishop, who, engrossed in dealing with the more important business of diocesan affairs, initially procrastinated over, then later chose to forget the 'temporary assignment' he had put in place at St Hildreth's.

When some two years later, he visited the parish to administer the sacrament of Confirmation to an accumulation of eligible children seeking spiritual reinforcement of their budding faith, he was reminded by his attendants of the unresolved status of the parish management, he was heard to respond casually that 'change for change sake' seemed unwarranted now. Dermot was both surprised and relieved at this pronouncement, for his dedication to his parish work had become entrenched, and he was reluctant to forsake the various projects he had initiated for his schoolchildren, the youth, and the needy of his flock.

His Lordship compounded his surprising statement when he went on to justify his new rationale, by adding that since, with the obvious exception of Bridgett, now the full time housekeeper, Dermot was no longer burdened by immediate family, which might distract him from his parochial commitments, there was no valid reason to uproot him a second time.

What he failed to admit was that Dermot's stewardship as parish priest was the main and unspoken explanation for this apparent magnanimity, because in his two years in charge, Dermot had managed to reduce the parish debt, incurred by the saintly but economically incompetent Father Docherty, to levels which satisfied the pressing demands of the local bank. This achievement alone, removing as it did the possibility of financial penalties for both parish and diocese, was the real factor, which influenced his lordship's decision.

In truth, the bishop was most happy to leave Dermot at St Hildreth's, in the reasonable expectation that he would continue to administer the parishes finances with the same conscientious frugality that he had so far successfully exercised.

His condescending assertion 'that under the circumstances it might be just as well to leave well alone' was music to Dermot's ears, whose joy in the news, left him feeling forever indebted to his hierarchical superior, blithely oblivious to the fact that his own financial proficiency had earned him this reward.

So Dermot stayed on, and in time was given a curate to help him as the numbers in his rapidly increasing flock expanded, and his happiness with his task was absolute, except at night when the memory of his father's unrepentant smile forever haunted his slumbers.

As for Michael, he prospered in Eastinglea, where his popularity got him voted onto the Union Lodge Committee, and his enduring standing amongst his fellows eventually eased him into the position of Lodge Chairman. In time he was nominated for a permanent position on the County Executive. His interview for the job became a formality in which his 'heroics' at the Empire Royal Theatre were regurgitated before an admiring panel of interviewers. His selection to the post was applauded unanimously. Shortly afterwards he moved out of the pit, then out of Eastinglea, and ultimately to Durham, where he revelled in his newly elevated status as he settled his family into life in the city's prosperous suburbs. As time passed and his career progressed, his sense of guilt for Tomas's death faded, as did his ties to Dermot and Bridgett, till gradually they became virtually strangers to each other. Eventually, all communications between them ceased.

Chapter 24

As Hope Dies

Bridgett had visited James just once after the disastrous events of the *Wings for Victory* Concert, at the local hospital into which Lady Jane had arranged his admission. It was known as 'The Sanatorium', but it had been built originally as a Victorian mansion by an ostentatious but philanthropic landowner, who bequeathed it to the local population when he moved with his family to the provinces of Greater London, where *'we shall cavort more regularly with our peers',* he is reputed to have said. The generous gift of this grand house became of huge benefit to a grateful community whose elected representatives on the urban district council swiftly converted it to a vital refuge for the sick, and rapidly staffed it with professional medical staff supported by able and dedicated volunteer carers and administrators, lest their eccentric benefactor should change his mind.

It stood on the cliff tops, which towered above the shoreline, and each of its wards was designed with a glass-walled veranda, kept tightly closed through the winter months against the worst excesses of the northern weather, but which were opened to let in the healing comfort of the sun's warm air in the balmy days of summer. On such days, patients could look out from their beds beyond the trimmed lawns and the manicured gardens to the sea and the distant horizon, while enjoying the healthy tang of a gentle offshore breeze. The Sanatorium was a tranquil place, in which broken bodies and confused minds could recuperate, and where problems of heart and soul were peacefully eased away.

Bridgett had heard of James's part in the theatrical nightmare that her father had created only when she read of it in the press report of the coroner's verdict. It had come as a grievous shock to her to know that his condition was a direct result of her father's actions.

As she followed the young nurse along a line of beds, made up in vivid red blankets that contrasted brightly with the brilliant white of the pristine linen sheets and pillowcases, her heart ached for her lover who she had assiduously avoided since her return from Ireland, unable to bring herself to explain the circumstances of her long absence to him. She believed that he would not want to hear that she had born and lost him a son, and even less the circumstances in which it had all happened. Now fate had caused their paths to converge again and all the dormant love she still bore for him had resurfaced.

The nurse smiled as she pointed to where James was sitting up in his bed. He was wearing a warm tartan dressing gown over his shoulders, and beneath it he wore hospital issue blue-striped pyjamas. He was freshly shaven and his hair was neatly combed, under the bandage that covered his damaged head. His carers had prepared him meticulously before the visit.

"Just half an hour", said the nurse as she turned to leave, "we don't want to tire him out."

She hesitated a moment, before she added quietly, "Don't expect too much. He may not know you immediately."

Bridgett pulled up the chair to the side of the bed and sat up as close as possible. She reached for his hand and took it in hers. James made no response and gave no sign that he was aware of her presence.

"Hello my love, how are you?" she said softly, and she gazed right into his eyes, which stared straight past her.

"Love you my darling," she added hopefully.

James still gave no indication that he was aware of her presence, as he gazed out beyond the garden to the sea. He made no movement at all, other than to blink now and then. He said nothing, and the heavy silence between them continued, till after thirty minutes, the nurse returned to tell a distraught Bridgett her time was up.

Bridgett left go of James's hand and turned to the nurse with a look of desperation in her eyes. The young nurse helped her to her feet, and led her from the ward, a comforting arm around her shoulders.

"It might be better next time," she said softly and proffered a handkerchief, but Bridgett shook her head and said,

"I can't live with this, unless there's hope!" She waved a despairing hand. "I need to know there's some hope!"

"We'll let you know as soon as he improves," said the nurse compassionately, and this time Bridgett accepted the handkerchief, which was still being offered.

So she left, and waited for word. But time passed and no word came. Then she phoned, and was advised to call the following week. When she did so, they told her there was still no change, and advised her to call yet even later. Then once more they promised they would let her know as soon as he improved, but no one called, not even once.

In the end, all hope within her died, and Bridgett never returned to the Sanatorium again.

Epilogue

The communion was over; the mass had ended. The excited children had departed to the celebration breakfast at the school, shepherded by their attentive teachers, while their parents and relatives wandered after them in casual groups, gossiping and exchanging idle pleasantries as they went.

For Dermot the end of the service brought blessed relief. He had struggled through the mass with increasing difficulty, stressed by the persisting memories of an unhappy past. Too weary to go to the school, he delegated to Father Kirby the responsibility for distributing the medals and certificates to the new communicants, the final ceremonial of the day. Heavy of heart he made his way back to his study in the west wing of the old presbytery. Feeling a little faint, he settled into his chair, glad to rest.

Bridgett heard him from the kitchen and brought him tea. Seeing his drawn face she scolded him gently as she placed the tray carefully on the table beside him.

"You don't look well brother," she said as she arranged the cups and saucers." You should have stayed in bed this morning. Father Gibbs would have happily come down from St Joseph's if you had asked him to, although I think Father Kirby, young as he is, would have managed quite well on his own." She began to pour as she chided him, concern in her every word.

Dermot heard her voice as a hollow noise, distant and indistinct. A great sadness welled inside him that turned to pain. It all seemed so futile, he thought, and the pain grew worse, burning his chest. Bridgett's voice faded and the room grew dark. His breathing became laboured and a chill came over him. Fear and panic seized him but he could not move.

I must sleep… I must sleep…. The pain seared through him, till he could bear it no longer. As he slipped into silent unconsciousness it stopped. All pain had left him, forever!

Bridgett turned to give him his tea and stood as if paralysed. She looked into the face of her dead brother and grief pierced her like a sword. She put down the cup and saucer, which rattled in her hands as she sobbed. She stood above him in confusion and cried her lonely tears.

'It's over' she thought, 'it's finally over.'

His face was serene; his brow was relaxed with no deep lines any more. He looked at peace. He was at peace. She felt consoled. Controlling her sorrow, she gathered herself. Kneeling down beside him, she prayed a wavering prayer. She looked into his face and the sight of him filled her with an aching love.

"Wherever you are now Dermot, you're with God. " she whispered as she got to her feet. "My work here is done. Our Lord has you now."

She leaned down to him and taking him in her arms, held him tenderly to her breast. Her tears fell on his face as she kissed his cheek, then she gently settled him back in his chair. She stood up again, and pausing only for a moment, turned and left the room, closing the door quietly behind her. In the hallway, she lifted the telephone, and called Dr James Nelson, Dermot's long time friend and medical advisor.

૯৲૩

At the funeral there was much whispering and head shaking in disbelief at Bridgett's absence. No one could understand how a sister so loyal for so much of her lifetime could desert her brother at the very moment of his death. Tongues wagged with malicious speculation as to the circumstances of her speedy departure. Only those who knew her closely and cared for her worried about her whereabouts.

On the deck of the ferryboat *S.S. Birkenhead*, which regularly ploughed its watery furrow between Liverpool and Dublin, Bridgett Mulholland, as she now called herself, stood peering out over the rail at the mist that shrouded the horizon. Through her hands she passed her rosary, pausing at each bead to recite a fervent *'Ave'* for her beloved brother. She was having difficulty praying as her mind flitted from her recent past to what she perceived as a bright new future. Dermot and she had often discussed her life long desire to live in Ireland (as Tomas had vowed they would all do one day) and Dermot had so often beseeched her to go with his love and blessing and live her dream - "before it gets too late" - he had said.

In the earlier years she had been tempted, but she couldn't bring herself to leave him to the ministrations of a non-caring stranger. She alone could share his thoughts, his confidences, and only she could properly serve his needs. So she stayed, time passed, and then they didn't discuss it any more. Except for that one occasion, when after the death of Padraig, the last of their sibling brothers, Dermot had taken her by the hands, sat her down, and made her swear that in the event of his own death, she would leave immediately, with not so much as a backward glance.

"Take me with you in your heart, he had said, so that I might know the old country too."

Bridgett had agreed to do it just that way. Now she was on her way to the ancestral past of which their father had so often spoken. She was going to cousin Elizabeth to live out her remaining days.

Elizabeth and she had been such great friends as children, sharing holidays when she came to England to visit. During these summers together, they and their friends would play games in a crowd on the slopes of the local pit heaps, known as the *'The Dillies'*, that lay around about the colliery perimeters. No one knew why they were called 'The Dillies', but they were a favourite haunt for little boys who played Cowboys and Indians, riding imaginary horses up and down them, like The Lone Ranger and Tonto, so that they became almost as black as the miners who passed by below. The "First Shift" workers back from the bowels of the earth waved to them smiling whitely from tired black faces as they trudged their weary way home in anticipation of a hot breakfast, a hot bath, and a comfortable bed, another hard shift behind them.

Elizabeth would always contrast these tired men to the ruddy and healthy farm workers who lived their lives so differently in the fresh clean air of Ireland. At such times her intrinsic talent for story telling, in her rich Irish accent, would fire Bridgett's imagination with impressions of green fields, fresh spring water, peat bogs and leprechauns. Bridgett yearned to see it all.

Elizabeth's visits ceased when her dad - Bridgett's Uncle Paddy – died suddenly of a heart attack. It was a loss from which her mother - Aunt Rose - never recovered, and Elizabeth spent the years that followed caring for her heart-broken mother. The task became a lifetime commitment that dictated the pace and tenure of Elizabeth's whole existence.

Through out this long period Bridgett and Elizabeth corresponded regularly, and Bridgett's taste for Ireland and things Irish never wavered, despite the torment she had endured as a distressed mother, bereft and alone in Dublin. Neither of them had married as they grew older, though each had endured the pain of an unfulfilled romance, which for Bridgett had led her to becoming her brother's housekeeper as she sought to restore meaning to her damaged life. They had much in common and lots to share.

Bridgett pondered on these things as she looked across the misty sea. She smiled a little at the happier memories, feeling sure that in the quiet beauty of an Irish countryside all her wounds would heal. She felt confident of her future.

Some four hours later, she walked down the gangplank and on to the dockside. Clearing formalities were minimal, and she passed smoothly through the dockyard area. She quickly picked out the excited face of her waiting cousin and waved enthusiastically. As she hurried to meet her, she noticed that there were others with her, and she was puzzled as to who they might be. There was a young man, a young woman, and two children, a boy of about eight or nine, and a girl about a year younger. Bridgett's curiosity was aroused as Elizabeth came towards her, beaming her delight.

"Bridgett, Bridgett, how lovely to see you." They hugged and kissed. Bridgett's hat was knocked askew, and the children behind laughed at her.

"Don't laugh children, it's not polite" said the lady who was clearly their mother. She spoke with an American accent.

"Please excuse them, they are a little excited to be here at the dockside, they've never been here before."

Bridgett found her familiar tone pleasingly disarming.

"Oh that's alright" she smiled "There are lovely children. I take it they are yours?"

"Yes, and I'm their father". The tall young man, who was also American, stepped forward and held out his hand to greet Bridgett. She took it uncertainly and glanced at Elizabeth for reassurance. Elizabeth responded excitedly.

"Bridgett, this is Robert, Robert Reynolds," she said, "and this is his wife Laura, and their children Terence and Jenny. They are from Boston, in America."

"Hello" said Bridgett still unsure, "It's very nice to meet you all."

Elizabeth took both Bridgett's hands in hers and clasping them joyfully she said,

"Robert is your son Bridgett, the baby you thought you'd never see again! And these are your grandchildren! Robert works at the American Embassy in Dublin. He's been looking for you for a year!

"Bridgett you have a family again!" she exclaimed excitedly.

Bridgett was stunned. She felt faint as the shock of what Elizabeth was saying hit her like a hammer. Her legs went weak beneath her and she swayed a little. She looked as if she might fall.

Robert Reynolds rushed forward and caught her. He led her to a seat nearby and as she slowly recovered, he spoke to her softly.

"*Mother*" she heard him say, "are you OK?" She studied the concern on the face beside her, and surveyed it closely.

'James - it's James,' she thought. 'He's his father's son, there is no doubt,' and tears slowly trickled down her cheeks, and for the first time in many long years Bridgett felt happy, totally and unreservedly happy.

☙

The pain had ceased, the heartache had gone, and the darkness had retreated from him. He felt warm again, peaceful and content, though curious of his surroundings, so calm and so quiet. A light appeared out of the diminishing darkness, moving it seemed towards him. He watched in awe as it approached, and a sense of elation filled his breast. It continued to grow, until he could clearly discern the outline of two figures at its centre. They were two men, shining silhouettes in human form. He could not clearly see their faces, but he knew they were smiling. One was tall and glorious in white robes. He did not speak, but raised his arm in a gesture of greeting.

"He's an angel," thought Dermot, but hesitated at the idea. The second was discernibly a man, with bright eyes that twinkled in a kindly face. He moved to meet Dermot who found himself drawn willingly and irrevocably towards him. As they drew nearer, Dermot gasped incredulously, as recognition dawned.

"It's you Daddy!" he exclaimed, "Can it really be you?"

The man spoke, soft in reply.

"It is Dermot, it is me." His voice was music in Dermot's ears.

"Welcome my son. Come. Let me lead you into Paradise."

Dermot reached forward and eagerly clutched his father's outstretched hands. Grasping each other round the shoulders they embraced with a fervour they had never shared before. Then turning, they walked together joyously into Glory. And the angel went before them leading the way.

In a different eternity, in a hell of his own making, the tormented spirit of Tomas Mulholland's primary ego meandered in a slough of deep despond. The vengeful hate that had brought him to death, as Michael Railley's bullet tore his soul from his mortal body, still possessed him now. So, with anger and hatred as his dark companions, he wandered in black futility through the corridors of Hell, seeking, never to find, the spirit of the man whose foul deed had projected him into hapless immortality.

For Heaven and Hell are prescribed differently for all men and for all women. Each person's infinity is forged in the substance of his or her own mortality, and each damned soul is condemned to drift in an eternity of desolation, tormented by the obscenities of a failed humanity. In splendid contrast, in the Heaven of the Just, the honoured soul experiences only infinite happiness and absolute joy, and everything that is good and virtuous is accorded them. And which good man could be fulfilled forever without the unqualified love of an admiring mother, or of a brother or sister, and yet more so, without the long sought approbation of a beloved father?

And so it was for Dermot Holland, whose eternal happiness was encapsulated in the approving smile in his father's eyes.

The End

About the Author

Peter Ward was born in Co. Durham England, the son of a coalminer. Of Irish pedigree he was raised in a disciplined Catholic household.

He was educated at a Jesuit College in Sunderland, after which he served in the Royal Air Force, Later, he too went into mining, working as a field research officer investigating the causes of pneumoconiosis, the miners' lung disease. After the research was completed, he moved into the synthethic fibres industry with IMPERIAL CHEMICAL INDUSTRIES. There he studied industrial chemistry, and working in product development, progressed steadily through the management structure.

Following ICI's sell-off of their synthetic fibres interests, Peter travelled abroad to join ARAMCO, the Saudi Arabian oil giant. This change of profession initiated a twenty two year career as a Corrosion Engineer. During this period Peter's work took him to locations as far apart as NORWAY, NIGERIA, THE MIDDLE EAST, and the PEOPLE'S REPUBLIC OF CHINA.

Recently retired from an engineering post in SYRIA, Peter has started writing, and 'TO A GREATER GLORY' is the first novel of this new career. His second book entitled 'PICK YOUR OWN STRAWBERRIES', based on the experiences he gained in his international travels, is being compiled. A third book, 'I KNEW MRS MINIVER' is also underway.

His chosen pen name *Peter Gartland* is adopted from his maternal Grandfather, who migrated to England in the latter years of the nineteenth century.

Printed in the United Kingdom
by Lightning Source UK Ltd.
123675UK00001B/224/A

To A Greater Glory

by

Peter Gartland

authorHOUSE®

AuthorHouse™ UK Ltd.
500 Avebury Boulevard
Central Milton Keynes, MK9 2BE
www.authorhouse.co.uk
Phone: 08001974150

First published by AuthorHouse 9/17/2007

ISBN: 978-1-4343-1497-0 (sc)

Library of Congress Control Number: 2007903677

Printed in the United States of America
Bloomington, Indiana

This book is printed on acid-free paper.